THE FOURTH KINETIC
CLAIRVOYANTS

BRADY MOORE

SURGE
Cayélle

THE FOURTH KINETIC

CLAIRVOYANTS

For permission requests, contact the publisher below:

Cayélle Publishing/Surge Imprint
Lancaster, California USA
WWW.CAYELLEPUBLISHING.COM

Orders by U.S. trade bookstores and wholesalers, contact Freadom Distribution:
Freadom@Cayelle.com

Categories: 1. Young Adult 2. Science Fiction 3. Fantasy
Printed in the United States of America

Cover Art by Carlos Quevedo
Textures by Sascha Duensing
Interior Design & Typesetting by Ampersand Book Interiors
Edited by Ashley Conner Editing

ISBN: 978-1-952404-38-2 [paperback]
ISBN: 978-1-952404-39-9 [ebook]
Library of Congress Control Number 2020949853

THE
FOURTH
KINETIC

CHAPTER 1

THE GIFT

I STARE UPWARD AT THE FADING STARS IN THE indigo sky. Soon, the morning sun will peak over the acres of rolling hills, and I'll have to wish the stars farewell. I don't know why I'm so fascinated by them. Maybe it's because, no matter how many times the angles change, the stars remain the same. Maybe it's because they're the only thing in my life that are consistent. It's like we're kindred spirits asking each other the same questions. *Why are you here? What is your purpose?*

I place my bulky, vintage headphones atop my curly, tapered hair and pull my cell phone from my jean pocket. A few taps of my finger against the screen, and a beat begins to swarm in my ears to match my heart. My eyes close and my head nods as the sounds of A Tribe Called Quest resonate through every pore like a warm cup of coffee.

I open my eyes just in time to see my mother pulling from the driveway in her crimson SUV. She blows me a kiss and waves. I can read the look of anxious optimism in her sparkling light brown eyes like a billboard. It only makes me shake my head and smirk as I wave back. What's there to worry about? New schools. New surroundings. I've done them so many times they've become as much of a routine as tying my shoes.

The school bus is pulling up over the hill just as my mother's car disappears. It's astonishing how few houses there are in the distance. Most of the ones I do catch seem far from lived in. It can only be a pain for the bus to pick me up so far off course. I quickly adjust the lone strap of my backpack that hangs over my shoulder, and tuck my hands into the pockets of my gray jacket. The weather in this tiny Missouri town doesn't seem too bad. Not too hot, not too cold. At least I know there is one thing positive about this place other than the clear skies.

I can already see the probing stares blaring through the bus windows. I try to conceal my rolling eyes as the bus comes to a halt. In this small town, everyone likely knows everyone and has known everyone their entire lives. I can imagine a seventeen-year-old stranger might be a bit intriguing to them.

I nod to the bus driver as I clump up the vehicle's grimy stairs. The whole interior seems as if it has just finished two tours of escorting soldiers in the Middle East. A light huff echoes through my jaws as I notice the only three black kids chatting it up in the back. Even they manage to glare at me like my chocolate skin is something abnormal. The only empty seat is at the very front, right behind the driver. I quickly sit, just as the vehicle rumbles forward.

I don't say anything to anyone, although I can feel the gazes scanning me. My stop is the last before we arrive at school. This is good and bad. Good because I won't have to worry about some awkward kid attempting to strike up conversation. Bad because I didn't get to finish my old-school hip-hop playlist.

A burly man with silvering hair tells me to take off my headphones the instant I step from the bus. I oblige, but his tone irks me. It's as if he's already determined I'm trouble just because he's never seen me before.

I stroll around the campus, taking in every hallway like I'm in a museum. It's surreal how eerily similar all of these high schools are. This is my sixth school in four years, and it's probably the most generic. The only

distinctive feature is the glass case draped with basketball trophies and plaques. I scan it for a moment, before
I realize just how many achievements the school has.

The information my mother was telling me while we
were moving begins to resurface in my mind. My new
high school is the best in the state at basketball. She
guesstimated somewhere in the ballpark of five champi-
onships in six years. It's actually seven in nine. Impressive. Maybe I'll stay long enough to catch a game. I
chuckle inside. Unlikely.

The morning bell sounds, and a flurry of people
bombard the halls. It takes barely a minute for me to
make it to my first class—sociology. The few students
who have already entered give a stunned scowl as I trot
in. I ignore them before heading to my favorite classroom position. Nothing says *don't talk to me* like the
back corner window seat.

Five minutes later, the classroom is filled. I ignore
each student's critical scan, and the childish snickers that come from over my shoulder. I can overhear
them making fun of my high-top sneakers, like wearing
anything that isn't popular automatically labels me an
outcast. Nothing new. I've met plenty of students like
these. The ones who like to mask their insecurities and
shortcomings by being obnoxious. People like this are
always easy for me to ignore.

Our teacher is the last one to enter. He's a tall, thin balding man with bifocals. His attire, perfectly pressed khakis and a tan blazer with elbow pads, looks like something straight out of an 80s movie. There's a friendly smile plastered on his stubbled face as he closes the door and moves to the white board behind his desk.

"The scientific study of society and human behavior!" He scribbles the same words in blue ink.

His gaze seems to fixate on me when he turns around. A hint of intrigue in his stare that makes my eyes roll.

"Good morning, everyone. My name is Mister Keenan, and welcome to sociology. Now I'm sure the reason you're all here is because all of the good electives were taken."

The entire class chuckles, but I just sit there with my palm on my chin. He waits for the laughter to simmer before he spends the next few minutes prattling on about his expectations for the course, and how we, as seniors, shouldn't be sluggish in our studies just because we're close to graduation. It gets me thinking about my own future. I've never given any thought to a career path. Mom wants me to go to college, but the thought of leaving her behind while she continues to migrate gives me a nervous itch.

Finally, Mr. Keenan takes up a clipboard and begins to call the roll. He runs down every name. A few students, who deem themselves the height of comedic timing, reply with anything but the *here* and *present* that is the norm. I can't help but groan and wait for the inevitable when he nears my name.

"Ree-on Grean?"

Everyone's eyes perk, and a few snide giggles fill the room. I give a deep sigh before raising my hand.

"It's pronounced just like Ryan," I reply.

"Oh! Okay. Sorry about that, Rion." He smiles apologetically before continuing the roll call.

It's funny—he hasn't taught any of these people before, but I can tell he's already sniffed out that I'm new here.

I give an apathetic nod, coupled with my best faulty smile, before turning back toward the window. I avoid making eye contact with any other student.

The chirping birds have my attention for the next few minutes, until something catches my ear. There's another new student. I can tell by the heightened tone in the teacher's voice when he calls her name.

"Danielle Young?" he says.

She quickly replies, as to not draw too much attention.

I look over at her. She is ironically seated at the desk in the opposite corner of mine. Her skin looks as delicate as an untouched pool of cocoa, and her eyes are large and round like coals. She's short. Very short. Even while she's sitting, I can tell she is no taller than five feet. Her coarse hair is crinkled into two poofs, and her modest outfit of a T-shirt and overalls seems just as outdated as mine. She glances at me, just as I ease my gaze away.

Mr. Keenan spends the better part of the next hour doing the same things every teacher does on the first day of school. Everyone groans when he starts passing out packets of reading material. And after highlighting specific sections on the syllabus, he talks about how the course will explore the nuances of human behavior. He starts asking the classroom questions, but I shrug and continue staring through the window. No way a new kid is going to raise his hand and volunteer on the first day.

"Rion?" Mr. Keenan says, and the entire classroom looks in my direction.

Son of a...you're supposed to be asking for volunteers! I turn from the window, realizing other students have already spoken and I haven't heard a single response.

"What's up?" I blurt.

The class snickers. Mr. Keenan gives me a look that clearly signifies my question wouldn't be necessary had I been paying attention.

"What are your thoughts on human behavior? A quote or an observation, perhaps?"

"Well…" I murmur, as I tap my fingertips against the cool veneer surface of my desk.

The entire classroom awaits my response with intrigued scowls. My eyes flutter, and I start to wonder if I should say what's really on my mind.

"Honestly…I think humans are full of sh—crap."

Laughter breaks out. Great. Just what I need. More attention.

The guys look at me as if I'm the new class clown. The girls look at me as if I'm the new bad boy. I'm neither. Just the new kid who wants to be left alone, and who would have loved it had the bell rang five minutes ago.

I look into the crisp frames of the glasses covering the teacher's light-brown eyes. He scowls at me just as he finishes calming the rest of the class. Surprisingly though, he seems more laden with curiosity than anger. So I reluctantly continue.

"People fear what they don't understand, hate what they can't conquer. Guess it's just the theory of man…"

The class looks around as if I'm speaking in some foreign language, but Mr. Keenan just looks on curiously, unable to take his gaze from me.

"'Hate Me Now'...by Nas." I scan the room with outstretched palms. "It's a rap song from 1999."

The short black girl in the corner is the only student who seems enamored by my response. The other wide eyes glaring back at me make it seem as if I've just uttered an Einstein equation. I take it their answers didn't stem from twenty-year-old rap lyrics.

"Very nice, Mister Grean," Mr. Keenan says, with a wily grin.

The bells sounds shortly after. It's as if the noise triggers memory loss, because nearly every student jumps from their seats and begins clamoring out of the room like I'd never spoken.

Mr. Keenan, still grinning from each ear, begins shuffling his papers and preparing for his next class. I shrug and grab my notebook to place it in my backpack.

"I look forward to more insight from you, Rion." He smiles just as I head for the door. "Welcome to Tyler High."

I trudge aboard the school bus and take a seat at the same spot behind the driver. The soothing vibes of

Run DMC blare into my eardrums to drown out the thoughts of another monotonous first day of sitting in classroom corner seats and eating alone in the cafeteria. I'm prepared to lean back and enjoy the brief trip home, but something catches my attention just before my eyes can shut.

There's a kid scrambling for the bus. I recognize him from my algebra class. He's slender, with untamed brown hair, but the metal boot on his right leg is easily his most recognizable feature. He's the only kid I spoke to today...sort of. I opened a door for him, and he thanked me.

He's still a few feet from the bus when I notice the driver preparing to close the doors. I'm not sure if he hasn't noticed the kid...or if he's seen him and doesn't care. I turn my apathetic glare to the other students. Virtually everyone who can see the kid through the window is laughing at his misfortune. I wish I was surprised. It seems that no matter where you go, high school students will always be at the bottom of the social maturity totem pole.

I shake my head when the driver reaches to clasp the lever and shut the door. Without hesitation, my focused glare takes aim at his hand. A deep scowl engulfs my face, and I become so focused that I refuse to blink. The driver pulls, but the lever doesn't budge. My nose twitches, and sweat begins to bead down my brow. My right palm widens, and my fingers unfurl. It's as if I'm standing beside the bus driver and tugging against the lever with all my might.

Finally, the kid clumps up the vehicle's stairs just as I release my mental hold on the lever. The driver yanks it so hard that I can hear the screech of the doors through the music that continues to swarm my senses. The kid nods at the driver and mouths a *thank you* before taking a seat behind me. A smirk fills my face when the driver looks around in a befuddled stupor, unaware of the special gifts of the silent newcomer behind him.

A breeze rustles the long blades of grass that dance around my jeans. I can feel a few pockets of air navigating through my bare toes as I sprawl out in my new backyard. Nights like tonight, when the sky is as clear and deep as a never-ending ocean, are always the most relaxing. Out here in the countryside, there are no city lights to mask the starry skies. No sounds of honking horns to pierce the soothing silence. Only the chirp of crickets.

Moonlight bathes one of the tiny insects as it inches toward me. I focus on the creature just when it makes a leap for my right leg. I hold out my hand, letting the cool air rush over my skin. The cricket stops midair, and its tiny appendages begin to wriggle in a frenzy over my open palm.

"Chill, bro," I whisper, as if it can understand me. "I'm not gonna hurt you."

My eyes never waver. I can feel them growing red as I make the insect hover to the other side of my legs.

"Rion!" Mom calls from the patio.

My eyes flicker, and the creature drops. It begins its version of an urgent scurry through the sea of grass as I turn to meet Mom's curious smile beaming from the back porch.

"Dinner," she says, as if she knows I'm guilty of something.

"Yes ma'am," I call back, before I lift myself from the grass and head inside.

I can't remember the first time I used my *gift*. There are a few hazy moments that still rest in the back of my head like clips of a movie I'd watched in the height of late-night fatigue.

Third grade, when Gary Moses pushed me on the playground, and I cried because I scraped my knee on a bed of wood chips. Gary laughed until he felt the air rush against his face, causing his nose to gush with blood. He told the teacher I punched him, but the other kids knew I hadn't touched him.

Then there was fifth grade, when Suzy Beamon kissed me on my cheek on Valentine's Day. She immediately toppled to the floor and hit her head on a desk before running to our teacher, claiming I'd shoved her. I got suspended for a week, even though my hands never budged.

But I specifically remember the first time I knowingly used my powers. It was five years ago, when I was in the seventh grade. I was sitting in my usual, chosen seat in the corner of Mrs. England's social studies class. I was bored, so I tried to make my pencil move. It did, and I remember my skin growing warm and my heart thumping like I'd just received a shot of adrenaline. I made the pages of my notebook flutter just to make sure it wasn't a fluke. I had wide eyes for the rest of the day. For so long, it had felt like a dream. But after that moment, the full realization that I was unlike any other human had fully set in.

Where my abilities come from, or why I have them, occasionally seeps into my thoughts. I come up with theories every so often. Could I be an alien? That's the theory that seems to hold up the most. It would certainly explain my mom always keeping to herself, and that we don't look much alike, aside from being African American. Although…it is certainly possible that I might be some sort of experiment gone wrong… or gone right.

Both ideas are aided by us constantly moving. Her career as a freelance researcher has the two of us rarely in the same city for more than a year, so I've never managed to make anything close to a friend. She tries little things to make me happy, like buying whatever I want. One time, she bought me a dog when we moved. I lost it after three weeks, and we moved after six.

As far as I know, my mother is oblivious to my gift. But I swear she's almost caught me a few times making quarters spin and causing curtains to waft when there is no air circulation. I often notice her in the corner of my eye, glaring at me as if she's waiting for me to move something. But I've never thought to tell her about what I can do. I can't imagine how she'd cope if she ever truly knew that her son had telekinesis.

She already thinks I'm miserable. Every day, no matter what house we live in, my mother walks by my room with the same wounded look in her eyes. She thinks I don't see her, but I always do. Even if it's not true, I always tell her that I'm content. I have no desire to waste time scrolling through social media accounts to forge phony relationships with strangers.

I've found other, little things to make the days and nights seem meaningful. I play games on my phone, watch an occasional action movie, or listen to music on my headphones.

But the only hobby I truly need…is my unnatural ability to move things with my mind.

CHAPTER 2

DR. DIANA GREAN

"HOW IS IT?" MOM SAYS, WITH A WORRISOME scowl.

I hadn't realized I'd drifted off in the middle of dinner.

"Do you not like it?"

"No...it's good." I stare down at my plate of baked chicken, spicy corn, and mashed potatoes.

I wonder how obvious it is that I have no idea which part of the meal she's talking about.

"I used some peppers in the corn. Just trying something new."

"Everything tastes great, Ma." I smile back.

I love her smile the few times I get to see it. It never fails to brighten the dreary atmosphere that seems to follow us like a shadow. A shame that it's only the two of us. My mother looks insanely young for a for-ty-three-year-old. Crisp, brown skin covers her face without a blemish or wrinkle. Her lips, like mine, are smooth and full. It's really the only trait we share. I can't help but feel jealous of her toned figure and pearly brown eyes, compared to my lanky frame and the list-less, dark spheres between my eyelids. Even her long, silky hair is nothing like the curly bush on my scalp.

She often passes for my older sister when we're occa-sionally out in public. This, of course, makes her feel celebratory. But I find it odd. Not once has she ever been on a date, spoken on the phone with people of interest, or even gone out with friends. She's also never mentioned any siblings or distant family. Dr. Diana Grean's life, for all I know, is shallower than mine. The only time she seems remotely content is when she's around me.

The thought of someone dating my mother makes me cringe, anyway. I don't want some stranger here pretending to fill a father role. Besides, who would even bother? Our lives seem to be locked away from the rest of the world.

"So how was day one?" she says, between bites.

My brow curls, and a smirk fills my face.

"Kids stared at me. Teachers mispronounced my name. Ya know...same 'ole, same 'ole."

"Try to look at the positives, Rion. At least it's August."

A light huff billows from my lips, and my gaze drifts to my plate. I hate to admit it, but it is nice to finally be entering a new environment at the start of the school year. Usually, Mom would have me dropped in at the middle of a semester, like the perfect stowaway.

"And as far as your name goes," she winks, "you should be proud. The spelling is unique...just like you."

"I'd be prouder if I knew it came from Dad or something." I bite my bottom lip.

Part of me didn't mean to say it aloud. I know what's coming next. I shovel a massive portion of mashed potatoes in my mouth, and look up with apprehension at her vacant stare passing through me.

Each time I bring up my father, or lack thereof, her good mood wanes. She never reacts with anger. In fact, anger would perhaps be normal to me. There are plenty of single mothers with deadbeat sperm donors. But the reaction she always gives is something curiously different.

"Your father's gone...but he was a good man."

I remember the words like yesterday, even though I haven't heard them in years. She has never given me any other details. I'd asked about his name, how or if he died, what he was like, where she'd met him...but no matter the question, her reply would always be the same. I told myself I'd let it go, but I doubt I ever will. It's hard to ignore such a gaping hole in my already melancholic life.

"Rion," her bright smile fades with guilt, "your father's gone."

"I know. Sorry."

The rest of dinner is shrouded in silence. By the time I'm done, I've zoned out so much I can't remember whether the food was delicious or not. I let out a deep sigh as I stare at my empty plate and push away from the table. I can feel my mother's sparkling brown eyes glaring at me as she simultaneously stands to her feet.

"Before you go to bed, make sure you pack away some of those boxes. I mean it."

"Yes, ma'am," I reply, in my naturally instilled, polite tone.

The sound of my mother washing dishes continues to resonate from the kitchen as I advance through the hall and up the stairs. I pass by a storage closet and the guest room we'll never use. It's always eerie renting furnished houses. I never feel like I'm truly home, and I can sense the ghosts of the people who used to live in them.

Eventually, I reach my room. My mother's latest attempt to ease the strain of our migration was to gift me with the master bedroom. It's a nice gesture, but it's not like I need the extra space.

I close the door behind me. The moonlight casts a calming beam through the window, and lights my surroundings. I plop down on my bed and glare at the empty corners. We've been here for two days now, and I still haven't put sheets on or unpacked my things. If it were up to me, I never would. What's the point? How long will I stay here? Six months? Eight? Maybe a whole year if I'm lucky.

I use my abilities to sift through the cardboard boxes on the floor like each garment is a member of the symphony orchestra, and I'm their conductor. It amazes me how easy of a task this is. By the time I'm done, the boxes are empty and clothes are sprawled against my closet floor.

A lion-sized yawn escapes from my jaws as I lean back and rest my hands behind my head. If she wasn't so exhausted herself, Mom would be in here yelling at me for sleeping in the grimy clothes I'd worn all day. I'm too tired and agitated to be tidy tonight, and as I begin to doze off, all I can think about are those words I keep trying to ignore.

"Your father's gone...but he was a good man."

Fifty-two, Mississippi. My bare feet are planted on the carpet like they've been welded to the floor.

Fifty-three, Mississippi. My keen glare focuses forward, and my fists are balled at my waist.

Fifty-four, Mississippi. My backpack remains still, hovering inches from my face as if held by an invisible rope.

Fifty-five, Mississippi. My lips tighten, and I can feel my pupils beginning to ache between my eyelids.

Fifty-six, Mississippi. Just a few more seconds, and I'll break my personal record.

Fifty-seven, Mississippi. The backpack begins to wriggle, and I can feel it slipping from my focus.

Fifty-eight, Mississippi. Streams of sweat start to career down my brow, and my forehead begins to ache.

Fifty-nine, Mississippi. I just need to hold on a bit longer.

"Sixty!" I shout at the top of my lungs, as if a massive crowd has surrounded my living room to cheer me on.

My backpack clumps to the floor, sending every binder fluttering from the opened zipper. A heavenly sigh flows from my chest as my knees wilt and I collapse onto the sofa. I can't help but break into celebratory laughter. Once again, I've accomplished another personal milestone.

The sun is starting to set, filling the room with a hollow, auburn glow. For hours, I'd been levitating everything. Books, lamps, chairs...whatever I could wrap my mind around. Mom didn't start trusting me to be home alone until my fifteenth birthday. Ever since then, I tinker with my powers every time I come home from school to an empty house.

My chest and limbs are numb and weary like I've just run a mile. My head feels like I've just eaten the world's coldest ice cream. Splitting migraines used to coarse through my skull whenever I'd levitate things for more than a few seconds. But I've never felt better after such extensive use of my powers than I feel right now. It's as if my body is starting to adjust, and I can't help but wonder just how much I can strain and stretch this ability before it reaches its limit.

A cold, unopened bottle of water sits on the dining room table. I'd almost forgotten that I'd pulled it out of the refrigerator a few minutes ago. But now, every drop of condensation that billows down its surface seems to be calling to me. I hold my arm up, not even bothering to fully turn and see the bottle. It zips into my palm like a paperclip to a magnet. I guzzle down every drop in one, long swig.

It amazes me how much better I've gotten with just a few years of private practice. When I was fourteen, moving an apple took all of my focus. But now I can move smaller objects flawlessly, without even looking straight at them. I want to start trying to lift larger, heavier objects. I slid the refrigerator in our old apartment once. But the last time I tried to mentally lift something more than a few dozen pounds, I ended up splitting my bedpost in two. That, and the following massive headache, were fun to explain to Mom. The fear that I might pop a blood vessel or fall into a coma also lingers in the back of my mind, no matter how unlikely it might seem.

I wish I knew more about this gift. The dangers. The limitations. As much as I want to keep it concealed, it's hard not being able to talk about it with anyone. This power is as dangerous as it is incredible, but there's no one to guide me.

Lights flash past the living room window, and the sound of tires rolling through gravel echoes from outside. I quickly rise from the sofa and scan the room to make sure nothing is too far out of place. With the swipe of my wrist, my books slide back into my backpack, and I rush toward the kitchen table. I mentally bring the backpack to my feet just as I take a seat. Reach inside to snag the first stapled stack of papers I can find, just as I hear the click of the front doorknob.

"Hey, Ma!" I shout, as she pokes her head through the door.

She turns and gives that warm smile while struggling to yank her key from the knob. The same tan bag she's had for years droops from her shoulder. She's barely able to adjust it before the hordes of thick books and folders filled with paperwork can spill out onto the floor.

The door closes behind her, and she releases a long sigh.

"Hi, sweetie," she says.

Her jet-black hair is pulled into a ponytail, with one strand managing to stream over her forehead. The blue pantsuit she wears makes her look like a lawyer on a crime drama.

"How was school?" she says, her high-heeled shoes clicking against the kitchen linoleum.

I slowly raise my head from the papers I was pretending to read. Mom places her bag against the countertop and washes her hands at the sink before she turns back to me with an intrigued smirk.

"Same 'ole, same 'ole."

I don't know why she always asks, when my answer never changes. One of these days I should say it was great, just to see her get excited.

She leans over my shoulder and plants a kiss on my forehead.

"Sociology, huh? Interesting stuff, right?"

I shoot my gaze back to the packet in front of me. I hadn't even realized what I'd pulled out.

"Oh...yeah. You should've seen all the looks I got yesterday when I spit Nas lyrics in class."

She shakes her head and laughs before taking a seat at the opposite end of the table. Even through her bright smile, I can tell she's tired.

"What about you? How was work?"

"Good." She nods, her smile fading.

I can always tell when she's lying. Her eyes seem to swim with reluctance, like she's afraid the full truth will only lead to more discomfort. I used to ask her more in-depth questions about the work she did for these random companies that hired her, but the responses were always filled with enough technical jargon that she might as well have replied in a foreign language. I guess we both have aspects of our daily lives that are too complicated to explain. Still, it seems strange that we don't at least confide in one another.

"What's for dinner?" I blurt out, to cut through the silence.

I immediately regret asking. She looks like she could pass out. The last thing she should be worrying about is feeding me. Hell, I could make do with a ham sandwich and a bottle of water.

"I can heat up leftovers, or whip up some spaghetti..."

"Ya know what? Why don't we put a pizza in the oven and watch a movie?"

"Hmmm..." She gives a sly smirk. "Did you do your homework?"

"Of course."

"What about the TV and the Blu-ray player?"

"Hooked 'em both up earlier." I omit that I did most of it by levitating chords into their proper outlets.

Yet another new skill I picked up today.

"Okay." She nods. "Let me change clothes, and I'll meet you in the living room in thirty."

I can tell she's relieved. She picks up her bag and bounces up the staircase like I've just surprised her with an all-expense-paid vacation. It's amazing how easy it is to make her happy. Maybe one day we'll go to the beach, and she'll actually relax. After my graduation, perhaps? Or maybe even Christmas break.

By the time she's back downstairs, I've already heated up a pepperoni pizza to perfection. She lets me pick the movie. I could've easily gone with a gory action film. But instead I find something we'll both enjoy. *The Breakfast Club*, an 80s classic. It's one of the few movies without a fight scene that I can sit through. Something about a bunch of misfits bonding after a day in detention intrigues me.

Mom dozes off about an hour of the way through. Her forehead rests against my shoulder, the light from the TV being the only thing bathing our surroundings. Darkness even spreads from the windowsill, but

I can still hear crickets chirping outside. I slowly grab the paper plate from her hand. There's still a half-eaten slice of pepperoni left behind, but I've already had my fill.

I send the plate hovering over to the kitchen table, but my gaze never leaves my mother's wilted eyelids. I think about pulling the phone out of my pocket and taking a picture to capture this moment. For whatever reason, she's always hated photos, and it's been years since we've taken one together. With her body resting over my arm, I'd probably have to mentally hover the camera above us, anyway. So I let her sleep peacefully. I even mute the TV and listen to her soft snores.

Part of me wants Mom to be aware of my gift. Lately, as I've grown stronger, I've contemplated telling her my secret. She's always been levelheaded, and prepared for everything. If anyone can handle this, it's her. I just need to find the right time.

My eyes begin to droop, and I can feel myself dozing off. The last remnants of the day are just about to fade, when I'm startled by an arduous buzz that abruptly courses beneath me. My first reaction is to glance down at my phone. I don't know why. The only number I have is my mother's.

I lean forward, making sure to keep Mom's forehead resting soundly against my shoulder. As the vibrations cease, I locate her cell phone wedged a few inches between the cushions beside her hip. The screen is lit up with a missed call from an unknown number.

A confused gnarl encapsulates my face, and my mind searches for a time when I've ever seen her phone ring. I think about using my gift to levitate it across her body and over to me, but the thought of the astonished gawk she'd have waking up to her cell phone in midair causes me to rethink the idea.

The screen goes black, and I turn my head back to the TV screen. The second I've faced forward, the buzzing begins again. I twiddle my fingertips and rub my lips. I can feel the anxiety beginning to pour through me with each second the phone vibrates. Do I wake her? Do I answer? Do I just sit here and ignore it?

"Oh!" Mom says, her eyes fully blossoming to shake off every ounce of weariness in an instant.

She leans up and snatches the phone into her grasp. She mouths *goodnight* to me as she stands, then taps the screen and brings it to her ear.

"What's wrong?" she answers, while sprinting up the stairs.

Her door slams shut the minute she is out of sight. I remain on the couch, the luminance from the TV cascading against my suspicious scowl.

After a half-hour of sitting alone, I finally decide to shut off the movie and go to bed. But the moment stays with me. As I lie on my uncovered mattress, staring up at the ceiling, I can't figure out which is more troubling—her receiving a call at this hour, from an unknown number, and knowing who would be on the other end. Or the look of sheer distress in her eyes when she answered it.

CHAPTER 3

THE OTHER NEW KID

I TRY MY BEST TO DISREGARD MOM'S BEHAVIOR after that late-night call. My dreams had run rampant with the ridiculous notion that it might've been my father on the other end. But in the following days, she doesn't seem to act any differently, so I reluctantly decided to chalk it up as some work-related issue that is none of my concern.

School has been an absolute blur. I've quickly gone from the new kid to the pessimistic know-it-all. My newfound moniker pours into my other classes, as teachers take turns testing out my wit. I wouldn't mind sharing my opinions and intellect if they'd come without the judgmental stares and under-the-breath whispers from my classmates. Sooner or later, though, the entire senior class gets wind that I'm not Mr.

Perfect. I'm terrible at math, and English class holds my attention even less than history.

Every school day seems to be more tedious than the last. But the highlight comes when school has finished, and I have a few hours to toy with my powers before my mother gets home. By the end of week two, things at school have almost completely died down. I have ceased being the know-it-all outsider, and molded into being just another quiet outcast. This, I prefer.

It eventually becomes evident that a few unenviable others share this same label, including the kid with the metal boot on his leg. He spends most of his time reading gamer magazines, and doesn't appear to have any friends. At least, not at this school. I always try to open the door for him when given the opportunity. He was missing from algebra class today. I find it odd that I care.

There's one kid who freaks me out. He sits next to me in English, and we always make brief eye contact. He has long, scraggly blond hair, and a thick patch of stubble on his chin. His hazel eyes carry an emptiness about them that make him seem neither lonesome nor anxious. His clothes are usually coated with a hint of dirt. All in all, his daily appearance makes me wonder if, and when, he ever bathes. After a few days, I over-hear that he belongs to a family of farmers.

There's a husky, blonde girl who always eats alone at lunch. Her meal is identical every day—a chicken sandwich, French fries coated with ranch dressing, and a carton of chocolate milk. I suppose I can't find fault with that. If pizza isn't in my daily intake, it's only because the line is too long, and I can't just levitate a slice from across the cafeteria. I heard this girl used to be sociable, until her best friend passed away from cancer two years ago.

For whatever reason, I relate to her. To all of them, really. I wonder if having a metal boot, belonging to a poor family of farmers, or losing a friend has made their lives as somber as mine. Maybe we're all just members of *The Breakfast Club,* waiting to be placed in detention together.

I'm startled when a figure plops down in the chair across from me, and I raise my eyebrows. I've been sitting in this exact spot since my first day, and not once has anyone come anywhere near me.

It's Danielle, the other new kid from sociology. She's wearing a bright-green T-shirt and a pair of tan capris. Her hair is coiled into the usual pair of poofs atop her head. I'm not surprised she's come. In fact, I wonder why she'd waited this long, when our gazes have met several times while in class.

"Military?" she says, in a mousy voice.

I scan around the cafeteria in confusion, then look back at her round eyes. She glares back at me like I should know what the hell she's talking about.

"I mean...that's why I move around so much." She removes a salad from her turquoise lunch bag. "You?"

"Oh...uhh...my mom is a freelance researcher."

I immediately question replying, as if I've just given away the password to my phone, or shown her the spare key to our house.

"Hmm...well, that explains a lot."

"Meaning?"

"You're smart." She giggles. "Well...smarter than most of these people."

I give her a scowl. Surely she can read my discomfort and tell I don't want to be bothered.

"Sucks, ya know. This is my third high school."

"My sixth," I blurt.

Why do I keep responding to her?

"Sheesh! All of yours been as lame as this place?" she mumbles, while glaring around at the cluster of students laughing throughout the cafeteria.

I do the same, and somehow let a conceding smile pierce through.

"Not quite. This school at least has some accomplishments."

"Yeah...but you can smell the arrogance on 'em."

She places her attention on her salad. I scan the area again. I don't know what I'm looking for. Signs that I'm being pranked, maybe?

"Where you originally from?" she says, between bites, not even bothering to lift her gaze to mine.

"You sure ask a lot of questions."

Her gaze shoots up, and an offended grimace fills her cocoa-brown face.

"Sorry." I sigh. "I'm not really used to this much interaction."

A sly smirk sprawls across her pouty lips. She digs her spork back into the damp lettuce in her bowl. I eagerly await a reply, but she remains silent for what seems like forever. She pines away at her meal until it's gone. My heart begins to beat slowly as I look away from her to pick at the cooling pepperoni on my pizza. Every so often, I glance back at her in hopes that she'll say something.

"Look," she finally grunts.

My gaze darts up, as if I can't wait to hear her response.

"We don't have to be best friends."

My brow curls. Somehow I find this reaction surprising.

"But there's no sense in pretending like we don't exist, when we've got something like this in common."

I nod. I can't help but agree. All the schools I've been to…there are almost too many to remember. And yet this is the first time I've run into someone I can relate to. Someone who knows what it's like to be a hollow shell in every yearbook they've ever appeared in.

My mind searches for a reply. I want her to know I agree. But part of me wants her to understand that she still needs to keep some distance. The last thing someone like me needs is a shadow. Or even an extra pair of watchful eyes.

"Deal," I manage to muster up, while reaching out my hand.

"Really, dude?" She laughs. "Put your hand away."

I retract my hand before looking around with flushed cheeks to make sure no one saw my dumb gesture.

"So…what does a *freelance researcher* do?" she says, making sure to put an extra-dorky inflection on my mother's job title.

"Companies hire her to do internal audits, or market research. A bunch of boring paperwork, really."

"And your dad?"

I freeze. Pizza crust is still dangling from my mouth, and I can feel myself staring blankly at her like she's just uttered a dirty word.

"Ah. Sore spot. Duly noted." She nods as she begins scraping the last remnants of her salad from her bowl.

I release my vacant trance and get back to chewing.

"So," she murmurs, "what made you want to take sociology?"

My gaze returns to hers. I don't know if she's truly interested, or if she's just that desperate to change the subject.

"Seemed interesting, I guess."

Danielle's hand pauses just as she tilts a bottle of water to her lips. She doesn't say anything, but her eyes thin, and a tickled smirk fills her face.

"My mom made me take it."

"That's more like it." She chuckles before guzzling half the bottle, while I toss the final morsels of crust into my mouth.

"You?"

It's funny. I can't remember the last time I asked someone my age a question and actually cared about their response.

"Thinkin' about choosing it as my college major. Studying people is kinda interesting."

"If you say so." I smirk.

The bell echoes through the cafeteria, just loud enough to drown out every student. We both start meticulously piling up our trash, like our parents are glaring over our shoulders. Danielle is the first to stand.

"Shall we do this again tomorrow?" she says, with an indifferent look glazed across her perfectly round face.

"Sure." I shrug, trying my best to seem just as nonchalant as her. "Danielle, right?"

"Yeah, but don't call me that." Her nose crinkles, and her shoulders shake like she's just seen a pool of vomit. "*Danielle* sounds like a prep school kid from the suburbs. Just call me *Dee*."

"Okie dokie, then. See you tomorrow, Dee?"

Okie dokie? Did I really just say that? I don't know if those words have ever come out of my mouth in my entire life. Danielle—I mean, Dee—just shakes her head.

"Good talk, Rion." She giggles before turning to join the masses by the trash cans.

And so it goes. Every day, Dee joins me at lunch. It's the only time we truly acknowledge each other, but I can't deny that it's the one thing I look forward to in school. It's the first time I've consistently talked to anyone other than my mother. Our conversations are usually short, almost like we're meeting for the first time each day.

One day, she tells me how much she hates being a military brat. Apparently, she can't wait to move away from her negligent parents. This makes me laugh. Me mentioning that I'd never want to be too far from Mom makes her eyes light up like I've muttered something insane.

Another day, we talk about music. She shares her favorite artists, none of which I'm familiar with. When I tell her that I like to listen to 80s and 90s hip-hop, she replies with a joke about how I need to update my playlist to something from this century.

By October, neither of us would admit to it, but we can probably pass a pop quiz on one another. I know her class schedule, where she lives, and what colleges she's applying to. And yet, when we walk through the halls, trot out to the bus lot, or even when we sit at opposite ends of sociology class…it's as if we've never spoken.

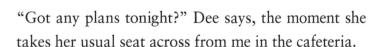

"Got any plans tonight?" Dee says, the moment she takes her usual seat across from me in the cafeteria.

My face gnarls. Somehow the words seem tangled in my head, like a phrase that doesn't quite compute.

"Huh?" I run my plastic fork through my plate of lukewarm spaghetti.

The pizza line is always long as hell on Fridays.

"Ya know...there's this magical thing called a *weekend* that kicks off every Friday night? It's all the rage with kids these days."

I chuckle at her sarcasm while she pulls a pair of perfectly sliced sandwiches from her lunch bag. I swear, her lunch always looks like something a third grader would have.

"Yeah, well, ya know...I usually just watch movies with Mom, or play video games."

"Well...if you'd like to interrupt the hermit life and get out of the house, we could go to the homecoming game tonight?"

My eyebrows perk up in surprise, and I stop chewing. A few weeks ago, she'd revealed how much she loved basketball. My food nearly launched from my jaws as I fought back laughter when she told me she had to stop playing herself, *because her legs stopped growing.* But I'd never gotten the vibe that she liked football, or that she'd want to attend one of the games at this school.

"Isn't the football team terrible?" I snicker.

Terrible is probably an understatement. There isn't a single plaque or trophy commemorating the school's football program, and apparently they only won two games last season.

"Oh, God," she replies. "They're awful! But popcorn, soda, people watching...it might be fun."

A lump fills my throat when I swallow.

"So you in?"

I can sense the look of reluctance pouring from my brow. I know I'd rather just spend another night levitating random things in the backyard. I've never been into sports. I've never even been to a school sporting event. Or any sporting event, for that matter. There's no point in purchasing cable packages when you're only in a house for a few months, so I hardly even watch games on television. It once crossed my mind to use my powers to play baseball, but I realized it would just be an easy way for someone to find out my secret.

"Maybe next time."

The sober words spout so quickly it feels like I didn't even say them. Dee casually shrugs and turns her focus to her meal. The remainder of lunch is filled with awkward conversations about homework. When the bell sounds, she gives me her usual smile and tells me to have a great weekend. As her tiny legs disappear down the hall, I can't help but think that my response bothers me more than it bothers her.

I sit along my open windowsill, tossing a stress ball out into the night air, and mentally retracting it back into my palm like a yo-yo. The bright lights from the school's football stadium shine from over the horizon to hide the starry sky. I keep telling myself that there's nothing wrong with wanting to toy with my unique powers rather than go watch my temporary high school lose a football game. Yet there's an emptiness in my stomach that even Mom's leftovers couldn't fill.

Is this how my mother feels when she refuses idle conversation with strangers, or politely spurns guys that ask her on dates? All I know is, I felt like a robot when I dismissed Dee, and every teacher's words after lunch went in one ear and out the other like gibberish. Maybe that's what I am—some stupid android with no father, no photos of friends to look back on...and no aspirations of the future.

The lights from Mom's car careen over the side of our house. I turn to glance at the clock sitting on my dresser drawer. It's half past nine. She seems to be getting home later and later each week. A deep groan skirts from my jaws as I toss the ball to the floor and listen to her trudge up the stairwell.

"Hi, sweetie," she says, as soon as she enters through my bedroom door.

"Hey, Ma," I reply, staring through the window.

"How was school?"

"Fine."

I can feel her disheartened glower bearing down on me, but I don't turn her way.

"Did you eat?"

"Yep."

I breathe a heavy sigh. She knows something is bothering me. Maybe she's too afraid to ask.

"Wanna watch a movie?"

I roll my eyes. Thank God she doesn't see me, or her guilt would turn to agitation.

"No."

I glance over my shoulder just enough to see her head bowing. I could easily just explain why I'm upset, but I want her to ask. Maybe if she doesn't force me to talk, she'll start to understand how frustrating it is to have a mother who rarely opens up.

"Well, we could..."

"I think I'm just gonna go to bed."

I stand and close my window before heading to the bathroom. I notice her in my periphery. I can tell that my words have only heightened her dejected state. It doesn't bother me much. She worries all the time. If she loses sleep over me tonight, it'll be no different than usual.

I plod through the cafeteria until I've reached my seat. It's been a Monday morning to forget. Not only did

I manage to bomb an English exam earlier, but every student has been buzzing about the exciting, upset victory at the homecoming game I chose to forgo. I pass a glance to the ridiculously outstretched pizza line before sitting and staring at the pale bun of the chicken sandwich on my tray. It might as well be prison food.

Dee comes trotting my way, and it heightens my mood. We haven't spoken since Friday, and I'm eager to talk about other things. I prattle my fingers harder against the cool table surface, with each of her methodical strides. It's been so long since I've found comfort in another person's presence that isn't Mom's.

She hesitates. My brow curls in confusion as she glances over her shoulder to the edge of the cafeteria. She turns back my way with a disheartened grimace, before continuing on her original path.

"What's up?" I say to her, before she even takes her seat.

She sighs, then looks back once more. I turn to follow her gaze across the room. I must be mistaken. Her gaze seems to be scanning between the farmer kid, the boy with the metal boot, and the husky girl who always sits alone, eating a chicken sandwich with ranch-drenched fries. It's funny, we're halfway through the semester, and I'd almost forgotten them.

"I think we should ask Jed, Brendan, and Alex to sit with us," Dee says.

The sincerity in her tone is one I've never heard from her.

"Say what?"

She turns to me with an offended sneer.

"What? Have you ever talked to them? They're such buzzkills, Dee." I scoff, as if I've ever made an effort to strike up conversation with any of them.

I haven't even bothered to remember their names. Yet here I am, acting like I've already crossed them off of my imaginary list of friends.

Her gaze switches back over her shoulder. Her eyes remind me of a child watching puppies at a kennel. None of them look lonely to me. On the contrary, they look like I did before Dee plopped in front of me two months ago—like they just want to be left alone.

"I mean…they look like they're fine by themselves," I say, just as a calming huff escapes Dee.

She turns back to me, for good this time, and starts thumping the containers of food from her lunch bag and onto the table.

"Why do you have to shut everyone out?" she says.

I look up just in time to catch her scathing glare. The morsel in my mouth lodges in my cheek, and I give her the most scornful look I've given anyone since Gary Moses back in elementary school.

"What?" she says. "Are they not interesting enough for you?"

"No…I just don't pity every quiet kid I come across, like you do," I growl, before taking a massive, angry bite of my sandwich.

Dee doesn't respond. She becomes stunned by the abrupt thump of the vending machine behind me.

Damn. Did I do that? I calm myself. My breaths steady, and I take a long sip of fruit juice. Dee gives me a cautiously bewildered look before bowing her massive eyes apologetically.

"I'm sorry," I grumble.

"I know. Me, too. I guess I used to be like that. And when it was me, I always wished someone would come over and talk to me."

We nod, then go back to eating our meals. After several minutes of frustration-quenching silence, that robotic feeling begins to hover over me again like a cloud.

"Basketball season starts in a few weeks," I say. "Maybe…we can all go to the first home game together?"

She looks at me with a large smile. It's the brightest one I've seen from her yet. Deep down, I think she knows I don't want to add to our circle, or go to the game. The thought of me considering it is what creates this gleam in her eyes.

I'm surprised at how much I enjoy making her smile. After all, she is my best friend.

Wait...it's finally hit me. I have a best friend.

CHAPTER 4

THE VOID

MOM IS LATE GETTING HOME TONIGHT...AGAIN.
She left a note telling me to fix myself dinner. It's nearly ten o'clock now, but I've tried not to spend my time worrying. Instead, I look back on the day's events. Specifically, I focus on when I managed to move the vending machine. I'd gotten perturbed with Dee, and I was able to move it without even focusing on it. Makes me wonder—is the key to lifting heavier objects in channeling my emotions?

An hour goes by. It appears my theory isn't far off. I spend the time turning my concern into focus as I beam at the living room couch for nearly fifteen minutes. It takes my head being drenched with sweat, and my eyes growing bloodshot red, but it manages to hover a few inches off the soft carpet. If it weren't for the throbbing headache that followed, I'd be in full celebratory mode.

Our only house phone blares from the kitchen, sending the pounding in my skull into an increased frenzy. The couch thumps back down. I snarl and head to the kitchen, holding my left temple. A relieved breath cascades through my lips as I bring the phone whirling across the room and into my hands.

"Hello?"

"Is Doctor Grean in?"

I scowl at the adverse tone of the woman on the other end. A proper greeting would've been nice.

"No, she isn't at the moment. Can I take a message?"

Click. I bring the phone from my face and peer at it with discontent. What a jerk.

I send the phone sailing back to the holder on the wall. It slams against it and topples to the floor. I chuckle, and my eyes thin like someone has just challenged me to a duel. It looks like accuracy will be my next lesson for the night.

I clap and rub my hands together. My face turns to a focused, but eager grimace. The phone is no longer visible. It has ducked below the wooden kitchen island, but I can still sense its location. With a flick of my wrist, I have brought it from the floor and into view.

I smirk as it whirls back into my hand. If I take my time, I could place it back on its white holder with ease. But I know that if I can become precise enough to put it in place in a mere second, there'll be no telling what I can accomplish.

My first attempt is a success, but it feels too easy. I need to do it faster. I close my eyes this time, and the phone retracts to my palm. My fingers dance around it. I bite my lip as I visualize the holder across the room.

Crash!

My eyes widen as soon as I fling the phone. Might as well have just fastball pitched it into the wall, because now there's a small crater where its holder used to be.

"Oh, shit!"

My heart races as I scurry across the room. The phone itself has shattered into pieces. I run my hands through my hair and glance around the room like I'm trying to make sure no one is here to see my blunder.

I have to focus. Panicking now will accomplish nothing. With my abilities, I collect the phone shards and fling the pieces into the trash. My mind is flipping between where to find another phone this late, and what excuse I can come up with to justify a hole in the kitchen wall.

Something catches my ear in the distance. I scamper to the window and peer through the curtains as delicately as I can. Please don't let it be Mom!

A massive sigh of relief courses through my chest once I realize it was likely a car passing by, or perhaps nothing at all.

I sprint upstairs to the utility closet beside my mother's room. If there is a spare phone, or something to make the hole less noticeable, it'll be in here. I nearly slip and fall when my socks glide against the firm carpet. When I reach the doorway, I give the knob a tug, but the door fails to budge.

"Oh, c'mon!"

I wriggle it a few more tedious times, like the lock will magically come undone after enough yanks. I squint toward the tiny keyhole embedded within the chipped golden paint. I have no idea where the key to the door might be. Hell, I don't even remember my mother ever locking it, let alone placing anything inside. But if there's a replacement phone, or even tools in this house, this is the only place I'll find them.

I take a deep breath and hold my hand beneath the rusted latch. I focus intensely. I imagine the inner workings of the lock—its molds, its ridges. With a twitch of my thumb, I am delighted to hear a light click.

My eyes widen. The lock is undone. I pump my fist and swing the door open. There is no time to celebrate my minor victory. Mom could be home any minute.

The closet is much larger than I'd imagined. It looks as if it could've been used as a bathroom once. It smells of old, damp cardboard and fresh plaster. A few useless, rusted tools are sprawled against the opposite wall. Boxes are scattered throughout. Half of them are the empty containers we used to move our things in.

"C'mon," I whisper, as I begin tossing the empty boxes aside with flicks of my wrist. "There's got to be something in here."

Sweat bears down my brow. What am I doing? What am I possibly looking for? Do I really think I have time to install a new phone, or fix a hole in the wall before my mother returns? Instead of trying to fix it, I should be thinking of an alibi.

My frantic movements stop as I realize that I am standing in the center of two mountains of toppled boxes. My feet are engulfed in a sea of cardboard. A deep sigh billows from my jaws. This was one long, fruitless endeavor.

I wave my hands, and the boxes separate in a circle around me. In my panic, I have created a new problem. Many of the boxes I mentally tossed like tissue paper weren't empty. Now, there are important-looking documents, receipts, and old folders scattered around the closet like dressing covering one of Dee's salads.

A smirk fills my face. Some of those boxes must have been heavy, and I moved them around without even thinking. Makes me wonder if the weight of the object even matters, or if such limitations are only in my head.

A light flashes through the window in the hallway, and I shake myself from my daze. No doubt it's Mom's car pulling up over the hill. The odds of multiple cars passing by our secluded home at this hour are slim to none. My gaze darts from side to side. This problem—at least, the bulk of it—will have to wait.

I step from the center of the dusty floor and back into the supple hall carpet. One last sight of the muddled closet makes me cringe when I slam the door shut. I almost forget to relock it before springing back downstairs.

"Hey, Ma!" I shout, the second I enter the living room.

Sweat flushes down my forehead, and there is a distinctive pant billowing from my chest. The front door shuts behind her, and she turns to look at me with a befuddled stare.

"Hi, sweetie. Everything okay?"

A distressing lump fills my throat. I look into her weary brown eyes. She looks beyond tired, like she could collapse onto the floor.

"Yeah. I was just doing some exercising."

I want to slap myself in the face as soon as the words flutter from my lips. She can't possibly believe that lame excuse. I'm still wearing my school clothes, for God's sake.

"Okay, honey." She nods before darting for the kitchen.

I curl my brow, and my cloaking smile fades as I hurry to follow her.

"I'm sorry about being late. I had a ton of work to get done."

"It's fine." I fold my arms as I stand in the kitchen doorway.

I watch as she places her bag on the kitchen counter and begins to wash her hands. My gaze drifts from her disheartening look to the glaring hole beside the refrigerator.

"I made myself a sandwich and chips for dinner."

"Good." She smiles.

My throat runs dry when she dries her hands and does exactly what I'd hoped she wouldn't do. I clamor forward with widened eyes as she moves to the fridge, right beside the man-made crater in the wall. I begin searching my empty mind for an excuse that isn't as dumb as my last one.

"I'm sorry!" I blurt out, as she opens the fridge, and closes it almost as fast.

She turns and gives me a startled stare while clasping a bottle of water. Again, I am confused. Surely she didn't fail to notice it.

"About what, sweetheart?"

"Umm...the uhh...the hole."

I point beside the fridge. The hollow cavern in our kitchen wall seems ten times larger than it looked fifteen minutes ago. I swear my heart is going to jump out of my chest.

"Oh!" Her eyes widen.

"It was an accident!"

"Well, I'll get it patched up this weekend." She turns away as if she's only seen a tiny scuff.

My scowl is more harsh than ever. She grabs her bag and approaches me. I think this must surely be some sort of new disciplinary tactic, until she kisses me on the cheek and nudges by me.

"I'm gonna shower and head to bed," she says, before reaching the staircase.

She doesn't even turn around to speak. I stand idle at the edge of the kitchen.

That's it? No questioning about how the hole got in the wall? No questioning why I was doing calisthenics late at night in my school attire? Not even one question about how my day was?

"Can you turn everything off down there?"

"Yeah...sure. Goodnight, Ma."

Her door shuts, but I don't hear a response.

The morning sunrise has barely crept through the kitchen windows to highlight the cracked void beside the refrigerator. My empty gaze is focused forward, oblivious that my cereal has turned into a soggy mess. My school bus will be here soon, but Mom has yet to emerge from her room. I keep hearing loud rumbling coming from her door, like she has woken up late and is rushing to get ready for work. Consistently coming home after nine, ignoring when I've done something stupid...in all the years, she's never acted like this.

"Yes. I know. I'll be there as soon as possible!" she yammers into her cell phone, when her door finally opens.

I look up, and she's scurrying down the stairs with her bag clutched over her shoulder. She ends the call and comes toward me. She isn't wearing her usual professional pantsuit. Instead, she's dressed in a white polo and khaki pants that are both wrinkled like she'd picked them up off of the floor.

"Sorry, sweetie. Work problems."

She rushes over to kiss me on the forehead. When she leans in, all of the folders and books in her bag spill onto the kitchen floor.

"Damn it!" she growls, and drops to her knees.

I've never heard my mother curse before. The words seem awkward coming from her, even in frustration.

"It's okay, Ma."

I rush to help her scoop everything up, keeping my gaze focused on her worrisome brow. Seeing her this way makes my heart feel like a weight is strapped to it. There are bags under her eyes, and her hair looks like it hasn't been combed.

After a few seconds, everything has been piled back into her bag. I can tell we've done a lousy job, because the bag looks even more full than it did before. Mom doesn't even bother to attempt another kiss before she hurries back for the front door, and I hurry behind her.

"I'll probably be late again tonight." She turns the knob.

"It's fine. I've got an exam to study for, anyway."

"Love you, sweetheart."

"Love you too, Ma."

The door slams shut. I want to rush after her and tell her everything will be okay, but I remember that the bus will be here soon. I stand still until I hear her SUV speeding down the road.

My body feels numb as I re-enter the kitchen. I don't bother to finish breakfast, or even pick up my bowl. I use my abilities to dump the contents into the trash and toss the bowl into the sink. Next, I send my chair scooting back against the table before placing my focus on my backpack resting beside it. As soon as I clench my fist to bring it whirling across the room, something catches my eye—a tiny object laying where my backpack used to be. Sunlight from the window bounces from its surface and springs into my gaze. I approach it with reluctance, as if it might be a disgusting insect that scurried in unnoticed. Only takes a few steps for the object to become clear.

A curious gnarl fills my face. The object is a thin flash drive with a rubbery, red covering surrounding its metal shell. It must've fallen from my mother's bag and slid underneath my backpack.

I hear the rumbling engine of a school bus echoing through the window. I shake from my stupor and hold my hand forward. The flash drive zips into my palm, and I shove it into my pocket before heading for the front door.

CHAPTER 5

THE FLASH DRIVE

"HEY! EARTH TO RION!" DEE SHOUTS, WHILE snapping her tiny fingers in front of my face.

My eyes flutter like I'm waking up from a dream. I glance down at the untouched pizza on my plate. I can barely remember entering the cafeteria, let alone sitting down.

"I'm sorry. What?" I gawk.

"What's up with you today?"

"Nothing."

"Does it have something to do with that flash drive?"

My gaze jolts up. Dee continues to glare at me with a raised eyebrow. I don't know how to respond. My hand begins to creep down to the protruding hump in my jean pocket like I need to make sure the flash drive is still there.

"Umm…"

"You were staring at it by your locker like a full-on weirdo." She laughs.

"Oh…uhh." My gaze shifts to the side.

"C'mon. Tell me."

The thought of being able to confide in someone is a foreign luxury that intrigues me. I pass several glances between her and my pocket before peering around to make sure no one else is watching. Dee is more attentive than I've ever seen her. I can see my reflection in those gigantic black pupils as we both lean forward.

"My mom's been acting weird lately," I whisper.

"Weirder than usual?" Dee chuckles.

I roll my eyes. "She's been coming home later and later every night. We haven't had dinner together in over a week, and last night I put a hole in the wall—"

"Wait. You put a hole in the wall?"

"Yeah. It was an accident. Long story. The point is, she didn't even get mad or punish me when she got home. It was like I'd only spilled a drink or something."

Dee leans back and mouths the word *wow*. She moves toward me with a hefty smirk when she realizes there's more to the story.

"This morning, she was rushing out the door and all of her stuff fell out of her bag. I helped her put everything back inside, but this flash drive got left behind."

I reach into my pocket and pull it out for her to see. She glances at it, then looks at me like I've gone crazy.

"Soooo...what's on it?"

"I don't know. But my mom doesn't even own a laptop. And these companies she works for don't let her leave with confidential information."

"Well...I think we should go find out." Dee snickers as she begins gathering her things.

"What? Like right now?"

"Uhh, yeah."

She grabs my wrist in one hand, and snatches her lunch bag with the other. I barely have enough time to grab my backpack and fling it over my shoulder. I have to twist my body several times to keep my knee from slamming against other seats as she pulls me past the table and toward the hallway.

"Where are we going?"

"Computer lab! It's open during lunch period."

I nod and follow closely. We head to the library I've never set foot in. Smells like old dictionaries, and every wooden surface looks like it was made during the Civil War.

A few faculty members pass curious glances toward us when we rush inside. I try to avert my gaze so they can't see the unnerved scowl on my face. Dee seems completely unbothered. She leads me to a small room in the back of the library, where desktop computers line the walls, with a few tables in the center. Once she's made sure no one else is inside, she shuts the door behind me and plops into a seat.

"What if someone comes in?" My eyes are wide, and my heart is racing like we're doing something illegal.

"Even nerds prefer lunch over the computer lab. We'll be fine." She shoves her hand into my pocket to remove the flash drive.

"Hey!"

"Shhhh. We're in a library."

I scowl, but the intrigue quickly returns. I make one more cautious inspection of the scenery before kneeling over Dee's shoulder. She leans over and gives me a wink as she plugs the drive into the side of the computer. My heartbeat thumps when she clicks the mousepad to open up a window on the monitor.

"Hmm," she grunts.

"What?"

"There's nothing really on here." She shrugs as she tilts the screen so close to my face that I can feel its warmth.

"What do you mean?"

I snatch the mouse from her hand and nudge her aside. The only icon on the screen is a folder labeled

FB. I click on it over and over again, as if each result will yield something different.

"You don't have to be a computer hacker to know when a folder is empty or not." Dee scoffs.

I stare at the screen. A deep sigh billows from my chest. Don't know what I was expecting to find. Something about my father? Something about my abilities? Hell, even boring details about Mom's job would have sufficed. At least I might've had a clue into why she's been acting so strange.

"What does FB stand for?"

I ignore her. I've been asking that same question in my head since the moment I saw the letters underneath the folder. That I don't know the answer infuriates me.

"Maybe the thing is for emergencies or something. I don't know." Dee stands.

I remain in a sulking position for several seconds. I can hear the faint hum of every computer in the room, like they're all taunting me. Dee looks back at me and hesitates before pulling the flash drive out of the computer and handing it to me.

"Here."

"No. You can keep it."

I shove past her and adjust the strap of my backpack. Dip my head low as I fling open the door to exit the computer lab.

"Hey, wait!"

I don't stop, or even slow my pace when she calls to me.

"What's wrong?" She scurries behind me. "What did you expect to be on there?"

I hear her words, but all I can think about is all the questions I still have. Maybe it was naïve of me to expect something more from a simple flash drive. But is it so wrong for me to want answers? Do I really have to go through the rest of this stale life without knowing anything about my mother, or about myself?

"Rion, will you please just talk?"

Her clamoring muddles my racing thoughts. I roll my eyes, curl my fists, and without warning or reason, I can feel my despair turning to frustration.

"Would you just drop it!" I turn and meet her massive eyes with a scowl. "It's none of your damn business, Dee."

I try to simmer my huffing breaths, when a table suddenly shakes in the corner of my eye. Dee freezes, her awestricken glare turning glossy with each second of silence. The few students and faculty in the library begin glaring in our direction.

I turn and clomp away as if nothing I've just said was rude and unnecessary. I hear no footsteps behind me, and I don't turn back. I'm too agitated to deal with Dee's prying questions. I don't want to get too angry and accidentally send a bookshelf toppling over. I just want to get through the rest of the day so I can go home and pretend like I never wondered about that stupid flash drive.

Rain is bearing down my windowsill when I wake up the next morning. It's the perfect weather for my mood. I spent most of last night making one of the kitchen chairs spin, while eating microwaved pizza rolls. For once, I actually wanted to talk to Mom about my day. I wanted to ask her about the flash drive and see if she'd offer up some motherly advice on how to address Dee. But once again, she was absurdly late getting home.

I was already in bed when she came and kissed me goodnight. She barely spoke, and went to her room without even mentioning the flash drive she'd left behind. I almost feel like she was afraid to speak. It's like she's hiding something from me. Well...more than she usually hides from me.

Mom rushes off for work as soon as I come downstairs for breakfast. This time, she blows me a kiss instead of placing one on my cheek. I try to ignore the gesture, but it stays on my mind all morning.

My sour mood carries over through each class. Instead of paying attention, I glare at the outside downpour until it's nearly noon and the sun is finally shining again. When the bell sounds for lunch, I gather my things. For the first time all year, no other student beats me through the door.

I stride toward the cafeteria in a hurry. Dee hasn't spoken to me all day. We briefly made eye contact in Keenan's class, but she looked the other way like I was a gnat fluttering in the distance. I know I need to apologize, but for some reason part of me doesn't want to. Part of me meant what I said. Dee can be annoying sometimes, but…she is my only friend.

I find her in our usual area of the cafeteria. She has already pulled out a bowl of pasta and a box of juice. With each footstep, my thoughts scurry with what to say to her.

"Hey," I murmur casually, as I take a seat across from her.

She shoots me a fierce scowl. Her usual wide eyes are thin and murky, but the glare doesn't last long. She looks down at her meal and begins rummaging through it with her fork as if there's a prize hidden within. I tap the table and think about what to say next.

"How'd you do on that quiz?"

That's it? That's what I came up with? I want to slap myself. But before I can, Dee slams her fork onto the table.

"I get it, Rion." She scoffs as our eyes meet. "You're not really good at friendship."

Her words are cold and distant, like she's talking to a stray dog, or someone that angered her at the DMV. I feel myself glaring off in the distance like a punished child trying to keep from whimpering.

"Neither am I. But there's a difference between being defensive, and flat-out being an asshole."

Before I can speak, she grabs her things in one scoop and stomps away. I can feel several gawking stares on me. Dee doesn't look back, and eventually takes rest just a few tables away...right in front of Alex. To my surprise, and slight embarrassment, the blonde-haired girl smiles at Dee in the midst of chomping on her usual French fries coated in ranch dressing.

I was expecting a look of shock on Alex's face, like the empty stare I had when Dee first sat in front of me. At the very least, I was expecting a relieved smile from a girl who was finally being acknowledged after months of sitting alone. But they immediately begin talking, like they've done this before.

That's when it hits me, and I feel my brown cheeks turning a scarlet red. Dee has already made other friends. And me...I might've just lost the only one I had.

I think about Dee the entire ride home, and about how I should've just said *sorry*. I ponder what I can do to make it up to her. I'm sure she can't stay mad at me for too long if I'm sincere. I've never had to apologize to a friend before. What do I do, exactly?

The piercing creak of the school bus sounds, and I realize we're at my stop. I've barely taken my last step from the bus floor and into the rain-soaked grass, when my focus shifts. I peer across the front yard and see Mom's SUV in the driveway. She has been coming home late for weeks. And yet here she is…home early?

My pace is rapid and direct as I clamor for the front door. When I move past her SUV, my hand brushes the shimmering crimson hood. It feels warm from the glaring sunlight, and virtually every droplet of rain has evaporated from its surface. How long has she been home?

Part of me is excited. I feel like we haven't really spoken in weeks. I need to talk about this Dee situation with someone, even if I'm not sure if Mom can actually help. I also can't help but be curious. She's been so visibly stressed lately, and I'm trying to fight the notion that she's home early because something is wrong.

As soon as I open the front door, my feet slam into a box that is sitting along the floor. My chest grows tight as I scan everything downstairs, from the living room to the newly patched wall in the kitchen. There are boxes everywhere. Every surface has been cleaned like a hotel maid has just swept through. My head whips from side to side. The dishes are all packed in a box on the kitchen table. The TV and the Blu-ray player are no longer resting along the living room entertainment center.

"Hi, sweetie."

I look up and see Mom at the top of the stairs. A hint of apprehension is evident in her tone. Her face appears blank and uneasy. I've seen this look before, far too often.

An overt queasiness fills my chest. Mom starts explaining, but her words barely resonate in my head. I catch the necessary details as I aimlessly glare at the wall. Apparently, she's been *reassigned* to some lab in South Dakota.

South Dakota? Oh, joy. I guess I'll pass the time by levitating buffalo through open fields.

I roll my eyes, and a soft, belligerent breath creeps through my lips. Mom has a dejected stare as I pass by her and stomp to my room. I use my powers to close the door just hard enough to show my agitation without being too disrespectful.

I don't come out for the rest of the night, not even for dinner. Mom doesn't bother trying to make me. The only time I hear from her before I go to sleep is when she taps on the door and whispers goodnight. I can sense the knot in her chest when I don't respond.

I'm able to finish out the remainder of the week at Tyler High. My last few days are like all of the other departures I've had in the past. I am told to clean out my locker, which is an easy task, considering there was never much in it. A few teachers give me a halfhearted hug and wish me luck, as if they'll remember me by the end of the school year.

I never tell Dee that I'm moving. She's still pissed at me, and I don't want her to feel as if I'm just trying to garner sympathy by giving her the news. Besides, after this week I'll probably never see her again. Why try to salvage something that has no future?

For us, Thursday began as Wednesday left off. There was some eye contact during lunch, but it lasted so briefly that it was almost impossible to consider it intentional. The farmer kid, and the kid with the boot, have now joined her at Alex's lunch table. I still don't know if Dee really enjoys their company. But their smiles and occasional laughter sure seem genuine. I find myself feeling appreciative as I sit alone and watch them. After how I acted, they deserve Dee's companionship more than I do.

By Friday, Dee has heard that I'm leaving. Mr. Keenan even makes an announcement to ensure everyone *wishes me Godspeed*. But Dee is the only one in the class who doesn't turn to acknowledge me. There are no goodbyes, and as I walk on the bus to leave on Friday afternoon, I'm left wondering how, and why, I let my only friend slip away.

CHAPTER 6

THE ROAD AHEAD

I'VE SPENT THE PAST FEW HOURS SCANNING THE warm, rigid asphalt as our crimson SUV flies across it. My gaze shifts to the rearview mirror and past the stacks of boxes that hinder our view of what's behind us. I stare at the open road as if I hope to see Dee driving after me in her parents' car, but all I see are rundown motels and gas stations.

"Why don't we stop for some food in a bit," Mom mutters, to break me from my trance.

She's had a pathetic tone ever since she told me we had to move, and I haven't spoken to her since we got in the car.

"C'mon, Rion. You have to talk to me."

A heavy sigh billows from my lips as I look at her. She has a hasty smile planted on her face that seems inviting. For a moment, I think about brushing her off, but I decide to change my tune. For years, I've been wanting her to fully engage with me. Now is the time to finally have the awkward conversation that's been building between us.

"Aren't you tired of this?" I groan.

"I...I thought you'd have gotten used to this by now, sweetie."

I remain silent and stare at the empty fields in the distance as if they are more interesting than anything she has to say. I can see her reflection in the window as her look grows more disheartened.

"I don't want to just get used to life, Ma. I want to enjoy it."

I can feel the knot in her chest when the words leave my lips. I don't want her to feel like I'm ungrateful for all of the things she's provided for me, but enough is enough. If I can't tell her how I really feel now, then I probably never will.

"It would be nice to have actual relationships with people that last for more than a few weeks."

My gaze shifts back to her as she shakes her head. Her palms seem to be gripping the steering wheel tighter with each frustrated breath.

"Rion," she groans, as our gazes briefly meet. "You could've gotten that girl's number and kept in contact with her, or anyone else you've met over the years. But *you* chose to be distant."

"Yeah, and who do you think I get that trait from?" My brow curls in frustration. "You think we're best buds because we watch movies together, but I don't know anything about you. I learned more about Dee in two months than I've learned about my own mother in a lifetime."

Another sigh brushes through my mom's lips. She doesn't look directly at me, but I can sense the thoughts swimming through her eyes.

"Is this about your father again?"

"Yes!"

Her brow coils, and I have to remind myself that I'm not talking to just anyone.

"It's about all of your secrets, Ma. Not just that," I say, in a much softer tone. "You never talk about your job. You come home late with no real explanation. You don't have friends, or talk about your life before I came along. How can you expect me to open up to you, or anyone else, when you don't do the same?"

She remains quiet. The sorrow seems to be building in her reddened eyes, but I don't know what to do. My arms stiffen, and my lips tremble. The sound of tires rumbling along rigid asphalt is the only thing I hear. Neither of us seems to know who should speak first.

"It's not that I don't want to tell you things, Rion," she murmurs, through a rigid tone. "It's just...there are certain things about my past that I don't understand, and things that I'm not proud of. I...I don't want you to see me how I see myself."

My throat tightens as she fights back tears. I want to look away, but the empty, woeful glare in her eyes won't let me.

"I wish you didn't have to live the way you do. That's why I want you to go off to college."

I roll my eyes and shake my head. Mom takes her hand from the steering wheel and wraps her fingers around my left palm.

"These next few years are so important, Rion. This is when you really find yourself. I'm not going to be here forever. I want you to create your own path and decide the type of person you want to be."

Again, a sigh pours from my belly. The thought of her acting like she's going somewhere without me makes my skin grow cold.

"So...say I go to college and hypothetically meet a bunch of awesome new people that make me feel like I belong. I'm just supposed to forget about you and ignore that if something happens to you, I wouldn't know who to call or what to do?"

"No...I'm not saying that, Rion. I just want you to..."

Her warm palm retracts and returns to the steering wheel. I glare at her with a confused scowl, waiting for her to finish her sentence, but her gaze is now glued to the rearview mirror. Her pupils are widened, and her mouth is cracked open like she's just seen a ghost.

"What's wrong, Ma?"

She doesn't reply.

Flashing lights begin to blare from behind us. I turn and peer past the horde of boxes until I have a firm view of the back windshield. A white and brown state trooper's vehicle is now speeding toward us with its siren blasting. I scan every part of the surrounding highway to see if some other car might've caught the officer's eye, but our SUV is the only vehicle on the road.

"Why are they pulling us over?" I grunt, as my vision whips to the speedometer.

We're barely going over fifty miles an hour, and I'm almost certain the speed limit is sixty.

I glance at Mom. She still has a nervous gawk, and her gaze hasn't left the rearview mirror.

Our SUV begins to slow down, and my heart starts to thump. I tell myself to remain calm. That we just have a broken taillight or something. When we pull over and come to a complete stop, Mom finally turns to me.

"Everything is going to be fine, sweetie."

I'm not sure what to make of her tone. Her voice is assuring, but her eyes are swimming with anxiety. I turn to the back windshield again, just as the lone state trooper steps from his vehicle and begins his methodical stride toward Mom's door. His uniform is a pristine light brown, and sunlight bounces from the gold trimming of his badge. He has a chiseled face and a slim, muscular build, like he was born to be a cop. I can already see our vehicle's reflection in the tinted shades that cover his eyes.

"Don't do anything unless I tell you to." Mom twists the key underneath the steering wheel to silence the SUV's rumbling engine.

I can't help but be confused. What exactly does she think I'm going to do?

"What's the problem, Officer?"

Her voice sounds polite as can be. But still, the officer stops and leans over the hood of the car with a vacant grimace. Slowly, he scans the inside of our vehicle like he's searching for something specific.

"Someone called in a stolen SUV," he grumbles.

My heart freezes. I can feel the nervous perspiration building along my brow. I've never been in a car that's been pulled over, but I'm pretty sure they're supposed to ask for license and registration first.

"There must be some mistake."

This time, there's an unsubtle belligerence to Mom's tone. It's the same familiar, faulty twinge her voice has when she's asking me a rhetorical question after I've pissed her off.

"Out of the vehicle. Both of you."

My eyes grow wider when I notice his hand hovering over the taser along his belt. Mom turns to me and our gazes lock. My chest continues to thump until she gives me a fervent nod and gentle smile.

"It's okay," she whispers, before opening her door.

The look in her youthful brown eyes is one I've never seen before, and I can't quite pinpoint its nature. Is she worried? Angry? Perhaps both?

"Hands on the vehicle," the state trooper barks, barely a second after I've stepped into the cool air.

I glare into his tinted frames with a fearsome snarl, but do as he says.

"Are you carrying any firearms?"

"No," Mom groans.

As soon as she has her palms placed against our vehicle's crimson shell, the officer begins rigidly patting her down from her shoulders to her ankles. I can feel my blood boiling every time his hands slap against her.

"You're under arrest," he says, as if Mom has done something to provoke his anger.

My eyes nearly jolt from the sockets when he pulls out his handcuffs and yanks Mom's wrists behind her back.

"What for?" I scoff as I release my hands from the car and rush for the other side of the SUV.

"Stop where you are, right now!" the officer shouts.

My footsteps cease. My intense glare hasn't diminished, and my fists are still clenched. I'm mere feet from Mom and the officer. He has one hand clamped around my mother's wrists, and the other clasping the handle of the gun inside its holster.

"Get on the ground and put your hands on your head!"

I don't budge.

"I said, on the ground, now!"

He yanks the gun from his belt and points it toward my chest. My heart is thumping, and my teeth grind between my tightened lips. I'm certain I could mentally rip the weapon from his grasp, but I don't want to risk Mom's safety. As I slowly un-ball my fists and begin to raise my hands , my gaze finally drifts to Mom. There's a strange look of stern desperation on her face, but I can sense a sureness beaming from her stare and into mine.

The sun bares down. There is still a chilling breeze in the air, but I feel like I'm in a sauna. I finally begin to lower my knees to the ground, but I keep my focus on Mom. Her eyes grow more fearsome as the state trooper steps forward, his gun still drawn. My head is fluttering with questions that I don't have time to ask. My heartbeat races more rapidly, and the sweat on my forehead seems to flood my face like I've been doused with a bucket of water.

Then…it happens. Mom makes one quick nod. It's the last gesture necessary to cease my frantic mind. The look in her eyes is as unrelenting as any look I've ever seen from anyone. She plants an elbow into the officer's nose. Once he clutches his face, she dives for the ground.

It's as if my heartbeat has ceased, and everything is moving in slow motion. My face molds into an intense grimace as I focus on the officer's frame like the rest of the world is a black void. He releases his hand from his bloodied nose and points his gun forward. A new sensation surges through my body. It is a feeling I've never had before when attempting to use my abilities. Fear, nervousness, desperation, even anger—they are all there. I can feel adrenaline coursing through my veins, and my insides flaring like my chest is an over-heated tea kettle.

Without hesitation, I fling my arms forward with fingers splayed. Invisible energy seems to shoot from my mind, and through my outstretched limbs, with the ease of a blink. The officer zings into the air like he's a baseball being smacked by the bat of an All-Star slugger. His body curls like a stuffed animal as he flies backward and slams against the windshield of his police car.

I am amazed and horrified by my own power. It's as if I was floating above and watching everything take place. I remain still, my knees trembling against the ground as I stare at the officer's body. His head trembles to confirm he isn't dead.

Mom snatches my outstretched wrist and pulls me to my feet. She doesn't even make eye contact when she opens up the passenger door of the SUV and shoves me inside. My body feels numb as I glare at the empty road ahead with a widened jaw. Confusion begins to set in as soon as Mom has slammed her door and ignited the car's engine.

How long has she known about my abilities? Why did she wait until now to acknowledge them? For years, I've practiced moving inanimate objects both small and large. For years, I've accidentally created destruction that I've attempted to cover up. But never have I done anything like this. And yet, as our car speeds ahead, I can't help but wonder why I'm the only one who is shocked by what has just transpired.

My limbs feel weary, like I've just spent hours in a gym. The dank sweat on my clothes overpowers the smell of dirt and oil that surrounds us. The questions continue to swarm in my head as we speed down a vacant road. My mother. The researcher. The silent woman with no friends. She just assaulted a state trooper. She watched her son use superpowers. And yet she hasn't said a word. It's as if she was prepared for this encounter, right down to the smallest detail. I realize, at this point, that no amount of time may be sufficient to answer all the questions I have hidden inside.

"Seatbelt!" Mom snaps.

Before I know it, the car is whipping around a corner.

"Mom! What the hell?"

I raise my arms above my head as if they'll protect me in the event of a crash.

"Watch your mouth!"

Really, Mom? I can't say *hell*? Even under these circumstances, the slight hint of a swear word irks you? I shrug off this notion and return my gaze ahead. There are a few service stations, what looks like an abandoned home, a few trees, but no real traces of mass civilization.

We speed through red lights and swerve around corners. I glance at the back windshield to count the inevitable pack of cop cars in pursuit, but there's nothing. No police sirens. No traces of any other vehicle. And yet my mother speeds forward and clings to the steering wheel as if someone is hot on our tails.

"Mom!" I shout.

My conscience is yammering. Enough is enough. There are just too many questions.

"Mom! Tell me what's going on."

"I..." Her voice is raspy and barely audible.

She continues to stare forward without blinking, and a red tint begins to spread throughout the once-fervent whites of her eyes. She wants to cry, but something inside her won't let a tear fall.

"Mom...please," I murmur.

She finally turns to face me, with a grimace that looks weary and dejected. This look—it feels new, and yet almost familiar. It's like every burden she's ever had has finally become too much. She looks as if she's ready to release every secret she's ever held. Her mouth opens to speak, but again, we are interrupted.

Her gaze darts toward the rearview mirror. My heart jumps with frustration as my gaze reluctantly follows hers. We are no longer alone on this open road. Three vehicles are now approaching at a ferocious speed.

In the center is a machine I can only describe as the unholy lovechild of a tank and a double-decker bus. It is a matte black with windows as dark as the Grim Reaper's robe. There are no SWAT logos or government tags along the doors or hood.

On each side are two black SUV's with windows as tinted as the hell machine in the center. The sun shimmers around their edges like a coat of polished armor. Looks like something out of a nightmare.

Mom jams her foot harder on the gas, and the engine starts to hum even more. I glance at the orange needle on the speedometer, shaking at its max. But the vehicles behind still move closer and closer. With each waning second, I make an attempt to peer inside their darkened windows, but I see nothing. I look back at Mom with a worrisome scowl. My inquiries have left me for the moment. Now, I only wish we could move even faster.

"Head down!" Mom shouts, just before a bullet hammers into the center of the back windshield.

I flinch, but Mom just grits her teeth and grips the steering wheel as if only a light mist of rain has clipped the glass.

My body shifts to the side as we make a sharp turn. Dust flares from beneath our tires like we're on a closed course racing track. I grasp the edges of the door paneling, and feel my teeth chatter.

"Holy shi—" I spout.

Our car crashes through a wooden fence that separates asphalt from grass. The vehicle jerks and bounces, but doesn't slow down. We rush ahead at a speed I've never remotely felt before. I am barely able to capture my surroundings as they whisk by.

"Hold on, baby!"

She makes another swift right turn. I reach for whatever I can, but it does little to keep my body from jolting to my left. My insides squirm as if I'm on a rollercoaster. We are no longer on the road, and our ride begins to bounce and shake with each yard against the thick grass beneath us. I glance at the side mirror. The black vehicles swerve. The towering middle one nearly topples, and has to break hard to avoid tumbling over. But the two SUVs have hardly wavered.

It seems that they are only about thirty yards away. I look to my mother and watch as the sweat begins to flood her brow even more. I look ahead and see a new road approaching. Beyond it, appears to be a small shopping center that looks like it's been abandoned since the 90s. I can't help but grip my mother's thigh as true fear finally reaches me. God knows what terrifying fleet is inside those vehicles that inch closer every second.

The thunderous shake of our car lessens once we finally reach the road. The piercing screech of the tires billows through our senses as my mother swerves into a lane. Seconds later, I hear the black SUVs' tires doing the same.

"I'm so sorry, sweetheart," Mom mutters.

I snap my head toward her. My brow now feels like a hardened mask. Her eyes are blinking uncontrollably as she fights back the tears. Buildings flash behind us, but I barely notice them as I listen to her words.

"I was so stupid to think that I could keep them from finding us."

"Ma...wha—"

"I need you to listen, sweetie!" She unglues a hand from the steering wheel.

Confusion rustles through me once again. It's as if she's already heard my objecting thoughts.

As I can feel the deep rumble of the enemy vehicles approaching, she does something I could never have imagined. She whips the steering wheel, and our car violently spins. My body careens against the door, and I hear a faint clicking sound. I look down at my unfastened seatbelt. My eyes widen in unrelenting shock.

"You have to trust me!" she shouts, as our car regains speed.

I can feel the tires underneath me beginning to dribble off-road, and my heartbeat matches its thumps.

"Do you trust me!"

Tears finally tumble down her cheeks with each of her vigorous wails. My mouth opens, but no words can escape. The black SUVs curl behind us, nearly crashing against each other.

"Rion!" she shouts, to regain my attention.

I look back, my eyes as wide as I can open them.

"Do you trust me!"

"Mom!"

She bites her bottom lip, and our car slows.

"Don't stop running!"

"Wha—"

The tires grind to a halt.

"Get out!" She screams louder than I've ever heard any voice reach.

And then, against every fiber of me that refuses, I feel my muscles moving on their own. I take in the warm steel of the door handle and the draft of the outside.

"Run!"

I take one glance and notice that the two vehicles haven't quite straightened. Mom has positioned the car just on the edge of a withered old building within the shopping center. If I escape now, they might not see me. I realize that this was a chance she knew she had to take.

"I love you," she says, with trembling lips.

She shoves me from the vehicle and slams the door. The tires rip against asphalt and fill the air with a thick fog of dust. I don't even have time to say goodbye before the car speeds off into the distance.

CHAPTER 7

THE FIFTH SOLDIER

RUNNING. I'VE DONE SO MUCH OF IT THAT MY
mind can barely fathom pressing on. My body feels
fragile and numb, but at least the sound of the SUVs
has disappeared down the road and away from the
shopping center. Every breath feels like a hammer
against my chest, and I know that if I don't rest soon,
I'll surely collapse against the dusty concrete.

The sun blares from above as I scan every building
in desperate hope to see one that doesn't have rusted
chains wrapped around its doors. One finally catches
my eye after several minutes of searching, and I stumble
toward it like my legs are made of sticks. The glass
doors nearly shatter as I yank them open and wilt
against the floor.

I rest my aching back against a crusty, dilapidated
wall, and gaze around the room. From the looks of
things, this was an old convenience store. Empty cab-

inets, filled only with dust and cobwebs, are speckled throughout. A long counter topped with the most
ancient cash register I've ever seen rests to my left. The
atmosphere smells dank and grimy, and the light from
outside barely seeps through the murky front glass. The
silence would be eerie if it weren't so calming after all
the chaos.

I'm grimacing, but I can't pinpoint my emotion. I
am angry at first. Angry at my abandonment and at
the confusion of it all. But soon, fear sets in. This is a
different type of fear. The kind of fear that can only
come from truly being alone.

Where do I go from here? I left my cell phone in the
car, and I don't know if Mom would even be able to
answer if I had it. What do I do? Do I wait for her to
return? Is she even coming back? Is she okay? Sorrow
wraps around me like a frigid blanket in a blizzard. I
wipe a stray tear from my eyes, but my scowl remains.

A massive cockroach enters the edge of my glare. I
turn just in time to see it scurry from the corner and
begin toward the front counter. I've always despised
these creatures. Their disgusting little legs and antenna
usually sicken me. Not today. Today, I envy their ability
to venture on their own and survive.

The creature gets to the top of the counter and
attempts to scale the protruding ridge. Its fidgeting
hind legs dangle until it falls back to the ground. The

soft thump of its body seems to echo through the empty room. It wriggles for a moment, then regains itself and continues again. Such persistence.

I raise my index finger, and the creature lifts into the air. Stupid little insect. It has no idea how much its life is in my hands right now. A light sigh billows from my crusted lips as I slowly raise it over the counter and lay it on top. It scurries on as if nothing happened.

It barely leaves my line of sight before I hear footsteps, several of them, coming from outside. I rise to my feet with so much vigor, it's as if I'm just now catching my second wind. I move my back against the wall and glimpse through the glass door.

There are five—no—six soldiers total, just one building away. Five are clad in all-black armor similar to a SWAT team's. They each carry a long, strange-looking gun that looks like something out of a sci-fi movie. Their faces are covered by black helmets equipped with tinted visors.

A slender woman in the center is the only one with her face exposed. A malevolent look is sculpted on her ghostly white visage. Dark bangs rest above eyes, which are bluer than the afternoon sky. The rest of her short haircut flows to the nape of her neck. A black catsuit hugs her frame from her neck down to a pair of thick boots. Two handguns are holstered at her hips. It's as if she knows she doesn't need to be protected like the minions that surround her.

The five soldiers listen to her attentively as she points to each edge of the empty outside square. She instructs them like they are pawns and she is their queen. I slow my breathing and place my ear against the glass.

"Search every corner until you've found him," she commands, in a tone that would be soothing if it weren't so malicious. "He couldn't have gotten far on foot."

Each of them nods, and the group separates. All of my senses return and remind me just how little energy I have left. I inch away from the window and turn to glare toward the back end of the convenience store. There's a thin wooden door that is marked with a rusted sign. It used to say *Employees Only*, but many of the letters have withered away.

The sounds of thumping feet come my way as I stumble across the room. Dust flies into the air when I scamper by. The fight to prevent a cough seems to take more focus than attempting to move my old couch with my mind. I hear them tugging away at the front door just as I've reached the edge of the room. I glance back and see two shadows stream against the murky floor. I turn and squeeze the doorknob. Shift it to each side as swiftly as my hands can manage, but it doesn't budge. A squeal escapes my lips as I tug. It's no use—the door is locked.

I shift my head back. Their masked faces have turned, and I know they've heard me.

Crash!

Shattered glass rattles the floor, and reflexes cause me to raise my arm over my face.

"We've got him!" one of them shouts, as he creeps through the jagged hole he's just created.

The other shoves him through with a heightened eagerness.

Instinct kicks in, and my arms fly forth, triggered by the renewed thumping in my chest. I can feel the invisible energy surge through my body and across the room like a tidal wave. The remaining scraps of the doorway explode into pieces as both armored men go flying outward. I don't wait to see their bodies scrape against the withered parking lot. I turn and refocus my attention on the locked door. I spread my fingers as I place my hand just above the knob.

"We...we've got...a...a Kinetic," one of them groans, while writhing against the dilapidated asphalt.

All other sounds are mute to me now. Every bit of focus is on this doorknob. I can feel the veins protruding from my brow, and my eyes turning a bloodshot red. My hands shake, and my teeth rattle. I think about the closet door at home that I unlocked with ease. I can't let my panic cloud my senses.

Slowly, the knob rattles as if stricken by a miniature earthquake, until finally I feel it rip from the crusted wood. Close enough. I glance back as I swing the rickety old door against the wall. Here they come. Two more soldiers join the ones I previously blew away. I fumble up a mucky stairwell. The smell of dust and poor plumbing fills my nostrils.

Voooom!

A sensation I've never felt comes rushing by. A powerful gust seems to clip my legs just as I turn the corner of the stairwell. It knocks me to my knees and sends a flurry of wood and dust scattering into the atmosphere.

My body slams against the wall, and I gasp for air. A powerful ache creeps into my skull, like I've just been thumped in the head by a baseball. What the hell was that? If that was the blast from their guns, I doubt I'll be able to withstand a straight shot.

Thunderous footsteps return as I regain my focus and begin stumbling up the stairs. There are only a few steps, but it feels like I'm crawling up thousands. I don't know what is pushing me. Fear, perhaps? Whatever it is, the adrenaline surging through me is incomprehensible.

Voooom!

The next blast comes just as I dive through a steel doorway. The door swings from its rusted hinges and smacks against the rooftop floor. A warm beam of sunlight flows into me as I cradle into the fetal position.

I just lie there, clutching my hands to my head. A piercing screech seers though my mind. My heartbeat is the only recognizable sound, and my entire body is numb. I peek out and see the open rooftop. The sun is glaring at me through a thin patch of clouds. My mind is yammering at my body to do whatever it takes to move. I have to get up!

The only thing I can muster is a limp crawl. It doesn't take long to realize that they have me. I can't hear, or feel, their roaring strides, but I know they're approaching. I begin to pray as my hands scrape against aged cobblestone. My mind begins to wander, and I think about all the times Mom used to read the Bible to me when I was younger. We never managed to make it to a church, but the memory still feels comforting now.

I reach the edge of the building. With the hint of strength I have left, I pull myself to my feet and glare out over the edge. My blurred vision begins to clear as the unruly shriek in my skull subsides. A heavy groan pours through my lips before a forceful, gloved hand grabs my shoulder and spins me around.

"We got him, ma'am." The soldier taps the right side of his helmet.

Four of them are there with their massive space-age guns pointed at my face. The idea that they haven't killed me isn't relieving, because I can only imagine what it'll be like to be their prisoner.

"Yes ma'am." The same soldier moves his hand from his helmet and grabs my wrists.

If they weren't still numb, I have no doubt that pain would be shooting through each pore.

One of the other soldiers reaches into a compartment on his black belt, and pulls out a device that resembles handcuffs. Its smooth steel surface shimmers in the sunlight, and a glowing red light blinks in the center. He hands it to the soldier that is still gripping me.

"Wait!"

The voice comes from the doorway. It's the last of the five soldiers. The others turn to look back at him, and although I can't see any of their faces, I can feel their suspicious snarls glaring back as he runs toward us.

"New orders," the fifth soldier says, his weapon wound across his back.

Pow!

The fifth soldier strikes the helmet of the soldier clutching my wrists, sending him tumbling to the edge of the roof. Even in my numbness, I can sense the excruciating strength of the punch. Everything happens so swiftly that I can barely follow each movement. The other three struggle to bring their guns up, as if they are just as confounded by their ally's betrayal as I am. By the time they're prepared to fire, the fifth soldier has already whipped his gun from his back and placed it into perfect position.

Voooom!

The searing blast sends the four soldiers flailing from the roof like confetti. I edge my body straight up against the wall as I collapse my palms over my aching eardrums. My feet seem welded to the rooftop floor as I gaze back with wide, reddened eyes.

When the screeching subsides, the fifth soldier snaps his hidden glare toward me. I wonder if I should raise my hand and send him flying over the edge with his colleagues. But when he moves toward me, I don't budge.

"Don't be afraid," he says, as calmly as one can through a huff of staggered breaths.

My God. How comical my confused, yet relieved, scowl must look.

"Follow me."

He turns and scurries for the doorway, but I remain frozen.

"I'm here to help you," he growls, whipping his head back toward me.

One foot moves, but the rest of my body is still reluctant.

"We don't have much time, Rion. Let's go!"

Huh? He knows my name? My eyes widen like saucers. All at once, the feeling in my extremities returns. Without any more notions of hesitation, I stumble to my feet and scramble behind him, down the stairs.

He stalks through the convenience store's shattered glass doorframe with his weapon raised high. With a jolt of his neck, he scans every inch of his surroundings before signaling me to follow. I match him, stride for careful stride, as we move along the building's edge. Our pace is slower than a run, but much more vigorous than a jog.

The sun is beginning to set just below a few rundown buildings in the distance, and the fifth soldier seems adamant on keeping us in the shadows. I march as closely as I can behind him without bowling him over, and all I can think about is how much I want this day to end. I've never craved sleep so badly in my life. A warm bed would be heaven. Hell, a pillow and blanket will do.

"Gamma Team, status report."

We both hear the buzz come from the earpiece protruding from the fifth soldier's helmet, but neither of us says a word.

"Gamma Team. Copy? Do you have the kid?"

This time, I realize it is the woman from before, who was giving the soldiers their orders. My mind begins to flicker with where she might be hiding, and how close we might be to her. The fifth soldier's stride only quickens.

"Ga…Gamma…Gamma Team is down," someone else replies.

My panic returns. We are only about fifty yards away from the building where the fifth soldier rescued me, when a deafening rumble careens into my senses like lighting striking the earth.

"Beta Team is moving in!" the woman shouts.

My knees shake, and the numbness in my body returns. I do my best to fight it, but it's no use. My feet buckle, and I tumble to the coarse gravel below. A cloud of orange dirt wafts into the air as I collapse. I hear the fifth soldier's boots scrape against the ground to halt before I make the mistake of turning around. That massive tank-bus that was pursuing my mother's SUV earlier is now stampeding toward us.

"C'mon!" The fifth soldier yanks me to my feet. "We gotta move."

We take off through the empty parking lot like we're in an Olympic track meet. The fear and desperation rushing through my veins is the only thing pushing my weary frame. The vehicle is easily a hundred yards away, but I have no doubt it will catch us if we don't do something soon. We have to find a place to hide.

"In here!" The fifth soldier points to a tiny building on our left.

It used to be a post office, but like every other building in this abandoned area, the signage is missing letters, and the paint has molded to a crusty beige.

I think to object when I first see it, because the front is nothing but dingy glass from one end to another. They have already seen us, and there's no way they can't catch us in here. But I say nothing to the fifth soldier. At this point, there is no use in arguing with him. Somehow he has rescued me. Somehow he has infiltrated this sinister squadron. Somehow...he even knows my name.

He swings open the door, and we rush inside. I have barely taken two steps in, when my heart freezes once more. There is another man in here. He is tall, at least six feet and some inches, with a chiseled appearance that reminds me of some NFL star quarterback. His skin is a pale, yet vibrant, peach that makes him look no older than thirty. His short, prickly hair shimmers with shades of golden blond and dark brown. Ocean-blue eyes sternly peer through a pair of glasses with crisp, circular lenses.

His body seems just as powerful as the gleam in his eyes. I can't see any muscles through his blue button-up and long brown coat, but I can tell that he could probably bench press both me and the fifth soldier with ease.

"Did you—"

"Yeah." The man darts his gaze to mine. "This way."

He turns and moves behind a dusty counter and through a doorway. The soldier quickly follows, and I find myself filled with the relieved sensation of knowing this guy is no enemy.

The rumble of the tank-bus grows faint as we dart through the old building's back corridors. I can barely keep up. My two allies jump counters and turn corners like they're in an obstacle course that they themselves constructed. By the time my frustration and confusion have begun to replace my fatigue, we have reached the back of the building. Just before the outside light of the opening back door can hit my face, a new voice screeches.

"Freeze!"

My two allies halt. I grimace, from behind them. Two new soldiers stand with their massive guns drawn. The man with the glasses, and the fifth soldier, raise their hands, seemingly to surrender. I pour out a dejected sigh as my quivering arms lift to the sky.

Part of me is relieved that I don't have to run anymore, but I don't want to give up. I want to use every ounce of strength I have to send all of them, including my allies, flying through the open doorway. But deep down, I know that doing so much as shifting a rock might send me spiraling into unconsciousness.

"We've got him, ma'am." One of the men places his weapon upward and moves toward us.

The other keeps his gun pointed at our chests, ready to squeeze the trigger at our slightest gesture. The enemy soldier approaches his former teammate and rips the weapon from his shoulder. But before he can turn around, the man with the glasses acts. His movements are so quick and precise that I can't help but think I'm hallucinating. He grabs the edge of the enemy soldier's gun, and without even the slightest effort, he turns and fires it.

Voooom!

Another blistering wave of force blasts the other soldier. One enemy has barely rammed into the side of the opposite wall before the man with the glasses begins a fistfight with the other.

I have collapsed to the floor. Once again, I'm covering my ears to counteract the wretched shriek of the blast. But I have not taken my gaze off of the action. The fifth soldier stands idly as the mysterious man with the glasses rejects every blow thrown his way. I have never seen anything like it. These aren't ordinary moves. The man with the glasses throws no punches or kicks. He just blocks. This enemy isn't some street punk, either. He is clearly a trained martial artist, yet he can't land a single blow. Every swing, every kick, is blocked or dodged, until finally the man with the glasses grasps the soldier's wrists and twists. An excruciating growl reverberates through the soldier's helmet as he falls to his knees. The man with the glasses swings his burly leg around for his first actual attack. It lands squarely into the soldier's head, sending him flopping to the ground like a sack of potatoes.

The ringing sensation in my head subsides, and the fifth soldier helps me to my feet.

"You all right?" he says.

I can't even bring myself to respond, because I'm still in awe. It was like something out of a Bruce Lee film. But the fifth soldier seems to brush it off as if it were expected.

"Let's go," the man with the glasses says, after grabbing one of the discarded guns and throwing it over his shoulder. "Our ride is just around this corner."

The rumble of the tank-bus resonates in my eardrums once again. I'd almost forgotten about it until now, but it is still coming. The fifth soldier is now carrying me like a wounded veteran. I can hear my numb feet dragging against the gravel as we trudge through the exit.

We turn the corner to see a shimmering black SUV resting in an alley. It's almost identical to one of the vehicles that was pursuing Mom and me. The barely present sun bounces off of its tinted windows and beams into my eyes. It should aggravate me, but I'm just thankful that I don't have to run anymore.

The man with the glasses opens the back door, and the fifth soldier lays me inside. My eyes widen as soon as I come to rest against the leather seat. There's an Asian girl, likely not too much older than me, laying against the window in a deep sleep. This moment can't get any more peculiar.

The door slams shut behind me before I can even turn to give my flustered look to my new allies. I glance back at the unconscious girl. Her skin is a beautiful porcelain shade, and her lips are a rosy, robust pink. Her jet-black hair curls into a long ponytail that drapes down her back. She is wearing a pink T-shirt and a pair of fitted jeans that creep just above dark sneakers.

The front doors shut, and the engine rumbles. The man with the glasses is in the driver's seat, with the fifth soldier on the other side. I have had it at this point. I am already mentally and physically exhausted. I'm done with being confused. I open my mouth to ask whatever angry question will fly first, but the man with the glasses speaks before I can.

"Here." He shoves one of the massive guns into my lap.

I gawk. I can barely raise my arms right now, let alone fire an unfamiliar weapon.

"What am I supposed to—"

"No, it's for her."

My face gnarls even further. I glance over at the fifth soldier, who has just finished strapping himself down. Somehow I trust him more than this other guy who has barely acknowledged me in the few minutes we've known each other.

"We're good to go." He nods through his black helmet.

His body flops against the door. He hits the soft surface with a thud as if he were a robot struck by an electromagnetic pulse. I find the energy to lean up, but before I can fully check if he is okay, movement in my periphery catches my attention.

"Cutting it close, aren't we?" The man with the glasses glances in the rearview mirror.

I realize his words aren't directed at me or the fifth soldier, but at the Asian girl.

"Relax." She shrugs while taking the gun from my lap.

I turn my astonished stare toward her. She looks at me with the brightest smile I've seen in weeks, like she wasn't just unconscious seconds ago. Her eyes are like nothing I've ever seen before. They are mostly brown, but there seems to be a faint sparkle of pink fluttering through them, like ink in water.

"Don't worry, Rion," she says. "You're in good hands."

CHAPTER 8

THE SAFE HOUSE

MY HEAD RESTS AGAINST THE WARM WINDOW as I gaze out at the fields whirling by. I can see the Asian girl's reflection. She peers out of the vehicle's rear as if we're still being followed.

It has been nearly a half-hour since we got in the car, and the fifth soldier still hasn't moved. Every so often, I try to listen for the hint of breath, just to make sure he's alive. The only thing I can make out is a faint flutter whistling from his helmet.

The man with the glasses hasn't said a word. The look of reluctant angst on his face matches the agitated grimace on mine. He takes his intense stare from the road only once. It is merely for an instant, but I catch the abrasive glance of his blue eyes through the crisp lenses above his nose. I peer back with a look of exhausted indifference. I should be thanking him, but part of me can't help but wonder why they've yet to explain who they are.

"Is he gonna be okay?" I glare out of the window.

The Asian girl and the man with the glasses both whip their gazes in my direction, and I can read a look of confusion on their faces.

"You should get some rest." The Asian girl returns her gaze to the darkening horizon.

I've reached my boiling point. Thoughts of my mother once again swirl through my mind, along with the well-being of the soldier that saved my life. I feel that if I don't get answers soon, I might lose my mind.

"Can someone *please* tell me what the hell is going on?"

"Trust me," the man with the glasses grumbles, as he stares at me through the rearview mirror. "We have as many questions for you as you have for us. Right now, all of that can wait 'til we get to our safe house."

"I highly doubt that!" I shake my head and ball my fists. "You have no idea what I've been through today. I deserve some answers."

"Ara," the girl says, in a soothing tone.

She lowers the gun and touches my shoulder. Her rosy eyes meet my scowl with a hopeful smile. The anger in me begins to subside. There is a calmness and nurturing tone to her voice that makes me feel like I know her.

"My name is Ara. And that's Leo." She nods toward the man with the glasses.

He still doesn't take his stern stare from the road.

"We know you've been through a lot, and you used a lot of kinetic energy. Which is why it's best you get some rest. We have a long drive ahead."

I glance over at Leo, who scoffs at Ara's complacent demeanor. I turn back to her and nod. I trust her. Not sure why, but I do.

My eyes flicker open at the sound of a few light rumbles. I can't even remember dozing off, and it takes a few seconds for my vision to clarify in the crisp darkness. The SUV comes to a halt. I scan the vehicle. The fifth soldier continues to lay motionless in the front seat. I can't help but maintain a scowl.

Meow.

The sound creeps through the window beside me, and my attention drifts toward it.

"Lyra!" Ara shouts, as she jumps from the backseat to caress the small cat running into her arms.

Its golden fur shimmers under the towering light post illuminating the area.

I turn my attention to a two-story farmhouse just a few yards away. Its surface is made of worn redwood, and there are tiny patches of light glowing from a few dusty windows. A pair of rocking chairs sit at opposite ends of a long porch. The house is the only building resting amongst a seemingly endless ocean of tall, green grass that spreads to each corner of the horizon. In the center of the driveway is an old sedan that looks like it hasn't moved in forever. The whole scene looks like the type of place Mom would move us to, and I can't help but hope she'll come rushing through the rickety front door any minute.

"I almost started to get worried," a raspy voice calls out.

A short, plump man comes slowly trotting across the driveway. His pale face is covered by a patchy brown beard littered with gray strands to match his shaggy hair. His attire looks like something a farmer in the old west might wear. He wears a calming grin as he approaches Leo, and gives him a hefty hug.

"How'd it go?" he says, as I slowly open the door. "You take out the car tracker?"

"Of course," Leo whispers. "Everything happened just like you said, right down to the smallest detail. What does it mean?"

The older man nods, and a pondering look replaces his deep smile. He scans the distant darkness before a sigh billows through his husky jaws, and his gaze darts toward mine.

"In due time. Right now, it's more important to be gracious hosts."

My eyes widen as he begins to waddle over to me. He stops close enough for his scent of dirty laundry, chopped meat, and light cologne to pour into my nostrils.

"No need to be afraid, Rion." He places a hand along my shoulder, and a smile spreads across his leathery, bearded mug. "You're amongst friends."

I can't help but internally scoff at his words, but I find myself slowly stepping from the vehicle and onto the soft lawn. The grass is even deeper than I thought, and it feels as if I'm stepping onto a bed of hay.

"My name is Pavo." He grins while extending his hand.

I grasp it and give it a firm shake. They feel rubbery, like they've been through decades of hard labor. I look behind him at Ara, with the cat clutched between her arms. Her smile seems sly, but welcoming. Leo, on the other hand, continues to glare at me with guarded suspicion.

"Let's get you into some fresh clothes, and get you a hot meal, shall we?" Pavo says, as I refocus on his murky brown eyes.

A restless sigh sifts through my nostrils, but this one is undoubtedly one of relief. Pavo begins his waddle toward the house. Ara rocks her cat between her arms. She patiently waits until Pavo has passed her, before she turns and follows him. I nod and move close behind.

"Leo! Take our other guest to the shed, please."

Other guest? Pavo's words seem as vibrant as the shimmering stars in the bright night sky above us. I can't help but look back to the fifth soldier's limp frame, still lying in the passenger's seat. More questions scurry through my mind with each methodical step toward the old house. I tilt my head to try and catch everything in my line of sight.

After nodding, Leo opens the car door and gathers the armored soldier around his burly shoulder.

"Welcome to, what Leo and Ara have dubbed, the Safe House. It isn't much, but it's home."

I shake from my daze and peer down into Pavo's wrinkly face. I try my best to match the gratifying smile he gives me.

"And it'll be home to you for as long as you want it to be."

As a whole, the Safe House is remarkable for its simplicity. I've never been in a home so large, but so empty. There are no pictures or decorative trinkets throughout its spacious interior, and all of the furniture looks like something out of a museum.

The backyard is mostly made up of farmland, with rows of vegetable plants that seem to stretch for miles. There are a few cows, chickens, and pigs separated between fences. I can't help but smile when Pavo tells me that they grow all of their food on the property, so they essentially never have to leave.

The brief tour ends with him showing me to my room. It's in an almost identical position to the one I had in Missouri. It even comes equipped with a personal bathroom, and I move toward it barely a moment after Pavo has shut the door behind me.

My shower lasts nearly an hour. It's been so long since I've bathed that it feels like the soothing soak from a downpour in the middle of the desert. All of the day's pain and frustration seem to wash away. I want to bask in the acute freshness of my own skin when I'm done, but the light chill of a breeze through the aged wooden walls changes my mind.

I stand in front of the queen-sized bed, with a feeling of indisposed relief. New clothes have been laid out for me. A smooth cotton polo goes over my face, and I am

stunned by the precision of its fit. The dark cloth seems
to cling to my frame, as if it were made just for me. A
pair of boxers are next, followed by some dark jeans
that look fresh out of a department store. Each fits like
I tried it on in the fitting room before purchase. I run
my hands along every inch of the fabric, and marvel
at how good it feels to finally be at ease.

The feeling doesn't last long. My thoughts shift to
my mother as soon as I've placed my feet into a soft
pair of white socks. I pace around the room, trying
my best to forget what happened today. The burgundy
walls are bare. Only a tiny dresser, equipped with a
wide mirror, rests at the opposite corner.

I want to scan every inch of the room. I want to
see what scars mark the walls, and what scuffs riddle
the floor. I want to know who was here before me,
and how these clothes were so perfectly prepared. But
before I can even place my hands against the wood, an
entrancing aroma spreads across the room.

My stomach rumbles and gurgles like it's revolting
against me. The scent only makes matters worse. It
smells of fresh beef and peppers, with a hint of chopped
onions to give it the perfect twinge of deliciousness.
I leave my room and inch down a long staircase. The
wood beneath my feet moans and creaks. Patches of
dust cling to my palms as I glide them along the railing.

The appetizing aroma grows stronger with each step. I start to hear whispers once I've reached the bottom of the stairwell. By the time I've rounded the corner leading toward the kitchen, I can clearly make out every bit of Leo's words.

"Why would Arkright be out in the open now?"

"I wish I knew," I hear Pavo reply.

"It must have something to do with the kid."

I know Leo is talking about me, and the use of the term *kid* causes me to snarl.

"Maybe so. But one thing is for certain—"

"The Predators," Leo says, cold severity evident in his tone. "If they find out that there's a fourth—"

Meow!

"What the hell!" I shout, while jerking upward.

I feel a warm, hairy touch sift through the bottom of my jeans and into my skin. I look down at Ara's cat gracefully stepping over my foot. The tiny feline gives what looks like a sly, boisterous grin at me before sliding onto the shimmering white tile of the kitchen floor. It's the strangest look I've ever seen from an animal. If I didn't know better, I'd say the cat was winking at me.

"Lyra says you shouldn't eavesdrop."

Ara's voice startles me, but I don't jump. The soothing melody of her tone seems to calm me, no matter how abruptly it may come. I turn to look at her gazing back at me with a wily grin. Her dark hair is still in a ponytail, but the style seems to have been fine tuned into a long, thicker tress that starts upward and falls just beyond her neck.

"C'mon." She glides by me with a giggle.

I turn the corner into the bright kitchen. The entire room is lit only by a single lamp that hangs from the center of the ceiling. A long, double-sided iron sink sits beneath a window at the opposite end of the room. Beside it is a refrigerator that seems like the oldest model still in existence. Its surface is a rusted crimson, and its shape reminds me of something manufactured in the 50s.

"Hello, Rion," Pavo grumbles, through his usual raspy tone. "Have a seat."

When he first spoke, I thought that he might be sick. But I'm beginning to realize that his grungy voice is just his natural tone.

Ara pulls out a chair from the rounded table. Leo sits with hands clasped together, like a teacher getting ready to have a conference with a student's parent. He is no longer wearing his coat, so his sculpted biceps bulge through his blue T-shirt.

I sit just as Ara places a large spoon and a bowl full of beef stew in front of me. I can't help but bask in the steam rising to warm my face. She sits at the last vacant seat beside me and pushes away a loose hair strand in front of her eyes. She smiles at me when she catches me staring, and like a dope, I dart my vision toward my meal.

"Ahem," Leo grumbles, from the opposite end of the table.

My gaze jolts upward, and I notice him staring at me. My brow curls, and my gaze shifts between them. Ara and I both start eating spoonfuls of stew. Her gobbles are nibbles compared to mine, as if she is trying her best to look more well-mannered. Pavo's elbows are rested on the table, and his gaze is fastened on me like I'm standing trial.

"So," I murmur, with a mouth full of food. "Are you guys some resistance group that works with my mom?"

I try not to make eye contact as I speak. Instead, I focus on the waning morsels of food left in my bowl. But I can feel the attentive stares blaring in my direction with each syllable.

"Your mom?" Leo scoffs.

I take a break from chewing and sulk as I look up at him. His tone sounds like he's disgusted, and I can't help but be annoyed.

"Do you know anything about the soldiers who were chasing you today?" Pavo lets out a deep sigh.

"Not really." I shrug before refocusing on the delicious broth in front of me.

I'm entranced by how good it tastes, and can't help but wonder if it's really the best stew I've ever tasted, or if I'm just that hungry.

"Well, what can you guess?" Leo asks.

Again, I stop eating. My scowl is reflecting back at me from Leo's glasses. How dare he? How dare he speak to me in such a hostile tone, like I'm some intruder?

My mood simmers when Pavo raises his palm toward Leo and gives a calming nod. Leo takes a deep breath and lowers his head apologetically.

"Please, Rion." Pavo returns his attention to me. "We just have some gaps of our own that need filling."

My fingers rattle over the smooth steel of my spoon handle, and I do my best to ignore Leo's anxious grimace. I glance at Ara. She nods toward me with gentle eyes as she chews.

"I guess those soldiers are some government agency sent to find people like me. Which would explain why my mom has been keeping me on the move my whole life."

Their demeanors change. Even with my gaze straying from them, I can sense them perking up with scowls, as if I've said some trigger word.

"So am I close?" I huff as I slide my bowl to the center of the table. "Or have I just been watching too many sci-fi movies?"

I finally look up at their blank faces. Ara's look seems passive. Nervous, even. Leo lightly shakes his head, as if his grievances have been replaced with a whole new batch of questions. But Pavo...Pavo looks at me with caution. As if he doesn't want to correct me.

"Well...you're certainly in the ballpark. But please tell us more about your mother."

Thoughts of Mom begin to flutter through my skull as if the image of her is locusts feasting on the fields of my other memories. The mental pain of her leaving me behind comes rushing back. I open my mouth, but I don't speak. It's as if the frustration and confusion have sent a sharp ache shooting through my head and down my spine.

"I don't know much, honestly. Her name is Diana Grean. She's forty-three. Umm...I thought she was a researcher, and that she didn't know I had powers. But now...I feel like the few things I thought I knew are all lies."

The room is eerily silent, and each of them stares back at me like a child being told about unicorns and fairies.

"She never had friends or talked about her job. Guess now I know why."

I bring my hands together at my chin and stare off into the pasty kitchen walls, wishing Mom would come bursting through them. Telling me not to slouch in my chair would probably be the first thing she'd say to me. A longing smile fills my face, but I feel the moisture building in my eyes. The refusal to cry in front of my new acquaintances stops them in their tracks.

"And...your father?" Pavo says.

"Never met him, or even seen a photo. And she never talked about him. I don't even know his name, or where they met."

Again, I catch them looking around and exchanging grimaces.

"One minute, we're on our way to a new house in South Dakota. The next, we're being pulled over by some asshole cop for no reason."

Ara begins to run her spoon along the stained sides of her bowl, as if the gesture will lessen her anxiety. A light sigh billows from Leo's cheeks that makes me feel as if he's finally ready to rule me out as a hostile.

"He tried to arrest us. Didn't even ask for Mom's license." I shift my gaze to Pavo's enamored, but empathetic, scowl. "I used my powers to help us get away. And minutes later, we're being chased by those soldiers."

A lump fills my throat. I keep whispering in my head to steady my voice so that they can't detect my sorrow.

"She told me to trust her. Then she pushed me out near that shopping center and drove off. Now, I don't know whether she's dead or alive."

The room is so silent you can hear the trees rustling outside. Even Lyra the cat sits quietly at the edge of the room, gazing back at me like she wants me to cradle her between my arms.

"I'm sorry, Rion." Pavo groans. "I'm not sure if we know who your mother is, or where she might be."

The words hit me like a gut punch. My head begins to bobble in a nodding motion as I fight back tears and the agonizing thump in my chest.

"But…"

My gaze darts back to Pavo, and he stares back.

"… we might be able to find her."

I don't know if he's telling the truth, but somehow Leo's silence and the hopeful gleam in Ara's eyes make me believe him. I want to thank him, not just for the effort to help me when I don't even know if he can actually find Mom, but simply for how much he's helped me so far. My life was saved. I have been clothed, fed, and given a place to sleep. Even if Pavo doesn't do anything else, he's done enough to earn my gratitude.

"I think you should tell him," Ara hums.

I turn to Pavo. Tell me? Tell me what? I don't need a mirror to know that my look suggests all of the intrigue necessary to avoid actual words.

Pavo lets out a deep sigh, and his gaze meets mine. I am relieved. I am relieved to know that my answers— at least some of them—are finally coming.

CHAPTER 9

THE FOUR STRAINS

MY EYES ARE WIDE LIKE TWO OBSERVATORY telescopes aimed at a distant star. Ara places a cup of steaming hot tea in front of me. I grasp it without displacing my attention as Pavo clears his throat.

"What I'm about to tell you might seem vague, but it's the truth. No matter how impossible it sounds," he grumbles, through an exhausted tone, as his gaze trails off toward the ceiling.

Leo leans back and runs his hands over his prickly chin. Ara holds Lyra tight in her bosom as she takes a seat. The light smile on her face makes her look like a toddler about to hear her favorite bedtime story. Lyra's purr is the only sound that breaks Pavo's brief silence.

"It was a little over eighteen years ago. I had no memories of who or where I was, but I remember lying in a glass chamber. Tubes are protruding from my arms. I don't feel like I'm breathing. But…somehow I am."

I feel a chill trickle over my skin as I begin to picture every moment.

"Suddenly, the chamber opens, and I'm yanked out by someone else. It's a woman. She has beautiful brown skin, long hair, and brown eyes that look just as frightened as mine."

I notice Ara's smile growing as soon as this woman is mentioned.

"She is wearing a long, white bodysuit. So am I. I look down at my hands, as if it's my first time seeing them. Then I look around the room. It's some sort of laboratory. There are computers and chemicals everywhere, but there's no one in lab coats, suits, or anything. I only see more chambers, just like mine. There are twelve in all."

I lean in, unable to keep myself from wondering if the woman he is speaking of is my mother.

"She looks into my eyes and tells me we have to go. That's when I finally realize that there is an alarm sounding. Lights are flashing everywhere, like a fire drill. Part of me is wondering how I even know what a fire drill is. I nod and say *okay*, and it feels like the first time I'm hearing my own voice. It takes me a few steps to get my bearings, but after a while my body feels fine. That's when I see her running around the room and unlocking the other chambers."

He takes a long pause, as if he hasn't gotten to the most troubling portion of his recollection.

"The first person we set free is another man. He looks the same age as me. Maybe mid-forties. But who the hell knows, right?"

A brief stint of boisterous laughter almost manages to creep from his lips, but the moment seems to dissipate like the warm vapors from my cup of tea. The next listless look that overtakes his eyes almost makes me want to tear up.

"But then...I look in the other chambers and...and see—"

"Kids." Leo stares down at his clasped hands.

"Leo and two others were teenagers. Another three were no older than five or six. The last three were..." Pavo shakes his head in disgust, his gaze flickering toward Ara.

"Infants," Ara says, with a fading grin.

A baseball-sized lump invades my throat at the sight of Pavo fighting back tears so he can continue.

"For a second, I'm wondering...what monsters could've been experimenting on children? Babies, even?"

He shakes his head in disbelief, like he is the one being told the story.

"The other man and woman grab two of the infants and yell at me to hurry and help, so I run over to the nearest chamber. I'll never forget Ara's eyes when I first approached. She was so tiny, so innocent. She was crying at first, but she stopped the moment I held her in my arms."

Ara reaches over to clutch Pavo's hand, and they each share a warm smile.

"The woman leads the way out of the lab. The kids… those frightened kids…somehow we convince them to come with us."

A long, dejected sigh pours from Leo. He has barely glanced up from the table since Pavo began speaking.

"I'm not even sure if the woman knows the way out, and yet we follow her down a hallway that feels like it'll never end. There's sounds of screaming and crashing behind us. Then chimes of gunfire. Eventually, we reach a door. My God. The light was so blinding. It was like we'd never experienced the sun before. But we don't stop running. The air is chill, and there's a forest in the distance. We run through it for what seems like an hour, until we reach a lone boat sitting on the edge of a lake. It isn't hitched to anything, and there's no one near it. Somehow I know it's meant for us."

Pavo turns to me with a smile, and nods as if his recollection is complete. I can't help but scowl. After a brief stillness, though, he continues.

"From there, we hid in a nearby town for a while, at a homeless shelter that thankfully gave us refuge. After a few days, the oldest of us got together to try to compile memories. It was all the same. None of us knew anything. But it didn't take long for us to realize our similarity."

My brow perks. Leo finally raises his head, and his gaze meets Ara's. They each sit ramrod straight before holding out their left arms.

"We each have a mark," Pavo says.

I look down as if I'm gawking at buried treasure. Each of their left wrists has a series of dots embedded onto their skin, like Braille. There is a different number of dots on each of them, and none are arranged the same. At first, I think they're tattoos. But as I look closer, these dots seem like they are a part of them. Almost like birthmarks.

"We were scared for weeks. We didn't know if we were born with the marks, or if they were trackers placed to find us. For days, we moved from town to town, and eventually settled in an abandoned library."

Pavo chuckles.

"The man who we first released from the chamber—that bright son-of-a-gun—he reads a few books, and is the first to realize that the marks are star patterns. The one on his arm is the constellation Auriga. So that's what he names himself. He convinces us to do the same."

Pavo looks over at the others with a smirk.

"The constellation Leo." Leo points to his arm.

"Ara." She does the same.

"And Pavo."

Awe rushes through me, and I realize that I don't have it as bad, after all. But my head is still swimming with more questions.

"Anyway." Pavo leans back and rolls down his sleeve. "We kept moving from place to place every few weeks. We wound up somewhere in North Dakota, and began raising the children as our own once we were sure we were no longer being followed. We started teaching them all of this knowledge of the world we, ourselves, couldn't quite grasp how we understood. And then everything changed."

My gaze jerks up to his. I hadn't even realized I'd been staring at my own arm, wondering if there should be a mark on my blank wrist.

"It was roughly five years after we'd settled, when our abilities started to manifest."

"Abilities?" I blurt, my mouth becoming dry, and my heart starting to rattle. "Abilities like mine?"

Pavo nods and smiles.

"Each of us belongs to one of the four strains." Ara beams at me.

"Four strains of what, exactly?"

"Clairvoyants." Leo huffs.

"The three oldest of us had always had a sixth sense we couldn't explain," Pavo says. "It's how we found our way out of that lab. How we found the boat. And how Auriga knew to settle in the library. After five years, we began to have intense dreams. At least, that's what we thought they were. It didn't take long to realize that they were actually visions of the future."

My body begins to grow numb with a sense of exhilaration that I can only recall once—when I first discovered my gift.

"Over time, the visions became much easier to understand," Pavo says. "And while they're still not voluntary, they always pertain to Clairvoyants. And that is how I found you, Rion."

A smile forges through my gawk.

"You see, we realized that the chambers had been grouped by our abilities in sets of three. Leo's strain has the ability of telepathy, or mind reading."

I curl my brow and glance at Leo, who is glaring back at me with a grimace. I find myself afraid that he is reading my thoughts right now, and I can't help but sweat.

"Ara's has the special gift of transferring their consciousness into another's body. Or what we like to call, aural projection."

My head darts toward her like a bulb has just clicked on in my brain.

"The soldier that saved me?" I say.

"You're welcome." She gives me a sly wink.

I can't help but return the gesture as I glare into those sparkling eyes of hers.

"And then there are those like you," Pavo continues.

I refocus my attention on him with a dumbfounded grin, like I'm receiving some sort of blessing.

"Those who are telekinetic, who can move objects and shift the air around them with mere thought."

"However," Leo says, as if he's been waiting for this moment all night. "Correct me if I'm wrong, Rion, but aren't you only seventeen?"

My smile fades, and my animosity toward Leo comes flaring back. I open my mouth, but don't respond. I hadn't even bothered to do the math when Pavo mentioned that their escape happened a year before I was born.

"Exactly." Leo sternly huffs, as if I've given a reply. "There are only supposed to be three in each strain of Clairvoyant. You, Rion, are the fourth kinetic. And you don't have a mark like the rest of us."

The rattle in my chest begins again. Everyone, including Lyra the cat, turns toward me. I no longer feel blessed, but like an intruder. Even Ara's smile has faded to a look of reluctant suspicion.

"Which begs the question." Leo leans forward and glares into my trembling scowl. "Where the hell did you come from?"

CHAPTER 10

LYRA

"WHY ARE YOU LOOKING AT ME LIKE THAT!" I slam my fists against the table.

Ara jumps back, and Lyra gives an ear-splitting howl, but Leo's glare never wavers.

"Those soldiers came after *me!* Not you."

"Psyriin has been hunting us since before you had hair on your junk, kid," Leo growls.

"Psyriin?" I huff.

"The Psionic Research and Intervention Initiative," Ara says.

"We don't know how they're funded, or what government agency they work for," Pavo says. "But we assume they're some sort of militarized version of the people that had us captive in the lab."

A hint of irritation in his voice as he raises his arm in an attempt to calm Leo.

"Yeah, well, they found me before you did. So clearly they know something you guys don't! My mom might be the key to all of this. Clearly, she's the one who helped you all escape. Once you see her picture—"

"She's not your mother." Leo laughs.

I snarl, and feel my body acting on its own. My brow hardens, and my arm raises toward Leo. I send him rushing backward with a burst of kinetic force. He slams into a cabinet with a *thud!*, causing Ara and Pavo to jump to their feet.

"Leo!" Ara runs to him, while Lyra gives me a scathing hiss.

"Say it again," I growl, as Pavo comes over to grab me. "Say it again, and I'll send you through the wall."

"Calm down, Rion," Pavo says.

"He wasn't trying to insult you." Ara passes a grimace between me and Leo.

She looks like a mom scolding her two kids.

"The woman who got out of her chamber first was a Prophetic Clairvoyant named Andromeda."

Once again, Ara's voice calms me. My furious breaths simmer, and my arm drops to my side, but I still feel like making Leo's body dangle from the ceiling.

"It's true, Rion," Pavo says. "Their ages and physical attributes might be similar, but Andromeda lived with us for years before she left.

"Use your brain, Mama's Boy." Leo scoffs from the floor. "If she and your mother were the same person, don't you think we would've noticed her being pregnant?"

"That's enough!" Pavo extends his arms between us.

His palm rests against my chest, and I'm certain he can feel my thumping heartbeat.

I stare into Leo's seething eyes, through his crooked glasses. He straightens them on his face while Ara grabs his arm to help him up. He stands and brushes the stray cabinet dust from his shoulders, like the mucking of his clothing is the only heinous act I've made. Then he does something that only rattles the protruding veins in my fists even further. He smirks. It isn't exactly a sly grin. It's the kind of smile you'd give someone whose ass you could kick if given the proper time and place. It isn't even the type of conceding look you might give someone as a silent *touché*. To me, this look, and the hint of laughter that follows, is unquestionably provoking. Leo is amused by my anger, and it's as if he was trying to bring something out of me. To test me, even.

"The most important thing we need to realize is that we are all on the same side." Pavo shifts his grimaces between us, like a mall security guard.

"I think we should all go to bed." Ara sighs as she pats Leo on the chest. "I think we've broken the ice enough for the first night."

Pavo gives her a nod. Before I know it, he's grabbed my arm and turned me toward the door. I don't know why, but I shrug him off as if the mere touch from his withered skin annoys me. Truthfully, I have no gripe with Pavo. As far as I know, he's a good man. I feel like I can trust him and Ara. As for Leo...everything about him just rubs me the wrong way.

I can't sleep. At first I think it's these uncomfortable, papery sheets I'm lying between that remind me of a hospital bed. Or maybe it's this surrounding quilt that seems thick enough to stop a bullet. Hell, with the last few days I've been through, I should be able to sleep on gravel. After a few minutes of squirming into the ideal position, I realize they aren't so bad.

Perhaps it's the unholy silence. At least in Missouri there were sounds of insects chirping, and the occasional rustle of tree leaves. Out here—wherever *here* is—the silence is mind-numbing. Even the animals out back seem like they're barely breathing. It's as if we're in some sort of alternate dimension, where no sound can pierce the acres of thick weeds surrounding this old farmhouse.

After a few hours of staring at the dried wood that covers the ceiling, the thought of my mother begins to creep back. Ever since we separated, my thoughts of her always begin with me wondering if she's okay. My throat runs dry, and my eyes water before the questions start to scamper in. Why? Why did she keep so much from me? Even if she isn't the woman who helped Pavo escape that lab, she definitely knew about my abilities, and about Psyriin.

A light rattle disrupts the silence and causes me to lift my head. I glare toward the bedroom window. Out here, I imagine that the sound of a squirrel running in the distance would be enough to catch my attention. But this is no squirrel. Someone else is awake, too.

I can hear light footsteps skimming the deep grass, and I edge onto the cold floorboards. I cringe at the thunderous shriek that follows my footsteps. I keep looking back, as if Leo will come bursting in to tell me to go back to sleep, but there doesn't seem to be a hint of movement coming from the other side of my closed bedroom door.

As I reach the window, I peek through the thin beige curtains that flutter with the calm wind. For some reason, I have my back against the wall like I'm spying. Nothing comes into view at first, and I begin to wonder if my imagination is attempting to create a reason for me to be up at this hour. I let out a deep sigh and look back to the loose bed sheets flowing onto the floor. I'm prepared to make another attempt at sleep, but before I take a step back toward the bed, the noise outside re-enters my senses.

It's Lyra. The tiny creature moves through the grass with an adorably fervent stride that makes her look like feline royalty. Her golden fur seems to shimmer with shades of orange and white in the full moonlight. A smile spreads across my face when she prances forward.

I rest my hand against my cheek and watch her like she's the star of a movie. Eventually, I have to move my body to keep her in my line of sight. She's so far out into the yard that she's now a furry, golden blur.

A shadow protrudes from beneath my view, and my body straightens. My smile shifts to a concerned gnarl, until Ara has completely appeared. Light glistens from her dark hair as she trots toward the cat with long, red pajama bottoms dancing around her bare feet. Her hands are tucked inside the pockets of a red hooded sweatshirt.

Lyra finally stops moving, and appears to take a solemn seat beside a withered old tree. It is the only thing in the scenery other than the tall grass. Ara is about halfway toward her before she stops. I adjust my body to get a clearer view. As I rest my elbows against the windowsill, she slowly turns and gazes upward. My eyes jolt like a burst of sunlight has bombarded my face. Ara is looking straight at me. I avert my gaze as if the starry skies were my focus the whole time.

"Psst," she calls out.

My gaze drifts downward at her tickled grin. An embarrassed smile drifts across my face when she nudges her head toward Lyra.

"C'mon," she says.

I turn to look at my closed bedroom door, as if I'm expecting Leo to be standing there glaring at me, like the eavesdropper I am. When I'm sure no one else is coming, I give a hefty sigh and turn back. Ara has continued her slow pace toward Lyra. I grab a sweatshirt from the closet and head down the stairs and toward the back porch.

"Didn't expect you to be awake." Ara grins as soon as I've exited through the screen door and stepped into the tall grass.

It feels prickly, yet soothingly cool between my bare toes.

"Neither did I." I give a sarcastic laugh while approaching her.

"Well, the silence can definitely take some getting used to."

We begin walking side by side. I turn back to glance at the farmhouse in the distance. I am amazed at just how far out we are. The air is brisk. Wind wafts through my face every few seconds, and makes me thankful that I grabbed the sweatshirt. The comforting material fits my body like I bought it myself. It's insane to me how much Pavo has prepared for my arrival.

"Sorry."

The word seems to squirt from my lips as if Ara had said something to provoke it. She turns to me with a confused stare.

"About what?"

"Well...ya know...about the Leo thing."

She laughs. We stop at the edge of a hill, and she plops down.

"Don't be," she says, as I take a seat next to her. "Leo is a bit of an acquired taste. But he's very brotherly once you get to know him."

I give a gratifying grunt. A strong gust of wind flows between us, and she scoots a few inches closer to me.

"So why are you up?" I say, as we look out over the hill, just beyond the old tree where Lyra sits.

"Oh, I always have trouble sleeping after I do an aural jump."

I nod toward her, as if I understand. She turns and takes a deep, calming breath. There is a gleam in her eyes as the moon reflects from them.

"So...what does it feel like?"

She turns to me with her signature grin, before wrapping her arms around her knees and coiling the edges of her sleeves around her fists. I can tell that she's been waiting for me to ask this inevitable question.

"It's weird. It's kinda like...stealing a car."

My eyebrow perks. This isn't remotely what I expected to hear. For some reason, I was expecting to hear some mind-blowing parable about inner spirituality, or some nonsense along those lines.

"The owner is in the backseat, tied up and screaming while you're driving. They're trying to wriggle free the whole time you're in the midst of a high-speed chase. And you're just trying to finish your task before they get free."

She looks over at my extended jaw and gives a soft giggle.

"Not what you expected, huh?"

"Not exactly, no." I laugh. "Sounds intense."

She shrugs.

Lyra creeps over and nuzzles herself between Ara's legs for warmth. I let another blissful breeze blow by before I continue my attempts to pick her brain.

"Earlier today, when you guys rescued me, Leo said something about cutting it close—"

She chuckles. "Well, it won't surprise you to know that Leo can be a bit of a worry wart. I've been *in* for longer than that."

"What's the longest?"

She ponders for a bit while rubbing Lyra under her furry chin.

"About thirty minutes, maybe?" she says, as if she's never calculated.

"And your body? What happens to it while you're in someone else's?"

"It's sort of…in a catatonic state. I can't be out too long," she pats her stomach, "or this ole girl won't be any good once I hop back in."

I pause to take it all in. All this time, I've used my powers and thought about the dangers that come with them. But the things Ara can do are beyond danger-ous. Every time she uses them must seem like a matter of life and death.

"What about the other guy?" I say, as my mind drifts to the body of the fifth soldier.

I realize I haven't seen him since we arrived.

"It takes some time for the original host to regain full control after I've left it. They're unconscious for a while."

I nod, but I can't help but feel foolish for even caring about the fifth soldier's well-being. After all, it isn't like the real person inside that suit would've been willing to risk his life for me.

"What would happen if you were in too long?"

Ara's smile dissipates, and she takes a prolonged look into Lyra's bulbous eyes. The cat gives a lengthy purr.

"You mean, if the driver ever gets free?" Her gaze tilts to the stars. "If we lose control...well, let's just say the mind was only meant to have one dominant consciousness."

Lyra lets out another soothing purr before crawling underneath Ara's leg and over to mine. I lightly jump, mostly because I'm shocked that this animal that hissed at me earlier tonight, now feels comfortable enough to brush her warm fur up against me.

I open up my legs more so that the tiny feline can get a comfortable position. She runs her paws up against my shirt and scrapes away at the layers of cotton like a scratching post. The prick of her tiny claws stings at first, but as I rub from her pointy ears down to her soft coat, I am distracted by something different. From the moment I first met Lyra, I recognized that her eyes didn't look like the eyes of an animal. I had ignored it before, but now, with a prolonged stare, I'm fully realizing it. Her pupils seem softer, clearer. Almost... human.

I look up at Ara, who is now glaring down at Lyra with a desperate look in her fervent eyes. As Lyra curls into my lap, I finally ask the obvious question.

"How long was she..."

"We were kids." Ara reaches over to caress Lyra within my lap. "Still learning about our abilities. We both started off jumping into animals. It was like a game. Pavo hated it, of course, so we'd always do it in secret. We used to sneak out at night and jump into birds. We'd fly around together, then hop back."

Finally, Ara's gaze meets mine again. A light smile has returned to her face, but her eyes are filled with glossy tears.

"One day, a stray cat comes roaming by. Lyra's eyes light up like she's seeing Santa Claus in the flesh. She asks me if I want to try first, but I'm petrified. Not Lyra. She was never scared of anything."

I look down at Lyra as her eyes drift shut, and my heart starts to rattle.

"We'd never been anything other than birds or lizards that crept through the yard every so often. For a while, it was Lyra, prancing around, running through the fields as fast as she could. I laughed and laughed. We even pulled pranks on some of the others."

There is so much sorrow in her voice. I want to give her a hug or rub her shoulder, but something in my head tells me to just sit there and cradle Lyra in my lap.

"But after about an hour, I keep calling to her, and she doesn't turn to me. A bird flies by, and she starts chasing it. I run after her, and...she runs from me. It takes me forever to catch her. By the time I bring her back, Pavo has her real body cradled in his arms. At first, he's furious. But then I can see the worry in his eyes."

She pauses for a moment. It's as if she's reached the part in her story that she always tries to forget.

"We tried for weeks, months even, but..."

I feel my arm reaching out toward Ara. I run my hand along her back as if I'm stroking Lyra's fur. She looks back at me, and the hopeful gleam returns to her eyes.

"She's still in there, somewhere. She's definitely too damn smart for a cat."

I release my hand and place it behind Lyra's warm ears.

"Any-who." Ara's original perkiness comes roaring back, like when our conversation had just begun. "After that, it took years for Pavo to trust us to use our powers. And even then, we always had to use them under the adults' supervision."

We? Us? Adults? The words spout from her so inanely. Sure, I remember Pavo's explanation, but I'm just now starting to come to the realization of it all. I haven't even been here for twenty-four hours, but it's become clear that no one else lives here other than Pavo, Leo, Ara, and Lyra. For the first time, instead of wondering about my mother and what will happen to me, I'm wondering...what happened to the other Clairvoyants?

CHAPTER 11

THE OTHER CLAIRVOYANTS

AN ADORABLE SNORE WHISTLES THROUGH Lyra's whiskers as she sleeps between my thighs. Ara stares off at the moonlit horizon, while my head flutters with calculations. Leo insisted that there were four strains. And before me, no strain had more than three members. There should be twelve of them—not including me—but there are only four Clairvoyants living here.

A yawn echoes from Ara as a breeze passes through the chilly, late-night air. It makes the questions sift through my head more rapidly. Could Psyriin have captured or killed the rest of them? It's easily the best explanation. But if it's true, then it is definitely an even touchier subject than how Lyra got trapped in the body of a stray cat.

The curiosity is killing me like the cliffhanger of a television show's season finale. I want to know. Need to know. I have to ask. But how? How do I ask without offending her? The last thing I want is to make her uncomfortable. I already have one person in the house who seems to despise me.

Ara's body shifts like she wants to get up, and I know that I have to come up with something soon. I take a deep breath and fine-tune the question in my head before I speak.

"So…" I make sure my tone is solemn and sympathetic, "you guys are all that's left?"

Her head jerks to mine. I just know she's about to give me a vicious scowl. But instead, I am relieved to be met with a contrite chuckle.

"Oh, no. Our lives have been gloomy. But not as horrific as we might've led you to believe."

I can't help but give a deep sigh of relief. I don't know what's more relieving—that she wasn't offended by my asking, or the idea that there are several others somewhere out there, alive and well.

"As far as I know, only one of us has been captured by Psyriin."

I want to know who, but my original reservations begin to creep back in. I try my best to seem less interested by twiddling my hands through a few blades of grass between my lap.

"Is that why everyone left?" I mumble.

She looks into my eyes through a few quick blinks. I can feel the disappointment flurrying through her face as she recalls the distant thoughts.

"I'd love to tell you that Auriga being taken is what separated us. But the truth is, we started collapsing way before that."

Auriga. I remember the name being mentioned in Pavo's story. He was the man who realized that the marks on their arms were modeled after constellations.

Ara looks down at Lyra and rubs her soft fur before returning her focus to me.

"I guess it all started after Lyra's accident. After that, we went from being a family to being more like students at a school. The Prophets—Pavo, Auriga, and Andromeda—used to train us at least four days a week."

Andromeda. When Ara says her name, a heightened sensation shoots through me. For some reason, I'm still hopeful that the woman who freed Pavo from the chamber is my mother. That perhaps, who they know as Andromeda was still Diana Grean, and they just hadn't put it together yet. Mom being a Prophetic

Clairvoyant would certainly explain how she knew when to move us to another town, and how we escaped Psyriin. But if she had been pregnant with me while living with the Clairvoyants, my existence wouldn't be so shocking to them. As much as I want Andromeda to be my mother, the timeline simply doesn't add up, and I hate admitting that Leo was right.

"Carina was actually the first person to leave."

Disdain fills Ara's voice, and I glance up at the look of agitation plastered across her face.

"She's an Aural, like me and Lyra, but she's way different. It's kinda hard to know how old everyone is, but she was a teenager when we broke free. She always treated us like little sisters, but we couldn't stand her."

My eyes widen, mainly because I can't imagine Ara disliking someone.

"Carina was always terrified of our powers. She pretty much never projected unless we were training. But that didn't stop her from being a snitch every time we did something remotely against the rules."

Ara rolls her eyes, and I can't help but chuckle. I couldn't imagine growing up with two Leo's in the house.

"Anyway. She disappeared about ten years ago. Didn't even tell anyone. We just woke up one day, and she was gone."

An astonished grimace covers my face. The thought of an Aural out there somewhere, with the ability to jump into anyone's body and control them, is unsettling. Especially someone bold enough to leave the only family they'd ever known.

"Andromeda left two years later. Which was a surprise, because her and Pavo were inseparable. She didn't say goodbye, either. Only Pavo and Auriga knew she'd left. Apparently, she'd had some mind-blowing vision that she'd become obsessed with. They told us she felt she had to leave and find out what it meant. We haven't seen or heard from her since."

Ara takes a deep breath as her look of dejection reappears.

"Next was Lacerta. She's around the same age as Leo and Carina, so she'd be about thirty years old now. She's one of the mind readers. Her and Leo always had a thing for each other, and she was the only one who could ever keep him calm. So when she left, the stick up his ass got shoved even further."

I can't hold my laughter this time. Even Ara snickers.

"Lacerta was also really close with Andromeda. So after she disappeared, Lacerta just didn't want to be around us anymore. She wanted a normal life. As if that's possible for us." She gives a sarcastic grunt. "We tried to convince her to stay, but Auriga insisted on letting her choose her own path."

A thought creeps through my head. All this time, I had been worried about my mother, the only family I'd ever known. But the Clairvoyants were a family, too. Theirs was much larger, but just as connected as mine. They, too, had broken apart, and it makes me see Leo in a different light. I understand now why he was so careless about me and my mother. He had also been abandoned by loved ones. And like me, he had no idea if they were okay.

"The rest of us forged along for a few more years. There were the three Kinetics—Perseus, Aries, and Aquila—who are all in their mid-twenties now. The third mind reader is Lupus, who's about nineteen, like me. And then there's the lovely people you've already met."

I nod as I mentally sort out the math. I notice Ara's mood beginning to shift once more. There is a look of fierce anxiety in her eyes. It is almost identical to Pavo's when he'd first shared his past. My stomach starts to churn as I wait for her to continue.

"Then, about five years ago, Auriga wakes us all up in the middle of the night. I know I was just a toddler when we escaped that lab, but I swear...it...it was like that night all over again."

Ara stares at the wafting grass in the distance, as if she is watching her memories play out. The glossiness of her eyes feels cold and unsettling.

"He tells us to grab whatever we can and get out. We got away just before the first Psyriin soldiers came. Auriga foresaw it in a vision. He stayed behind so we could escape."

A deep silence follows, and for the first time, I feel guilt. I'm not sure why. None of this is my fault, but I can't help but wish that I could've met Auriga. I can't help but want to thank him. Without his sacrifice, Leo, Pavo, and Ara wouldn't have been able to rescue me, because they wouldn't have been saved themselves.

"After that, things kinda got rocky. Perseus…or Persey, as I like to call him—he hates that, by the way—wanted us to go back and save Auriga, but Pavo wanted no part of it. We moved here, but things just weren't the same. The Kinetics wanted Pavo to start training us to fight. They were hellbent on going after Psyriin, but Pavo was just trying to keep us safe. Then, one night at dinner, Persey goes on a tantrum about how he's tired of us being prey. He says we should be Predators."

My brow perks. Leo and Pavo had mentioned them earlier tonight. I can tell by the way Ara talks about this Perseus guy that she isn't too fond of him. But me?

I can't help but be inspired by this guy's vigor. If I knew Mom had been taken by Psyriin, I'd want to fight, too.

"A few days later, Persey tells us he's leaving, and that all of the *Predators* should come with him. Sure enough, the other two Kinetics go with him, and Lupus's impressionable ass goes, too."

"Wow."

"Yeah." She huffs, with another eye roll.

We sit in the grass as a light red hue begins to cascade over the peaceful horizon. We both yawn, and after a conferring nod, we rise to our feet.

"And you haven't seen any of them since?"

"Actually, every once in a while, we run into the *Predators*," she says, in a mocking tone. "Hell, you can probably catch some of their exploits in the tabloids."

I scowl as we walk side by side, back to the farmhouse.

"Pavo sends us out whenever he has a vision about them. We keep them from drawing too much attention to themselves. They want to draw out Psyriin, but they're incredibly reckless."

We reach the door at the back porch. Before Ara opens it, we give one last look at the soothing image of the sun beginning to rise over the hillside. Lyra squirms to get comfortable in Ara's arms, with her tiny eyes still shut.

"In many ways, they're just as dangerous as Psyriin. They don't care about regular people. And that scares us."

The door shuts. Creaks and groans echo against the walls as we walk up the staircase. I try to hold back another yawn, to no avail. We stop at the end of the hallway between each of our bedrooms.

"Luckily, you aren't like them." She grins.

I return the gesture, trying my best to conceal that I don't agree.

"Goodnight, Rion," she whispers, as she turns and heads for her room. "Thanks for listening. It feels nice to let it all out."

"Any time." I smile.

Her bedroom door quietly shuts.

A *thump!* shakes me from the most indulgent slumber I've had in weeks. My eyelids tighten as I wrap the sheets around my shoulders in an attempt to ignore the jarring sensation. Another *thud!* shakes the bed. I growl and crack one eye open. My vision is blurred, but I can still make out Leo standing over me through a few streaks of brisk daylight.

"Rise and shine, Mama's Boy." He huffs as he kicks the bed again.

"Seriously?" I mumble, in a groggy haze. "What time is it?"

"Nine a.m." He opens up the curtains to let a flood of sunlight bathe the room.

I groan and shut my eyes to the point of ache, but he just yanks the sheets from me.

"You'd be well-rested if you weren't up 'til the crack of dawn, flirting with Ara."

I prepare to give him a piercing stare and a snide remark about how he's a sneaky prick for reading my mind, but he speaks again before I can even open my mouth.

"I know that because you made a ton of noise coming back in the house this morning. Not because I read your mind."

I roll my eyes. My hands blanket my face to shield the room's glowing luster.

"Why so early?" I snap.

Leo grins and saunters toward the door. "You'll be happy to know that our other guest has regained consciousness."

My eyes widen, as if a cool glass of water has doused my face. I rise from my bed and stare through Leo's thin glasses. He looks back with a wily sneer.

"I have no problem interrogating him without you. But Pavo insists that I bring you along. So get your ass up, put some clothes on, and meet me in the shed out back."

I scowl at him, but I can tell he's reading all of the expletives being thrown from my mind to his. He cracks a snide smile before turning and leaving.

"Five minutes!" he yells, from the stairwell.

A refreshing breeze surrounds me as I step out into the back lawn. I'm still insanely drowsy, but the thought of seeing the fifth soldier—the real fifth soldier—seems to fill my veins with an extra ounce of adrenaline. I am excited to know what we can find. But more so, anxious for any clues that might lead to Mom's where-abouts.

I'm a few feet from a fence that encompasses a horde of cows when I see Leo. He's wearing a tight gray T-shirt that clings to his chest like another layer of skin. You'd think the guy was some sort of professional model with the clothes he wears.

"About time." He marches up to me with a stern look in his eyes.

He's holding two steaming Styrofoam cups. He hands me one, and I place it to my face. The soothing, warm scent of hot cocoa billows into my nostrils and wakes me up just a tad more.

"Follow me," he grumbles.

I can tell he's *thrilled* to bring me along.

We walk about twenty yards from the corner of the house, to a tall burgundy shed. The wood is crusty and looks far from its original hue. For some reason, as I sip my delicious beverage, I keep waiting for him to apologize for being such a jerk last night. It takes only a few more seconds of awkward silence to realize that it's a farfetched notion. Funny. I guess my talk with Ara made me sympathize with him more. But I'm quickly realizing that Leo is just easy to dislike. Silly me for thinking that he might let his guard down as easy as Ara did.

We come to the shed's towering double doors and halt. A large iron lock is draped across the handle.

"Hold this." He bombards me with his cup, just as I am tilting mine to my lips.

I grab it and scoff at him, but he ignores me. He pulls a set of keys from his jean pocket and sifts through them until he has picked out the most rusted one.

"How'd you sleep?" He unlocks the door and shoves.

"Fine, until you—"

The doors screech open, and Leo heads inside without even waiting for my reply. I grunt, before scanning the crisp blue horizon. I'm hoping to see Pavo or Ara. Even seeing Lyra trotting through the lawn would be a welcoming presence to break the tension.

I turn to look into the shed. There is nothing but a heavy flow of darkness glaring back. It looks like something straight out of a horror movie.

"You comin', Mama's Boy?"

I give a heavy sigh before stepping inside. The doors grind behind me, dousing the remaining fragments of light. The dank scent about this place reminds me of a sewer. Patches of dust cling to the bottoms of my shoes. I take a few more tiny steps and notice that there's no wood beneath my feet. The floor seems to be coarse like concrete.

Leo's footsteps scrape against the dusty floor, but the emptiness of this room makes it difficult to pinpoint exactly where he is. I move a few more steps before his cup is snatched from my hands, and I can't help but jump back.

I hear the flick of a switch, and cringe when the burst of a fluorescent light illuminates the room. I was right about the concrete, but it isn't just beneath my feet. It's everywhere. The walls are decked with thick layers, like we're in a bunker equipped for a nuclear war.

I take another sip of cocoa to ease my thumping heart as I gaze around.

"Welcome to the interrogation room."

I turn around and see him leaning against a concrete slab that stretches across the wall like a shelf. To his right is an iron door with a small, closed window at the top. Beside it is a lever that I'm guessing is used to open the door into the next room. After taking a long gulp from his cup, Leo places it against the slab and examines something that I can't make out until I move closer.

It's the fifth soldier's attire. His large weapon, helmet, chest plate, pants, and boots are laid out in a row. I stand in silence as Leo picks up each item, one by one. He studies them, as if there's some sort of clue to be found. He pulls a knife from the boots. It's the sharpest knife I've ever seen. Looks like it could cut through bone with one swing.

He tosses the boots to the side and picks up the pants. Pulls two loaded handguns from them and growls before taking the weapons apart like they're made of cheap plastic.

"They never carried handguns before," he whispers, as if he's talking more to himself than to me. "You're lucky we found you when we did, kid."

He sets his hands against the slab and glares at the gear. The enraged look in his eyes makes me feel uneasy.

We hear clambering through the walls. It isn't loud, but in this silence, it's hard to miss. My eyes widen like a child hearing a bump in the night, but Leo just shifts his scowl toward the door. I swallow a glob of thick saliva as my lips rub together. Leo stomps by me, to the door, and yanks its square window open so strongly that it seems like it might break.

He gives it a callous, almost murderous, glower for several seconds. The sound of movement in the next room is replaced by a few groans that I can faintly hear. I set my cup against the concrete slab and take a step forward. Leo turns to me and nudges his head to signal me in closer.

As I approach the window, Leo moves to the side so that I'm the only one who can see through the small space. I know the unarmored fifth soldier is there, but my heartbeat rattles like I'm about to see an alien or something. I stand on my toes to get a clear view. There he is, sitting in a chair that doesn't look the least bit comforting. The tip of each chair leg appears to mold with the stone floor, making the soldier's frantic movements seem even more useless than I'd imagined. His hands are tied behind him, and his feet are bound by a thick wire. Nothing on his body but a thin, sleeveless shirt and a pair of pale boxers both dampened by his own sweat. The room itself seems endless, thanks to a flood of hollow darkness. A small lightbulb a few feet from his head manages to illuminate him, and only him.

My gaze flows from the piercing stream of light to his balding scalp. Sweat drenches his brow so much that it looks as if he'd just been swimming in a pool. A rag protrudes from his mouth, secured by thick tape that is wrapped so tight around his head it makes his skin a blistering red.

Our gazes meet. His black pupils look like frigid coals. The look in them seems both ferocious and desperate. Apprehension grips me, and I can't turn away. Neither of us moves or blinks, until Leo slams the window shut.

I jump back.

"Okay," he says. "You saw him."

I turn and scowl at Leo, uncertain of what is next to come. Surely we aren't going in there? Even though this beast of a man is nearly naked and bound to an immovable chair, I can't help but feel uneasy going anywhere near him.

"You ready?"

My gaze meet Leo's. He doesn't need to read my thoughts to know how uneasy I feel.

"We're going in there?"

I feel stupid and weak as soon as the words limp from my creaking voice, but Leo remains focused. He heads over to the protruding concrete slab and kneels beneath it.

"Not exactly."

He retrieves two steel folding chairs and moves toward me. My brow curls. My heartbeat moves to a steady thump as he unfolds the chairs and places them in front of the door. He gives a solemn glance at the door before cracking his thick neck and moving his shoulders in a circular motion.

"We're not going into the room." He looks into my anxious brown eyes. "We're going into his mind."

My eyes widen, and my heart pounds harder in my chest, like it's performing a drum solo. I'm trying to fight my own thoughts, which I'm certain Leo is reading and mentally laughing at. I need to get it together. It's no big deal, I tell myself, while failing to notice Leo roaming behind me.

I'd barely taken a seat when I felt a prick against my arm.

"Ow!" I grasp the sore area and glare into Leo's haughty smirk. "What the hell did you stab me with?"

"It's a sedative." He places the needle on the table before ambling over to the other seat.

"Sedati...sedative...fo...for...wha...what?"

Leo's lumbering frame becomes a blur before I can even begin to make out any reply. The room spins. My body feels heavy. And then...everything fades away.

CHAPTER 12

INSIDE THE MIND

I DON'T REMEMBER ARRIVING HERE. I DON'T even know where *here* is. It's like a dream. Colors whirl around me in streams, like speeding bullets. The atmosphere is hollow. I can't feel myself breathe, and for a moment I'm frightened.

I look at my hands. At least, they look like my hands. But…I can't feel them. I can't feel anything. I wiggle my toes inside my sneakers. No sensation. And yet, somehow, I know they're moving. I swallow a thin layer of saliva, and the same awkward sensation follows.

My eyes are wide like saucers as they drift upward. The streaming colors are everywhere. It's like an infinite patch of shooting stars sifting through an endless sea of bright, white space. My awestricken gaze drifts down to my feet. There is nothing beneath them. I take a step. Then another. Somehow I am on solid ground, but the emptying white seems to have no contours or edges. Everything just...*is*. It's both terrifying and over-whelmingly beautiful at the same time.

"Trippy, right?"

I slowly turn my head over my shoulder, and there is Leo, right behind me. I glare into the back of his dirty blond hair as he stands in the nothingness. His arms are outstretched, and his palms are open wide. The streaming colors appear to be flowing around him, like ocean currents being manipulated by the wind. I creep toward him as if my footing could give way at any moment.

"Where are we?" I marvel at the lack of sensation from the movement of my own lips.

"We're inside the human mind."

Leo's voice seems to echo. His lips hardly move, and his eyes remain fixated forward. I marvel at the streams of light reflecting from his glasses before I finally turn and look up at the same thing that has his attention.

They can only be described as television screens shaped like storm clouds. Dozens of them appear each second. They come, stop for an instant, then whiz around us. I follow one, and it sends my body whirling.

It all rushes back to me. It's as if I've finally realized I am asleep. We're inside the soldier's mind. But I'm not a Reader Clairvoyant. How am I here?

"I've linked our minds telepathically," Leo says, his pupils scurrying around to capture each image before they go flying over us.

"I'm using the Psyiirin soldier's mind as a meeting point. Not easy, by the way. Don't let anyone tell you different."

A smile splits across his face, and I know he's laughing at me. I can't blame him. I probably look like someone high on mushrooms for the first time. I find myself scanning each of my appendages like a newborn baby. I know I look ridiculous, but I can't help but be astonished at this feeling. It's a feeling of being present, and absent, all at once.

"Is...is it always like this?" I say.

At least, I think it comes from my mouth.

Leo chuckles again. "Not exactly. Concurrent thoughts—things on the mind, at the moment—I can read those like they're being written across a person's forehead. If someone thought about throwing a punch at me, they might as well say it aloud first."

My thoughts trek back to the moment when Leo and Ara saved me from the Psyriin soldiers. Leo took down those armed men so quickly, and with such ease. Now I know why.

"But memories, secrets..." He squints. "I have to go deeper for those."

"Does he know we're in here? I mean, what if he was to escape from the wires?"

"You mean, if he somehow managed to get through the wiring around his ankles and wrists? Then got through the locked steel door? Well, then Ara and Pavo would be waiting on the other side for him."

"Okaaayyyy." My eyes cross to stare at the edges of my protruding lips.

It's the last thing I do before I feel myself start to normalize, and my gaze lifts toward the flowing images above us.

"So is this kind of like what Ara does?"

"I'm sure she's given you the car analogy, right?"

I nod, but my attention remains engrossed in the fluttering lights and pictures.

"Well, I can't drive the car. But I can see where it's going, read the instruction manual, pop the hood, and get all the car facts."

Even though my gaze remains on the impressive atmosphere, I catch Leo's agitated grimace in the corner of my eye. Apparently, I was supposed to be more impressed.

"In other words," he groans, "she can manipulate the body, but she has no access to the core subconscious. Reader Clairvoyants can do the opposite."

My head snaps toward him as I come to a realization. He's read my mind. He has to have. There's no way he would've brought me to the farmhouse, or saved me from Psyriin, unless he'd read my thoughts. And now, I can't help but wonder if while I sleep, Leo is scanning my brain, just like he's sifting through the fifth soldier's.

"So...you can see anything in his mind?" I try to deflect his attention, as if I'm able to defend my own brain.

"Anything and everything." He smirks. "Thoughts, ideas, dreams, fantasies, memories...they're all here. I can find things that he doesn't even remember."

If I could feel my chest thumping, it would probably be going a mile a minute. My fingers begin to twitch, and I find myself looking away.

"I could even make him forget things, if I wanted to. It'd be as easy as pulling a book from a shelf."

He speaks like he's tinkering with a toy, not talking about tampering with someone's brain.

A thousand thoughts scurry through me. I glance around, like a toddler that's gotten lost in a shopping mall. What if he's doing this to me right now? What if we're in my head, and not the fifth soldier's?

"Relax, Mama's Boy." He laughs, as my irked sneer darts in his direction.

"You'll be happy to know that I can't see anything in your head. I had to sedate you just to pull off this link. Clairvoyants have some type of psionic barrier around our minds that makes it painful and virtually impossible to read. Prophetics, like Pavo, are the only ones without it. But their minds are like beehives."

A sigh of relief—or the mental animation resembling a sigh of relief—cascades through me. Leo gives another hearty laugh before turning toward me.

"But you don't have to be a telepath to read body language and facial expressions."

I snarl.

With each second, I can feel myself growing more and more comfortable in this psychic plane.

"So what are you looking for?" I grumble, as I cross my arms.

Leo's eyes return to their stern state. His pupils begin to dance around once again.

"We're looking for any images of you and your mother. So if you're done being mystified, you can give me a hand."

A seismic groan echoes from my chest as I approach his side.

Even as I begin to come to terms with the idea that I am no longer in a physical realm, I can't help but stay awestricken. The intense tapestry of images and light feels like I'm inside of a prism.

I shake my head, trying to regain my focus. Leo peers into one particular image, then growls and sends it whirling by.

"So how do I do this, exactly?" I foolishly hold out my arms, like his.

"I'm going to sort the streams and send them your way."

I nod as if I fully understand. I can tell he's trying his best not to take his gaze off of the cluster of clouds bombarding his gaze. His body shifts, and his fingertips curl like he's directing a series of intricate puppets in the distance.

"Here."

He points, and my gaze follows.

"Memories will be red. Fantasies, purple. Dreams, blue. Nightmares, black. Ideas, green. Got it?"

I mumble everything to myself, reciting them like a poem, so I can't forget.

"Got it!" He huffs.

He looks at me, and the images around him come to a rigid halt above us, like they're cars screeching at a stoplight.

"Memories, red," I repeat. "Fantasies, purple. Dreams, blue. Nightmares, black. Ideas, green."

"Good."

His gaze returns forward, and the thought clouds begin scurrying once again. I turn and take a deep breath to prepare to receive my share, when something else catches my eye. A large bubble, just above the whirling colors in our periphery. The view inside this cloud is much clearer than the others. My glare fixates on it as a pair of bound feet come into view.

"What about that one?"

"His current thoughts?" Leo replies, without even following my gaze. "Keep an eye on them, if you want, but don't get too distracted. He's not going anywhere."

My brow curls as the soldier's feet continue to squirm.

"Ready or not, Mama's Boy."

My gaze darts down, and I regain my focus. My fingers dance around. I twitch my neck, as if I'm stretching my muscles in preparation. Leo shifts his arm toward me, and before I know it, the images stream into view. They come about a dozen at a time. Leo sends them grouped together, as promised. They move steadily, but he has slowed them far more than the images he sifts through. I feel each hue bathe my face in light as they surround me. It is overwhelming at first. But the thought that Leo is brushing through almost three times as many clouds as I am motivates me to increase my focus.

First, come the ideas. There aren't many. And perhaps it is my own arrogance, but I don't think it takes a telepath to understand the hollowness of the soldier's mind. These ideas are vague and shortsighted. What to eat for dinner. What to grab for the next mission. What to do in case of mission failure. Perhaps he should've taken longer to foster this idea. He was supposed to take a cyanide pill, but he doesn't seem to remember where he put it.

I'm not surprised by the soldier's lack of imagination. To be a soldier— a pawn in a much larger scheme such as this—there is no time for forward thinking. There is hardly any time for free will at all, it seems. So I move on.

Here come the fantasies. I scan through them like websites on a search engine. None of these seem relevant. The soldier appears to want to become a high-ranking general of some sort. There are also some dumb images of him sleeping with his superior officer. I recognize the woman from the abandoned shopping center. I discover that her name is Nastacia Arkright. It doesn't take looking through very many fantasies to realize the fifth soldier has a particular fondness for her. His vision of her is far less vicious than the woman I briefly saw. Her blue eyes and soft, clear skin are mesmerizing up close. Her body, at least in the soldier's mind, is a picturesque physique meant for a supermodel.

"Don't get distracted, Mama's Boy," Leo grumbles, over my shoulder.

I roll my eyes before I send the patch of purple images zooming away.

Next, are the dreams. Initially, I can't understand why Leo would even send me these. The soldier's dreams are so abstract, so unusual, that I feel like I'm trying to read Mandarin. After I remember what I'm looking for, I sift through each one, making sure there is nothing resembling me or my mother within them.

His nightmares are next, fittingly draped in black. There aren't many, but it takes only a few violent deaths and disemboweled corpses before I am ready to move on. The only one that garners my attention for more than a split second is a horrific image of a man attacking a woman. Chills shoot down my spine, and my outstretched hands begin to shake. I want to close my eyes, but after a deep breath, I gather myself and focus. Once I'm sure it isn't my mother in the image, a sigh of relief flows through me.

How does Leo do this? Gazing into someone's nightmares, examining thoughts that a person himself doesn't want to see. How does it not shake him?

I look over my shoulder at him. A horde of nightmares are blanketing his view, yet he scans them restlessly, like a businessman studying his profit margins.

The look in his eyes is so focused, so calculating, that I can't help but gain more respect for his calm restitution.

Finally, I receive the memories. I am glad they've come. To me, nothing is more important. There are ten red clouds around me, each one displaying different sets of images, every thirty to forty seconds. I start from the top and catch a glimpse of the intense military training he went through. Then there are memories of his time serving as a special ops member of some sort of US Strike Force in the Middle East. As fascinating as the images are, they aren't what I'm looking for. I brush them off and move on to the next.

"Careful," Leo's gaze continues to blare forward. "You aren't watching TV, kid."

I scoff and try to continue my examination, but Leo isn't done talking.

"You're looking for a face, or something you find familiar. Leave the research to me."

I reluctantly nod, and move on to the next row, ignoring the extraneous images of his rough childhood and schooling. It isn't until the bottom row that I finally see something that catches my eye.

It's Nastacia Arkright. She is wearing the same sleek bodysuit that I first saw her in. Behind her are images of that old, dusty square where the soldiers had found me. I glare through the soldier's viewpoint as he leaps from one of those daunting vehicles and stands in attention.

"*Search every corner until you've found him!*" Arkright shouts, glaring through the soldier's visor with her blue eyes. "*He couldn't have gotten far on foot.*"

This is it! This is the moment they came after me. My eyes widen as I stare at the image, like I'm a kid watching a movie on the big screen for the first time. The soldiers run forth, kicking in old doorways and breaking glass with their large weapons at the ready. Then the image wriggles and becomes foggy. The soldier's viewpoint seems to thrust forward like he is being shoved from behind. And then it just disappears.

I shake my head, and my eyes flutter. It only takes a moment before I realize what happened. This had to be when Ara took control of the soldier's body. Anything that happened from that point on, now belonged to her mind, not his.

Grrrrglll!

I stumble forward, barely managing to catch my balance on the invisible floor. My face molds into a confused gnarl, and I twist my head around to meet Leo. His normally stern and assured visage appears to be as distraught as mine.

"What was tha—"

Grrrrrrgggllllll!

Everything shakes again before I can even finish my sentence. The second rumble lasts a few seconds longer. I can feel my metaphysical heart trembling through my chest.

"Move!" Leo huffs as he darts past me.

He focuses his worrisome grimace upward, toward the image of the soldier's current viewpoint. I'd probably be agitated with him shoving by me if I weren't baffled and terrified.

I follow Leo's scowl, just as the image of the soldier's view begins shaking uncontrollably. It's as if we're watching a camera caught in an earthquake.

Our surroundings start to violently tremble once more. Leo stumbles forward. I fall to my knees and grasp the invisible floor as dizziness clouds my senses. I try to get my bearings, but the sensation feels like I've been spun around for several minutes.

Leo grabs me and lifts me to my feet. Our gazes return to the image.

"Leo!"

It's Ara. She is standing inside the interrogation room, right in front of the soldier's quivering view.

"He's going into cardiac arrest!" she shouts. "Get out of there, now."

"Damn it," Leo growls.

He turns to the horde of images at our backs, and gestures like he's shooting the world's most accurate dart. A flurry of red images spews forth like a gust of wind. There seem to be thousands of them, and they now surround us in one massive cloud of bright crimson.

He brushes me to the side and begins whipping his hands all around him, as if he's chucking ninja stars at targets. With each movement, the images begin to turn black, like the collection of nightmares we'd just spent unnecessary time mulling through. I want to ask what he's doing, but the nauseating sensation keeps my lips from moving.

"Hurry!" Ara darts from the room.

I just barely make out Pavo in the interrogation room doorway, with an equal look of apprehension.

"Wha...what's happ—"

"What do you think?" Leo scoffs as he continues his gestures with ferocity. "He's dying!"

"What happens if we're still in here when he dies?"

"We lose all of this info. And you slip into a coma."

His tone is far too casual, like the second half of his statement shouldn't horrify me.

"A coma!"

Leo extends his arm toward my astonished gaze. I look around at the images, attempting to make one last observation amidst the chaos.

One of the red memory clouds snags my attention. It is only for a moment, but the image is as clear as day. The fifth soldier is standing amidst a sea of others like him. Above them, on a platform in front of a large screen, is Nastacia Arkright. On the screen behind her is a picture of my mother.

"Time for you to go," Leo says.

"Wait. Wha—"

I feel an intense shove, like I'm being pushed from an airplane. I spiral downward for several seconds, hellishly screaming the entire way. Eventually, everything shatters around me, as if I've just fallen through glass.

CHAPTER 13

THE CHARON

"MOM!" I RISE FROM MY BED.

My heart is thumping so fast it feels like I might hyperventilate. My extremities ache like I haven't used them in weeks.

"Calm down, Rion."

Ara is sitting in a chair beside me. There is a worrisome look in her pearly eyes, but her presence calms me and settles my thundering chest. Lyra leaps into my lap and lets out a soothing purr. I scan the room, realizing it is nighttime now. The orange flare of a lamp at the edge of the room barely manages to light my surroundings.

"What happened?" I turn toward Ara.

"Arkright must have implanted something in the soldier's chest to make him go into cardiac arrest in

case of capture." She sighs. "We've never had something like this happen before, or we would've been
more prepared."

I continue to pant, and my head begins to shake. My
body feels cold. My skin is coarse and ashy. Ara hands
me a glass of water. I gulp it down so fast you'd think
I'd just wandered through the desert.

"How long was I out?" I say, as soon as the last drop
of liquid has billowed down my throat.

"About twelve hours."

There's a glower on my face as I hand her the glass
and wriggle my extremities to assure that everything
is still in working order.

"Where's Leo?"

"He and Pavo are downstairs in the—"

I leap from the bed, and nearly tumble as soon as I
take my first step toward the door. After being inside
the soldier's mind, it feels incredibly weird to move my
limbs. Every step takes more focus, and it feels like I
am acutely aware of each appendage and pore.

"Rion, wait!" Ara calls, from behind.

I do my best to ignore her, and stagger to the stairwell. Lyra rushes ahead of me, nearly tripping me
when I reach the bottom. As soon as I'm clear of her,
I stumble toward the kitchen, where I can hear Leo
and Pavo talking.

"I saw her!" I blurt, as soon as they've come into view.

They're sitting with folded hands at the kitchen table. There are uneasy gleams in both of their eyes.

"Rion," Pavo grumbles, and sighs. "Come. Have a seat."

I clamor for a chair. Lyra jumps into the other empty seat beside me as Ara creeps to the doorway. Once I've settled inches from the table, my fierce glare meets Leo. There's a look of indifference on his stern brow.

"I saw my mom. Right before you pulled me out. I saw her in a memory. She was on a screen, in some sort of meeting they were having—"

"Slow your roll, kid." Leo extends his hand. "I saw it, too."

His tone is anything but assuring. Pavo lets out another unsettling sigh, and his fretful grimace drifts downward.

"And?" I huff.

"Well..." Pavo's scowl passes by each of us. "There's some good news, and some bad news."

"More like, bad news, and not-so-bad news," Leo says.

My insides churn, and I can't help but contemplate the worst-case scenario. Is Mom okay? I want to ask this question first, but I am terrified to know the answer.

"The memory you saw was a Psyriin briefing," Leo says. "The only information they were given was your mother's name, appearance, and whereabouts."

"But weren't they after me?"

"Their original mission was to apprehend your mother," Leo says. "They didn't even know you existed until after they'd sent that cop to arrest her."

My eyebrow curls with worrisome intrigue. I fixate my bulbous pupils on Leo's crisp lenses. I have to know. Is she okay?

"Well, what's the good news?" I say.

I can't help but cringe when Leo huffs before responding.

"The not-so-bad news is that the soldier broke off to find you after you and your mother separated. Ara took control of him shortly after, so there's no way he knows what happened to her after that. For all he knows, and for all we know, she is far away and safe."

A sigh of relief embellishes me, but it's only for a moment. I know now why Leo called it *not-so-bad* news. She could be far away from all of this, and perfectly fine. Or...

"So..." I whimper, as I my limbs grow rigid again. "What's the bad news?"

There are only seconds before his response, but the time feels like agony. It doesn't help that Ara is standing by with a somber grimace. Pavo is struggling to look directly at me, and Leo takes a deep breath and glances toward him for last-second approval.

"If your mother was captured, she would've been taken to a Psyriin prison called the Charon."

Tension fills the room. They are familiar with this place. Or at least, the idea of it. And whatever it is, the look on their faces assures me that the Charon is nothing short of a nightmare.

"It's not a normal prison," Leo continues. "It's some sort of aerial vehicle that is constantly mobile—making it impossible to locate. It's where they took Auriga."

My mouth becomes dry, and sweat beads down my forehead. Part of me is thankful that my mom is possibly alive. But the sheer dread and despair on their faces envelopes the room and makes me tremble.

"So...what do we do?"

"There's not much we can do, son," Pavo murmurs.

My jaw widens, and disbelief replaces my solemn scowl.

"There has to be something." I grind my fists against the table. "You can see the future, right? Can't you see if she's okay. Or find the Charon somehow?"

I know it's somewhat of a dumb question. If there were a way for Pavo to find this mobile prison, they'd surely have used it to find and rescue Auriga by now.

"My visions, for whatever reason, only pertain to myself and other Clairvoyants." Pavo frowns. "So I can't use them to find your mother. And I haven't been able to have a vision about Auriga since the night he was taken."

"And they're involuntary, remember?" Leo grunts, as if it's his mission to make me feel as miserable as possible.

I sincerely wish anyone other than him would speak.

"Well, go into Pavo's mind, like you did the soldier's. Find a vision or something."

"It doesn't work that way, kid." Leo gives a dejected laugh. "Prophetic Clairvoyants can't exactly pick and choose what they can predict—"

"And," Ara says, from over my shoulder, "a Prophetic doesn't know a vision is a vision until after it's happened."

Leo nods. "So hypothetically speaking, even if I were to spend days, or weeks, searching for a vision, Pavo's mind wouldn't be able to differentiate it from an infinite flood of ideas or fantasies. It'd be like trying to find a specific snowflake in a snowstorm."

I want them to just stop talking. I know they are just telling me the truth. But they're too honest. Why can't they humor me? Why can't they at least give me some sort of hope?

"I'm sorry, Rion," Pavo murmurs, through his raspy voice. "But we can't risk our lives on hypotheticals. Especially if we aren't even sure she's there."

My scowl hardens. My wooden chair screeches as I stand to my feet and snarl at each of them.

"Well, what about saving Auriga?" I huff. "He's on the Charon. Is there a way you can force Pavo to have a vision about him?"

"Scale it back, kid," Leo growls.

"No! I'm not going to sit here and do nothing. We have to try and draw them out. And...and Ara can try to infiltrate the Charon as another soldier."

"Even if he had the perfect vision," Leo says, "*forcing* Pavo to have one could kill him."

I can tell from his tone that this isn't the first time the idea has been tampered with.

"There are only two members of Psyriin that are even given access to the Charon. Some guy the soldiers call Bard, and Nastacia Arkright. None of the soldiers we've interrogated have ever met Bard. And Arkright has gone out of her way to avoid us, because she knows what Ara and I can do. Now that she knows you've met us, she isn't coming anywhere near you."

"So I'm just supposed to *hope* my mom is okay." I scoff.

I shake my head and tighten my fists. I feel Ara's soothing scent come over me. She's resting one of her soft, porcelain hands on my shoulder.

"We all want to do more, Rion," she says. "But we just have to be patient."

No. A disgusted frown is plastered on my face.

I shrug her away, then storm out of the kitchen before any of them can mutter another demoralizing word. My feet thunder up the stairs so hard it feels like the brittle wood will shatter beneath me. I reach my room and telekinetically slam the door.

I can't recall ever being this saddened and angered all at once. All I can do is think about Mom. Sure, she could be okay. But the thought that she has been taken…that she could be in any pain because of me… it is too much for me to just sit back and hope. I am not like Pavo, Leo, and Ara. I can't just wait idly by for the worst to happen. The slightest possibility that she isn't safe is enough for me to act.

And there's nothing they can say to sway me.

That eerie silence surrounds my room again. Only the sound of rustling grass creeps through my window. The stillness reminds me of the nights when I'd sit outside of our short-lived Missouri home, staring at the stars and wishing I could move them.

I cram a backpack with clothes, and throw it over my shoulder. I pass a glance at the empty room, before sliding the door open with my mind. The hallway is bathed in blackness. I give a brief minute for my eyes to adjust, before creeping down the stairs.

Meow.

The sound startles me as soon as my feet have touched the bottom of the stairwell. I look down. Lyra is rubbing against my leg and staring up at me with those eerily human eyes.

"Lyra, what are you doing?" I whisper.

She reaches up and paws at my pant leg, as if she is trying to stop me from making the decision I've already made. I roll my eyes, but still pick her up to cradle her between my arms.

"Fearless little Lyra. I bet you'd help me if you were still human."

"You're probably right."

The scruffy voice chills my skin and sends my heartbeat into a frenzy. When I whip my head around, Pavo is standing in the kitchen doorway with a halfhearted smile. When my senses have fully recognized him through the crisp darkness, my chest starts to settle.

He flicks on the kitchen light, and the golden hue billows down the hallway to brighten my nervous scowl. Lyra jumps from my arms and scurries toward him.

"Listen, Pavo, you're not gonna—"

"Come on. Let me fix you some food for your trip."

Before I can even reply, he's turned his back and sauntered into the kitchen. I let out a dejected sigh and slowly follow. My eyes widen as soon as I step foot into the brightly lit room. Laying at the center of the kitchen table are four containers of food. There is some leftover stew, soup, dry cereal, sandwiches, and my favorite snack—a pack of peanut butter and cheese crackers. I look up, and Pavo is standing over a pot of freshly prepared coffee. The steam billows from the counter and clouds his subtle grin.

"You had a vision about this." I huff.

"To know you were leaving? That was intuition. But yes, I had a vision." He chuckles. "You like two creams and two sugars, right?"

I smirk and nod. He doesn't even look back at me to see my response. I take a seat at the table and begin removing clothes from my backpack to make room for the food.

"So how do your powers work, exactly?" I lay a few poorly folded shirts on the table. "The visions about yourself. Like, if you've seen this moment, doesn't that mean you can change what happens?"

Pavo snickers as he continues stirring the steaming liquid in a tall Thermos, without turning toward me.

"It's a bit complicated. It's almost like a sixth sense that turns on and off. Watch your lap."

Before I can fully grasp his casual words, Lyra leaps into my thighs and then jumps on the table. My eyebrows curl as she coils her tiny frame into a ball and rests beside the pile of shirts.

"I can see everything that happens next. I know you would've knocked those clothes over if I didn't tell you to watch your lap. And I know that you wouldn't have knocked them over if I said something."

My mouth drops as I peer at his short, husky frame in sheer amazement. With a bright grin glowing through his scraggly beard, he turns and moves toward the table. He has the Thermos in one hand, and a mug in the other.

"I know every reaction to every word I say. But like I said, the feeling comes and goes."

He screws the lid on the Thermos and slides it toward me.

"And the ones that aren't about you. What are those like?"

"Well..." He takes a deep breath.

A scowl begins to harden across my face.

"Those are a bit more jarring for Prophetics, unfortunately. It looks and feels like we're having seizures."

I'm horrified. Here we are, using our abilities like toys, but Pavo has seizures every time he experiences his *gift*. I can see why Leo was so hesitant about the idea of trying to induce a vision out of him to find my mother. I imagine their first attempt to find Auriga wasn't the most pleasant experience.

"So," Pavo says, to break the obvious tension, "what's your plan?"

I can't help but scoff. He already knows what I'm going to say. Then again, he actually doesn't. In his mind, there are infinite responses to his question. But each one, he will undoubtedly be prepared to answer. The whole concept gives me a migraine.

"I'm gonna retrace my steps. Go back to Missouri, and try to find some clues, I guess."

I know it's a lousy plan. Part of me is ready to admit that to Pavo.

"It's not a lousy plan."

My head jerks back.

"It just needs a little steam." He takes a sip of coffee.

My face gnarls as he pulls something out of his pocket and slides it in my direction. It's a car key. Not just any car key. It's a key to the old sedan that had been sitting in their driveway. It's the only vehicle they had that hadn't once belonged to Psyriin.

"She's gassed up and ready." He smiles.

"Wait. You're giving me the car?"

Pavo nods and takes another sip.

"Won't Leo be pissed?"

"He'll live." Pavo chuckles.

"Thank you." I grab the key and glare at my skewed reflection bouncing from its silver surface.

"And here's one more parting gift."

I give him an intrigued stare as he reaches into his other pocket to reveal a small piece of paper.

"It's an address and an account number for a bank in Siler City, about a few hundred miles off the north highway exit. It's a bit out of your way, I know. But it will give you access to some funds that should help you on your journey."

I have to fight to keep my jaw from dropping to the floor. Somehow *thank you* doesn't seem to be enough to show my gratitude.

"No need to thank me. Soup and sandwiches can only take you so far."

I think of replying, but there's no point. A simple hug will suffice.

"It was a pleasure to meet you, Rion." He grins as he taps his hand against my back.

"I'm sure we'll see each other again."

"I'm sure we will." He winks.

With a gigantic smile draped across my face, I pack up the supplies, hop in the car, and disappear down the road. Pavo, with Lyra asleep between his arms, is the only person waving from the driveway as the Safe House disappears in the rearview mirror.

CHAPTER 14
BANK ROBBERY

THE SUN HAS JUST BEGUN TO RISE OVER THE horizon, and I can feel my eyes growing heavy. A yawn billows from my cheeks. I finished my Thermos of coffee hours ago. Snack wrappers and containers full of crumbs are scattered throughout the passenger seat. The intense desire to find the Charon and reunite with my mother seems to be the only thing fueling me now.

Buildings finally come into view and fill me with relief. I glance down every corner. If only I'd had a GPS to help me navigate the winding streets of Siler City, Oklahoma. It's called a city, but it feels more like a rickety old town. The buildings are mostly dilapidated structures ripped straight out of one of the black and white gangster films Mom and I used to watch. Still, it's easily the most populated area I've seen since leaving Pavo's farmhouse in Middle-of-Nowhere, Kansas.

There is a quaint collection of causal folks strolling down the sidewalks, each with their own wholesome hometown appearance.

I finally reach the street that matches the address on the slip of paper. I'd memorized it the moment Pavo placed it in my palm. After spending several minutes making the worst parallel park in human history, I exit the car Pavo graciously let me borrow. I wish I could've seen Leo's face when he woke up this morning and found both me and the vehicle gone.

I pinpoint the bank across the street, and flip the hood of my sweatshirt over the scraggly coils of my unkept hair. I take a moment to scan my surroundings, making sure there are no onlookers glaring my way. The few folks who had been staring at me while I struggled to park have now disappeared down the sidewalk. Once the last few nonchalant people pass me by without batting an eye, I advance to the tall glass doors at the front of the building.

A security guard standing near the entrance, tips his tan cap and gives me an inviting smile when I step foot inside. His belly protrudes over his belt. He looks like he wouldn't be able to stop an unarmed teenager if he had to run more than a few feet. I give a halfhearted smile and nod before looking away just as quickly. There are only a few people inside—three bank tellers behind the counter, and five patrons. I can't help but feel gratified that the line isn't long. The sooner I get out of here, the better.

I remove the slip of paper with the account information, and wait behind a slender, raven-haired woman dressed impeccably in a navy business suit. She turns to me, and her hazel-eyed gaze meets mine. I try to look down at the paper, but I don't want to seem rude, so I look back and return her gesture with my most hearty grin. All of this smiling makes me nervous and causes my mind to race with all of the questions I should've asked myself before now. Don't I need some form of identification linking me to the account? All I have is this slip of paper with Pavo's handwriting. Surely the teller isn't going to just hand me money when all I have is an account number.

Pavo foresaw this…right? He must have called ahead and connected me to the account, or something along those lines.

I reach into my back pocket for my driver's license before I remember my wallet was left behind in the car with Mom. Sweat starts to protrude from my brow. The woman in the business suit is called to the next available teller, and my heart begins to thump.

I try my best to remain calm. Pavo wouldn't have put me into this situation if it wasn't going to work…

would he? My stomach starts to rumble. I can feel all of the sandwiches and coffee I consumed on the road beginning to force their way up.

"Next, please," a man calls, from the edge of the counter.

My body freezes. I look around in a dumbfounded stupor, as if there is anyone else he could be talking to. I turn around, desperately hoping that there is an old lady waiting to my rear that I can send in my place. At least then I could buy time and pass off my anxious fear as chivalry.

"Sir?" the man says.

I turn forward and smile. I can only imagine how dumb I look while pacing forward.

"How are you today?" he says, with a massive grin on his face, like his job is the most fulfilling thing in the world.

Does everyone in this town smile?

I glance down at the golden nameplate sitting on the front of the counter. His name is Matt.

"I'm good."

I slide the paper onto the counter, my palm covering the writing, as if that is somehow going to matter.

"How can I help you?"

"I, uhh...I need to make a withdrawal?"

I keep trying to keep my voice from shaking, but I'm failing miserably.

"Alrighty. Do you have an account with—"

His warm smile has been replaced with an unnerved scowl. For a second, I think I'm already busted. My imagination has already pictured Nastacia Arkright and a horde of Psyriin soldiers bursting through the ceiling with rifles and tear gas. Once I've checked back to reality, I realize he is looking at something behind me.

"Can we help you?" the security guard at the door barks.

My head swivels to follow the teller's gaze. Two men and a woman stand in the doorway. Before I can fully examine them, the woman waves her hand and the security officer goes flying across the room. He slams against the wall with a *thud!* and immediately loses consciousness.

"Everyone on the ground!" the woman shouts.

My body slides to the floor, and my palms scrape against the cold linoleum. What just happened? My eyes saw something that my mind hasn't fully comprehended. I look over in shock at the security guard's burly frame lying still against the counter.

"Tellers. Hands where we can see them!" Her voice echoes through the room.

My heartbeat hammers through my chest as I peak at each of the assailants. The woman's skin is a deep, shimmering ebony tone that is a few shades darker than mine. Her light-brown eyes would be mesmerizing if they weren't wedged within a terrifying scowl. Her hair is closely shaved to her scalp, even thinner than mine has ever been. A round, silver ring sits pierced between her nostrils, fittingly like a fierce bull.

The man to her left has golden-blond dreadlocks, with a matching bleached patch of hair protruding from his chin. The shoulder-length locks have been pulled back into a ponytail, except for one strand that dangles over his left eye. The bright tint of his hair seems to glow in contrast to his dark eyebrows and chocolate brown skin. His coiled fists are surrounded by black gloves with the finger holes cut out of them, like something an 80s biker might wear.

The last guy looks Hispanic, with tan skin and oily black hair that twists over each ear. He appears to be younger. His boyish brown eyes don't appear as menacing as the others, despite also carrying a deep scowl. He looks anxious compared to his associates. Each of them wears tattered garb with their left arms exposed to reveal an intricate and distinctive tattoo that spreads from their shoulder down to their wrist.

"Everyone just chill," the woman snarls. "Remain silent, and this will all be over soon."

The whimpers and squeals from all of the frightened patrons flicker across the room like a flurry of mice. The raven-haired woman in the business suit is crying in the corner, her fingers clasped around her scalp.

"Go," the female assailant barks toward the Hispanic guy.

He nods and moves toward me. My gaze darts to the floor, and my throat tightens with every footstep. His worn-down sneakers are inches from my face when he stops over my shoulder and glares at Matt.

"Please...don't hurt—"

"I said silence!" the woman growls.

My unnerved glare gradually lifts to the Hispanic guy grabbing Matt by the jaw and peering into his frightened eyes. It is a strange scene. Even Matt's fear begins to waver, and gets replaced with sheer discomfort.

After a few awkward seconds of staring, he violently relinquishes Matt's chin and stalks to a doorway just a few feet to my left. The door has a coded lock with a patch of numbers above a long steel handle. The Hispanic assailant taps eight numbers, then turns the doorknob to enter like he's a welcomed guest. The robber with blond dreadlocks comes thumping behind in a pair of dark boots that are covered in dirt. I focus on their movements as they go behind the counter and shove Matt to the floor.

"Hope everyone is having a nice day." The woman wears a devious smile. "We're just here to make a quick withdrawal. Then we'll be out of your hair, and you can enjoy the rest of your day."

She paces around the room while the Hispanic guy types away at Matt's computer. She folds her arms behind her back and turns to glance through the front doors in anticipation.

"He's got a safety deposit box," one of the men calls out, in a sly tone.

Judging from the more youthful voice, I garner that it's the Hispanic one.

"Nice." The woman smirks. "Let's make it quick. I'm sure one of these heroes triggered the silent alarm."

A drawer opens, and they begin pulling loads of cash from it. My frigid fingertips start to rattle. I just want this to be over. I close my eyes and try to think of the days when my biggest worry was Mom catching me using my abilities. The thought manages to soothe my heart, even if only for a few seconds.

Movement catches my eyes when they creak open. The husky security guard is conscious. His eyes are open just wide enough for me to notice them glaring toward the female robber as she stares through the glass doorway. His body remains limp, but his arm begins to drift toward his side.

No! Don't do it, I mentally scream at him, as I watch his hand hover over the gun at his hip.

I try to make eye contact, hoping that my adamant glare will prevent his next move. I think about using my abilities to whisk the gun from him, but I can't fully see the weapon. Deep down, I know I haven't honed my powers nearly enough to manage this without causing more of a commotion.

The clump of boots billows into my ear, and I can't help but look up at the blond, dreaded man's scowl. He is clasping a bag full of cash. He looks down and makes eye contact with me. His brow curls into a confused gnarl as we both hear the click at the same time.

"Yo!" the blond, dreaded robber shouts, as his free hand rises faster than I can comprehend.

Bang!

My eyes shut. My hands dart behind my head. Each curl of my hair has been dampened by nervous perspiration. Blood curdling screams echo against the walls. My mind is howling for me to keep my eyes closed. And yet I open them. I open them before anyone else can.

The woman with the shaved scalp and the nose ring is still standing. Her eyes are bulbous, and her fists are balled so tight it looks as if her palms might bleed. Her chest is pumping. Her lips are clenched between her teeth, but she isn't looking at the security officer. She is glaring at the tiny silver bullet hovering mere inches from her face.

My jaw droops to the cool floor tiles. I shouldn't be amazed. Everything is becoming more coherent by the second, but my eyes are still as large as hers. My view shifts to blondie. His hand is stretched forth. A look of intense focus is curled across his face. The Hispanic guy stands near Matt with his mouth wider than mine.

The other Clairvoyants Ara had told me about. The Predators. It must be them. She always said they caused trouble. Now, I know what she meant. I can't remember their names. It would be easier if my mind and heart weren't thumping a mile a minute. But it's surely them.

The Hispanic guy must be a Reader Clairvoyant, like Leo. I'd watched him sift through the contents of the computer like he was a well-trained employee. He must've read Matt's mind to gain access behind the counter. The other two—they are Kinetics like me. Somehow the blond dreadhead was quick enough to mentally stop the bullet just before it reached the woman.

"Someone…always…has to try and be a hero," the woman snarls.

Her huffs of breath between words are so heavy it sounds like she might pass out.

She glares over at blondie and gives a sinister nod. I glance toward his snarl, and notice that he is breathing just as heavily. As he lowers his arm, there is a foreboding look in his eyes that seems to be trying to calm her.

"Guess I'll just have to set an example." She shrugs.

The bullet begins to turn, but it isn't a smooth one. When it first revolves, the tiny object seems to wriggle as if it's being tugged by two separate forces. My gaze shifts to blondie, whose look hasn't wavered.

"Quila," he growls.

She looks back at him, and an eerie smile creeps across her face. Her tattooed arm lifts. Slowly, her fingertips shift into the shape of a pistol, like a small child playing cops and robbers. My head whips between her sneer and blondie's disappointed grimace.

"Bang," she quips.

Sssffick!

This time, my eyes don't close. I see it all as if it were in slow motion, even though the bullet darts at near light speed toward the security officer. I sense his horrified squeal, but my focus remains on the bullet. It whistles through the air before I swipe my arm to shift its path, and watch it hammer into the wall.

"The hell?" The woman's jaw widens, and her gaze snaps toward me.

Those fiery pupils are glaring directly into mine. For a moment, I wonder why she's looking at me. After all, the feeling was fleeting, like an idea that had no intention of coming to fruition. But as my gaze scales to my outstretched right arm, the decision I've made comes fully into focus.

A faint shriek squirts from my throat. My arm remains extended, and my fingertips are spread wide like I'm trying to catch a baseball. I don't know what to do. I want to turn away, but I can't take my gaze off of the woman's astonished glare.

Blondie reaches down and pulls my arm so hard that my entire body turns to face him. He drops his sack of money to his side and pushes his knee against my left arm. The pain should feel excruciating, but my senses are preoccupied.

My eyes flutter, and I let out a yelp. I can hear the woman and the Reader Clairvoyant scrambling toward me. All three of their grimaces come into view as soon as I force my eyes to stay open. Blondie yanks my left sleeve down, and his coarse gloved hand shifts my wrist into their view.

A startled look spreads across their faces. Their bodies shift as soon as they've seen the unmarked, brown skin on my wrist. Should I speak? Should I tell them who I am, and why I don't have the distinctive constellation that all Clairvoyants are supposed to have? Should I mention that I know Pavo and the others? Hell, will they even listen?

My mouth opens, but before I can speak, blondie and the woman whip their heads toward the mind reader.

"I...I can't read his mind?" the Hispanic Clairvoyant says, with an unnerved twinge in his voice.

Wheeeewwww! The sound of police sirens whistles through the air, and all of our gazes shift to the glass doors.

"Get the money!" the woman snaps.

"What about him?" says the panicked Reader Clairvoyant.

"He's coming with us." She snarls before staring into my frightened scowl.

I'm about to plead my case, but the last thing I see is blondie's fist barreling into my face.

CHAPTER 15

PREDATOR OR PREY

"AAAHHH! OHHHH MY GOD!"

A sharp sensation shoots from my forehead down through my extremities as soon as my eyes open. My heart feels like it's being dribbled like a basketball. I grip the edge of the wooden chair beneath me. I manage to peer to my side and see the back chair legs barely touching the edge of a rooftop. I must be at least four stories up. The cracks in the asphalt below look like a lightning storm against the weathered gray concrete. Sweat pours from my brow as the sun beams through the clear sky.

"Wakey, wakey," a deep, sly voice says, from behind me.

The other Kinetic Predator—the one that wasn't at the bank. It must be him. I can see his daunting shadow, but his frame is shrouded and I don't dare turn around.

"What's your name, kid?" he growls.

"R-Rion. Rion Grean!" I clasp my hands tighter, and try to avoid looking down.

"Rion Grean, huh? Where ya from, Rion Grean?"

"Umm…that's kind of complicated."

"Simplify it for me!"

"Ahhh!" I shriek, as I feel the chair nudge. "Uhh…uhhh…Missouri. Uhhh…Indiana. Virginia for a little bit. Uhh…"

"What were you doing at a bank in Siler City, Oklahoma?"

"I was sent there."

"Sent there? You part of Psyriin?"

"No! I was sent there by Pavo."

"Pavo?" He laughs. "You know that old geezer?"

"Yeah. I'm…I'm a Kinetic, like you guys. You're the Predators, right?"

"Oh. So you know us now?"

"Yeah. Ara told me about you."

"Well, then, what's my name?"

My heart freezes. Damn it! What's his name? Ara told me, but the fear coursing through my every pore won't let me remember it. It's something that starts with a P. Pegasus? Proteus? If only I'd taken a high school course on constellations. Think! What did Ara call him?

"Persey?" I blurt, my eyelids shut tight.

"Ohhh. Not a good answer, kid."

"Wait!"

The chair drops, and my heart sinks with it. I feel myself slip, and I reach out as if there is something in front of me to grab. My body feels numb as gravity sends me beckoning for the concrete beneath.

I think about Mom. Think about how I got here, and how all of this happened. I feel terrified and angry all at once. I close my eyes and reach forward, as if they can somehow protect me from imminent death. And then...

Then I feel a push through my limbs, like my body is being pulled by wires that have reached their full length.

It is all instinct, just like when I curved the bullet at the bank.

My eyes open to the concrete just a foot away from my face. My breaths are heavy enough to push the stray dirt into a cloud around me. I stopped myself! Thank God, I stopped myself.

I feel my body swing around. I am back in an upright position, but I'm still hovering midair. I gaze around in confusion at the fields of gravel and weeds in every direction, as the sound of sinister laughter echoes behind me.

The excruciating creak of sliding rusted metal bombards my senses. Before I can even turn around, I feel myself being yanked backwards like I'm being sucked into the world's largest vacuum. I enter the inside of a large warehouse. There are a few windows speckled about, each with murky glass that is impossible to see through. From the looks of all of the rusted machinery, it's a place that has been abandoned for quite some time. There's a grotesque scent that smells like a mixture of steel, lumber, and mildew.

The large doors slide to a close with nothing pulling them shut. A few patches of daylight flow through the windows, but darkness surrounds me to the point that I can barely see my own sullied sneakers. Another flood of nervous perspiration begins to careen down my face once I clump to the concrete floor. I take a deep breath and try my best to ease my yammering heartbeat. Several devious cackles echo through the room. As my eyes begin to adjust to the intense blackness, the four Predators emerge from the shadows.

The memory of my conversation with Ara comes flooding back like I'm watching it all unfold on a TV screen. Perseus! The leader of the Predators is named

Perseus. If only I had remembered on the rooftop that he hates being called Persey.

My eyes quiver, and I wipe my damp brow. Once I remember his name, they all come rushing back to me. The young Hispanic Reader Clairvoyant is Lupus. Blondie is Aries. And I remember him referring to the woman as Quila, which must be short for Aquila.

"What'd I tell you, P," Aries says. "You gotta trust your boy. We got ourselves another Kinetic."

"A lousy one," Aquila gruffs.

"Lousy enough to curve a bullet," Aries replies.

"Chill, Aries. He isn't out of the woods just yet." Perseus grunts.

His ferocious tone makes me cringe. My blurry vision fully settles, and I examine him from a few feet away. He's a tall, chiseled white guy with ferocious brown eyes and short, prickly, jet-black hair. He has clean-shaven cheeks, with a small patch of hair protruding from the center of his firm jaw line. I remember Ara telling me that the Kinetics are all in their mid-twenties. But Perseus's face carries a war-torn weariness that makes him look much older than the rest of them. There is a thick scar above his right cheek that makes it look like he is always snarling. His upper body is covered in a black leather jacket, but the edges of a tattoo manage to peek just above the constellation marking on his left wrist.

Lupus is standing closest to Perseus's left. The other two are standing just a few feet behind them, with their arms crossed. Behind the Predators is a long, winding staircase leading to a loft.

"Okay, Rion Grean," Perseus says. "You're a Kinetic. So why don't you have a mark on your wrist?"

"Look." I take a deep breath. "All of this—Clairvoyants, Psyriin—it's all new to me."

Their eyes flutter with intrigue. I can't tell whether they believe me or not.

"I was raised by my mom."

There is a noticeable perk to their demeanors when I mention her. They pass glances to one another, with scowls that look both bewildered and uneasy.

"My powers manifested about a decade ago, but I kept them secret. I had no idea there were others out there like me."

"So how'd you meet the Phantoms?" Aquila says.

"Phantoms?"

"Pavo, Leo, Ara…and the cat," Perseus says.

I'm offended that he doesn't refer to Lyra by name, but I have to remind myself to stay focused.

"Well…a few days ago, my mother and I were moving, and Psyriin came after us. We separated, trying to escape them. Pavo apparently had a vision about the whole thing and sent Leo and Ara to rescue me."

I pause to examine each of their calculating grimaces.

Perseus gives a deep sigh. "Mom, huh." He twiddles the hairs on his chin. "And your dad?"

"Never met him. And don't know anything about him."

"Andromeda?" Aquila says, her sneer turning to meet Perseus's.

"Maybe," he replies.

"I'm pretty sure Andromeda isn't my mom."

"How old are you, kid?" Perseus says.

"Seventeen. Eighteen, in a few months."

His scowl hardens, as if he thinks I'm lying.

"Ever seen your birth certificate?"

"No."

"Any pictures of you being born in a hospital?" Aquila says.

"No, but—"

"Then how do you know this mother of yours is your birth mother?" She scoffs, her face curling to a skeptic frown.

"What else would she be?"

"I don't know. But for all we know, you could be some engineered Psyriin spy trying to infiltrate us."

When Aquila says this, the others give a gentle nod, as if it's a notion worth taking seriously.

"Look, I'm not some spy!" I ball my fists, and my fiery stare meets theirs.

"And yet you just happened to be at the bank at the same time as us?" Aquila says.

"I told you—Pavo sent me to that bank."

"And why would he do that?" Perseus laughs.

"I don't..."

That's when it hits me. Pavo never intended for me to withdraw any money. That bank account number he gave me was probably not even real.

"Because he foresaw the robbery and wanted me to meet you!"

The Predators all gawk at one another. I take their moment of silence to continue.

"We interrogated a Psyriin soldier. Leo figured that my mom might've been kidnapped and taken to this prison called the Charon."

Their scowls amplify, and their deep groans echo through the hollow building.

"It's the same place Auriga is. Right?"

"You got any proof of this, kid?" Perseus says.

"Yeah!" I shovel my hand in my pockets and pull out the key to the sedan. "Pavo gave me their car to drive to the bank."

"Ohhhhhh, snap!" Aries says, with a wily grin as the key rips from my hand and zips through the air, into his palm. "They got a mind reader and a body snatcher, and these fools are still rollin' around in the same ole busted ass, '97 sedan? Same, corny-ass Phantoms, all right."

"See!" I stand to my sore feet, and a relieved smile begins to protrude from my exhausted jaw. "Pavo must've known that we could help each other find the Charon."

"Cool it, kid," Perseus replies. "You think you belong here just because Pavo sent you our way?"

Aquila and Lupus nod with intense glowers, like they're still skeptical. Aries just rolls his eyes, the car key twirling above his palm.

"Please! I'll do whatever it takes to find my mom. I encountered Nastacia Arkright."

Their faces gnarl, and their gazes bore into mine.

"If I can draw her out somehow, we can find the Charon. Just...just give me a chance to prove myself."

My chest begins to thump, and heavy breaths pour from my nostrils. A sinister grin supplants Perseus's perturbed scowl. Aquila and Lupus garner the same reaction. There is an awkward silence that makes my stomach churn.

"Okay, kid," Perseus says. "You want to be a Predator? Then you gotta go through initiation."

"Whatever it is, I'll do it."

I sound like a child trying to impress the big kids on the playground. What am I saying? These people just robbed a bank. Aquila was ready to kill a guy without hesitation. The longing to see my mother, the thought of getting revenge on Psyriin, and the evident fear of what the Predators might do to me if I'm rejected, are all causing adrenaline to do my talking. What am I getting myself into?

Perseus nods toward Lupus, and the Reader Clairvoyant turns to head for a small padlocked door at the edge of the massive warehouse. I notice Aries shaking his head, while Perseus and Aquila glare at me like I'm fresh meat. I keep my fists balled. No matter how afraid or nervous I might be, I can't let them see it.

"I'm not like Pavo, Leo, and Ara," my anxiety makes me utter. "That's why I left. I don't wanna hide. I wanna fight."

"We'll see, Rion Grean." Perseus chuckles. "We'll see."

Once Lupus has disappeared inside the room-sized storage closet, I follow Perseus and Aquila up the warehouse stairs. Aries follows close, his arms crossed as if this entire process annoys him. The sun is beginning to set in the distance, and the air is growing colder by the second once we exit through the rooftop doorway. I fold my arms to keep warm, but I can still feel the goosebumps poking through my thick sweatshirt.

"Wait right here," Perseus says, through a sly tone.

He and Aquila have had conniving smirks on their faces ever since he told me about *Initiation*. I stand a few feet from the edge of the building, trying my best to make my nervous scowl seem like a look of eager anticipation.

Lupus emerges from the rooftop doorway, with a limp body dragging behind him. The man in his tightened grasp is wearing nothing but a T-shirt and a pair of white boxers. Both are covered in patches of blood. There is duct tape around his mouth, and his arms and legs are bound by thick plastic wire. Almost every inch of him is covered in sweat. A faint groan is the only thing that lets me know he's still alive. Reminds me of the fifth soldier.

Lupus drops him inches from the edge of the roof before joining the other Predators next to me. A lump fills my throat as I examine the man's damp brown hair and coarse, pale skin. I can't help but jump back as he staggers to his knees and starts to tremble.

"Okay, Rion." Perseus snarls.

With the swipe of his hand, the man's ankle and wrist restraints snap and wilt to the rooftop floor. The man's mouth remains bound by tape. I look on with tightened fists as his eyes flutter in disbelief. He refuses to move once our gazes meet, like he isn't sure what his next move should be.

"We bagged this piece of Psyriin garbage a few weeks ago, and Lupus removed his suicide patch." Perseus gives a menacing sneer.

I scan the man's chest, until I notice a thicker splotch of blood just beneath his left breast.

"Never gave us any info on the Charon. But we were able to steal some money from his account."

Aquila and Lupus both grin. But the look on my face is anything but amused.

"And now, he's pretty much useless."

My hapless gaze turns to Aquila, who pulls a gun from behind her back. It's the same one the security guard at the bank had used to try to shoot her. Chills run down my spine, and my fingers begin to twitch. Perseus, sensing my anxiety, stomps over to Lupus and brings the Reader's arm into my focused glare.

"You see this?" he snarls, while pointing to Lupus's tattoo.

It's a design of a fierce wolf snarling through a deep forest.

Next, he grabs Aquila.

"Look!"

Her arm is draped with a screaming eagle swooping down through a lightning storm, with its razor-sharp talons ready to snatch up whatever may come.

"This isn't preschool." Perseus huffs. "Predators are hunters."

He flings the leather jacket from his back so that his muscular arms are visible. Stylistically emblazoned from his left shoulder down to his wrist, is a statuesque figure clad from head to toe in golden armor and a helmet that obscures his face. The man on the tattoo holds his arm up high to show the severed head of a woman with snakes for hair.

"Perseus—the demigod who killed Medusa." He points to Aries, who moves his arm into view, with a forewarning glower.

His tattoo is of a ram battling through a brick wall with fire surrounding it.

"Aries—God of War!" Perseus's gaze darts back to mine. "These aren't just some stupid constellations. This is fate, Rion Grean. We're here for a reason. Why are *you* here?"

The gun hovers from Aquila's grasp, and comes to rest on the rooftop floor. My eyes are like saucers. My lips feel brittle.

"It's kill or be killed!" His fiery stare is focused on me. "Time to decide if you're Predator, or prey."

The Psyriin soldier dives for the gun. I whip my head around and fling out my hand. His body glides against the concrete floor. He swipes toward the weapon, but I've already snatched it from the ground with my abilities.

I've never held a gun before. Mom never even let me play with toy guns when I was little, no matter how much I begged for one. The handle feels awkward in my grasp, like a foreign animal that might bite me if I hold it too tight.

My heartbeat seems to freeze. The wisps of air that flowed from my nostrils have ceased. The soldier's weary gaze shifts to mine. I try to keep my hand from trembling as I inadvertently point the gun at his face.

"Now or never, Rion Grean." Perseus's voice echoes into the evening air. "Whatever it takes, right?"

My teeth grind. Another downpour of sweat drifts from my curly scalp. I want to refuse, and plead for another trial. Let me steal something. Let me do anything but this. I try to avert my gaze from the Psyriin soldier's horrified stare, but Aquila and Lupus are looking at me as if they're both waiting for me to resist. I keep telling myself to think of this soldier as one of those that attacked me in that abandoned square. If he'd gotten to the gun first, he wouldn't have hesitated. So why should I?

The Psyriin soldier takes a step back and stumbles. His back rests against the edge of the building. His eyes shut tight like he's preparing himself for my deadly shot. My index finger begins to dance around the trigger. I have to do it. Don't think. Just do it.

"Predator or prey!" Perseus shouts.

My palm loosens. It's as if I can feel my mother creeping up behind me to wrap her warm touch around my shoulders. I can hear her whispering that no matter what happens, everything is going to be okay.

The gun drifts from my palm and collapses to the stone rooftop surface. My head droops with it, and the grunts of all four Predators start to resonate in my clouded senses.

"I'm sorry," I whimper, still focused on my feet.

"No!" the Psyriin soldier screams.

My head jolts upward. My eyes widen, and my heart skips a beat. The Psyriin soldier is no longer on the roof. He is dangling midair, several feet from the edge of the building. I reach out, as if I can grab him from yards away. The second I step forward, he plummets.

The Predators each scurry to the building's edge, but I remain frozen. My heavy breaths could douse an inferno. I cringe as soon as I hear the thunderous sound of the body hitting the ground below.

"Daaammmnnn!" Aries places his fist over his gawking mouth.

My face gnarls in confusion. Aries is the first one to turn around. There's an enamored grin on his face, like he's just heard the funniest joke imaginable. The other three turn toward me, each of them with equally confused scowls.

"Now that's what the hell I'm talking about, kid!" Aries yells.

His dreadlocks bounce along his back as he sprints over to me. My body nudges forward when he slaps my shoulder. A hesitant smile creeps across my face as I let him wrap his tattooed arm around my neck.

"You actually let him think you weren't gonna kill him." Aries cracks up, while the others trot toward us. "That's some ruthless stuff right there, my boy."

They each surround me, but I don't know what to say. Perseus steps forward until he is towering over me. He seems to be scanning my brow, as if he's waiting for a sign of reluctance.

"Yeah, well, he had it comin'." I scoff, trying to replace my confusion with bravado.

Laughter echoes through the air. A few words follow, but I can't hear a thing as my mind still swims with anxiety. Perseus snatches me up like a proud father congratulating his son after a game-winning shot. Aquila comes over and thumps me on the back, and I smile at her.

"Welcome to the Predators, kid." Perseus grins as he relinquishes his hold on me, and my senses return. "Lupus, take care of the mess downstairs."

Lupus rolls his eyes before walking away. He is the only one who doesn't seem delighted by what has just transpired. I know he isn't able to read my mind, but I still can't help but think he can see right through my faulty smirk.

"Quila, get our rookie some grub, and make him a bed," Perseus says. "He's gonna need his strength."

Aquila nods and curls her arm around me. My feet drag alongside her rapid footsteps as we head to the rooftop door.

I turn around just before we exit the rooftop. Aries is standing in front of Perseus. Our gazes meet just before the door closes. His arms are crossed, and there's a dubious smirk across his face.

CHAPTER 16
TRAINING DAY

RAINDROPS RATTLE THE GRIMY TINTED windows. A patch of moonlight creeps through and paints my face in an orange glow. My hands rest behind my head, and my weary-eyed gaze fixates on the rusted tin ceiling. Lupus cooked up some spaghetti, so I've at least managed to eat something. It wasn't much, but it was my first real meal since leaving behind the packed food from Pavo. My body feels full and tired, but my eyes won't even tremble.

I wish I could sleep. Part of me wonders if I'll ever sleep again. I keep trying to tell myself that lying in the same sweatshirt and dirty jeans from the bank robbery is causing my discomfort. But deep down, I know that the sound of that Psyriin soldier falling to his death is tormenting me.

I keep mentally retracing every move I'd made. I didn't do it...did I? Maybe in my frustration, I'd accidentally—no—I couldn't have. I know I didn't do it, but that can only mean one of the Kinetics made the heinous move for me. But why would they do that?

Footsteps creep from behind me, and I quickly rise from the set of old couch cushions that Aquila has fashioned into a makeshift bed. When I turn, Aries is inching over toward me, his hands raised like he's approaching a stray cat he doesn't want to startle.

"You good, bro?" he whispers, as he moves beside me.

I'm thankful it's him. The other Predators terrify me. Even Lupus, if only because he hardly speaks.

"Can't sleep." I lean over the cushions and wrap my hands around my knees.

"Yeah." He laughs. "Been a rough day for ya."

He plops down right next to me, and we both gaze at the rain-soaked windows for a few silent seconds.

"Sorry about knockin' yo ass out at the bank. And danglin' you from the roof. Perseus can be hella dramatic."

"It's cool." I shrug, even though I'm still irked.

They fed me, gave me a place to sleep, and didn't kill me. I pretty much have no choice but to let the ordeal slide.

"Well...Perseus wants me to start trainin' you tomorrow," Aries sighs.

My gaze drifts downward to the end of the loft, where the other three Predators are sleeping soundly on much more comfortable mattresses.

"Actually, I volunteered. I know if I didn't, Quila would do it. And I'm not a hundred percent sure you'd survive her."

I grin, until I notice the serious look on his face, which makes me realize it wasn't a joke.

"Uhh...thanks?"

"Don't mention it." He slaps my already aching back. "Bright and early. So try to get some shuteye."

I nod as he rises. He takes two steps forward before I finally ask the question that has been on my mind for the past few hours.

"It was you, wasn't it?"

Aries turns around and tucks his hands into the pockets of his tattered gray hoodie. A wily grin cascades across his face.

"C'mon, bro. I knew you didn't have it in you as soon as P gave you the order. So I did you a solid."

Relief rushes throughout my body. Deep down, I'd known it. But hearing it from Aries is enough to lift the heavy burden from my shoulders.

"We do what we do because we have to. It's survival. Bet money homeboy would've killed you if he had the chance."

A smile drifts across my face. I want to hug him, or at least shake his hand, but I just give a thankful nod instead. He finally turns to head back to the end of the loft. I prepare to lay back down with a new sense of gratitude and relief, but before I can, Aries says one last thing.

"You ain't a killer, bro."

There's a forewarning tone to his voice. It makes my smile disappear as fast as it came. I lift my head and turn to meet his intense glare.

"But bes' believe, if you're gonna find this mom of yours...if you're gonna face Arkright and Psyriin... you're gonna have to become one."

The sun has just risen over a collection of large metal shipping containers in the distance. A chilly breeze wafts into my weary face. I tuck my hands into the warm pockets of Lupus's black hoodie. Turns out, we're the same size. I'm still exhausted, but it feels good to be in fresh clothes.

As I walk out into the damp gravel, Aries is smoking a cigarette and standing in the center of some rusted train tracks. I can tell the tracks haven't been used in years. Patches of thick moss fold around the auburn steel, making some areas virtually invisible.

A thick cloud of smoke flutters from his lips.

"Ahh, there he is!" Aries yells. "Sleep okay?"

I shrug as he flicks the cigarette to his side. I can't help but be enamored when he curls his fist, causing the cigarette to coil into a tiny ball just before it hits the ground.

"So what can you do?" he says.

I stop a few feet from him.

"Well, anything I can carry, I can move pretty easily."

"What about big stuff?"

"Uhh...I've moved a fridge and a couch."

"Like, moved it a few feet off the ground? Or..."

"Inches," I reply, with obvious embarrassment.

Aries's face curls into an unimpressed gnarl. He runs his hands through his blonde dreadlocks and glances off into the horizon.

"Can you move multiple objects at once?"

"N-no. Not really."

"Okay." He lets out a deep sigh. "So you're pretty trash."

My gaze darts for the gravel. A few days ago, I thought I was pretty good at this whole telekinetic thing. Now, I just feel like I'm riding on training wheels.

"But it's all good." He slaps my shoulder and gives me a confident smirk. "The first thing you gotta realize is that your power doesn't come from here." He taps his finger against his forehead. "Well...it does. But you can't think of it that way."

I try to hide my confusion, but I can only imagine how dumbfounded the look on my face is.

"Your mind automatically defers to the restraints of your physical body. But you don't know something is heavy until you've actually lifted it, right?"

I look on as Aries turns and reaches out.

"When instincts and emotion kick in, that sense of limitation is replaced with adrenaline."

I marvel as one of the massive shipping containers in the distance rises to the air. My mouth drops and my eyes broaden. I glance at his focused glare. There is a slight snarl on his face, but it doesn't look like he's even trying.

Clung! The shipping container slams onto a different pile.

I shake my head and laugh. Aries drops his arm and turns to me with a hearty grin.

"Ever been mad and moved somethin' you can't physically lift?"

"Sort of." My thoughts scurry back to a few days ago, and a scowl replaces my impressed grin. "I moved a vending machine when I was mad at a friend. And I made a state trooper slam into his cop car when he pulled my mom over."

"Nice! See that's the adrenaline. But unlike your physical limitations, you can manipulate your emotions. You can focus on anything you want when you're using your power. Once you focus on the occupied space of the object, instead of the weight, you can trick your mind into believing it's whatever weight you want it to be."

"Like, *light as a feather, stiff as a board*." I reminisce on the joyous days of playing *Ouija* with Mom, as a child.

"I don't know what the hell that means. But sure. Whatever helps." He shrugs while pulling another cigarette from his left pocket, and sets the tip ablaze with a lighter from the other. "So for the rest of the day, I want you to try moving that box back where it was."

I nod, and a focused scowl spreads across my face. I jump up and down. Even wriggle my neck and limbs, like I'm about to exercise. Aries just stares at me with a comedic grin.

"Just remember to focus on the scope of the object you're trying to move. If you don't, your power is gonna try to grab everything around it, and you're not gonna lift a damn thing. Can't try to move a book if you're focused on the whole shelf. You feel me?"

"Yeah. Yeah, I got you."

"Aight then, rookie." He smirks. "Good luck."

The sun is high in the cloudless sky, and my clothes are doused with sweat. I've been at it for six hours, and the most I've been able to accomplish is lifting the shipping crate a few feet. I have a throbbing headache, and I've had my arms outstretched for so long it feels as if they might crumble off my shoulders like dried clay.

My only break came when Aries brought me a ham sandwich and a bag of potato chips. I'd expected him to have a look of sheer disappointment on his face, but he only carried his usual crafty smirk when he saw me. This isn't remotely as easy as he made it look. Every time I try to move the crate to the side, an uncanny sense of nervousness kicks in, and the fear of dropping the massive object creeps into my mind.

"Okay, bro."

I let my aching arms droop to my side as Aries strolls up with his hands tucked in his pockets. My gaze darts toward the ground in an attempt to hide my disheartened scowl.

"Let's take a break and work on somethin' else." He smuggly snickers. "Follow me."

I groan and stride behind him. We stroll from the railroad tracks to an empty field that has been untouched by last night's downpour. We halt in the middle of a dusty patch of dead grass and auburn dirt. The warehouse is barely visible in the distance. Aries pauses and stares toward the empty horizon, then nods like he's just found the perfect site for my next lesson.

"So you said movin' small things was nothin'. But have you ever tried movin' a bunch of small things at the same time?"

My brow curls, and I search my memory. I try to come up with a scenario that might make the perfect example, but as I finish recollecting, I realize there isn't one.

"Never thought to try that."

"It's actually pretty simple. You focus on multiple things all the time, right?" He shrugs as he pulls his hands from his pockets, and points in all directions. "I don't just see what I'm lookin' at. I see everything in my periphery, too. I can hear what's behind me, even if I'm not tryin' to."

I gaze around and nod, before watching Aries ball his fists. A trio of dirt clods rise from the ground. He places one over the palm of his hand, while the others hover over each shoulder.

"Hold out your hand."

I oblige.

"Now, put these in the same position around your body."

I focus as one of the ping-pong-ball-sized mounds flows from his palm to mine. The others flutter to my shoulders. An immense smile protrudes from my face. Finally, something I'm decent at.

"Nice. So back in the day, when all us Clairvoyants were under one roof, the Kinetics used to play this game called Dirt War."

My eyebrow raises with intrigue as his body slowly spins in a circle. Orange dust wafts into the air. A thick line surges against the ground around us, forming an oblong ring, as if someone dragged a pole against it.

"The object of the game was to hit your opponent three times without leaving the circle. Ever noticed that scar Perseus has near his eye?"

A grin appears on his face when I nod. He looks off, like he's recaptured a fond memory.

"I popped him in the face with a clod that had a rock in it." He laughs. "It was an accident. But after that, Pavo and Andromeda made us stop playin'. Auriga just thought it was funny."

His gaze drifts downward for a solemn moment. His confident smile disappears before he shakes his head and replants his glare on me.

"Anywho. The game taught us how to use our powers with quickness and precision, not just brute strength."

I can't help but snicker at the image of seeing Perseus getting smacked in the face with a stone. I imagine him crying and running to Pavo, but I doubt the uber-tough Kinetic would ever let a tear trickle from his eye, even if he were in pain.

"Now…" Aries grunts as he takes several steps back. "Try to hit me."

I barely let him finish speaking before I send the three clumps of dirt hurling toward him. I call myself trying to catch him off guard, but he sends each one swirling away without lifting a finger.

Smack! A piece of dirt smashes into the back of my head. It doesn't hurt, but I still flinch like I've been punched.

"Don't forget about defense, rook," he barks, and gives a hearty chuckle. "In this game, you gotta knuckle-up and protect yourself at the same time. And don't just send your ammo in a straight line. These ain't bullets. Frisbee those bad boys."

My eyes widen as the other two dirt clods I'd thrown come hurling back from different directions. I dodge one, and send another fluttering by with my out-stretched hand. Just as I feel secure, the one I'd just avoided belts me in my cheek. Aries laughs, until the clod I deflected smashes against the side of his chest.

"Nice one, rook! So I guess you're ready to play?"

I smirk and ball my fists. Aries backs up and spreads his fingers. Three fresh balls of dirt fling into the air and orbit around him.

"New score. Zero, zero!" He cackles. "Let's get it."

We've been at it for about an hour. I've lost every game we've played, but I don't care. My body is tired, but adrenaline has kept my pace surprisingly fresh. For the first time in ages, I'm having fun. With each round, I feel myself getting better and better.

I know Aries is going easy on me. Actually, *easy* might be an understatement. The closest I came to winning was the third game, when Aries beat me after the score was tied at two. He demolished me in the next game, three to nothing, to douse any idea that I might be getting as good as him.

We prepare for one last round. My sneakers scrape against the dirt. My fingers twitch. I spin six dirt clods around me, like they are planets and I'm their sun. Aries sneers back and waits. Feels like a Wild West showdown.

"You guys playin' Dirt War, and you didn't invite me?" a feminine voice says, from behind me.

My face gnarls as I turn to see Aquila strolling toward us.

"Just doin' some trainin'," Aries replies, a hint of apprehension evident in his tone. "Kid is pickin' up pretty quickly."

"Well, then," she says, with a sly grin, rubbing her closely shaven scalp. "Let's see what you got, rookie."

She steps into the circle, her tongue sweeping across her upper lip like a lioness about to pounce on an unsuspecting gazelle. She wears a thin black tank top that lets the firm, brown skin of her strapping arms glisten in the sunlight. She looks incredibly attractive. I'd been so intimidated by her that I'd never really noticed that she is gorgeous when she doesn't look so murderous.

"Hold up," Aries says.

"No," I grunt. "Let me take her on."

Aries is clearly surprised by my response. He leans his head back and shrugs, before he and Aquila share an impressed stare.

"You heard the kid." She laughs.

I grunt and smile. I crack my neck and get into a calculated position, like I'm about to do an Olympic long jump. For the first time since seeing her at the bank, I'm not afraid of her. I can't wait to get her form-fitting dark jeans covered in dirt.

"Thirty percent," Aries says to Aquila, as she brings a slew of rough clods hovering in front of her chest.

"Fifty." She scoffs.

"Thirty!"

She rolls her stunning brown eyes. "Fine!"

"Okay, then." Aries stares at me with his worrisome gaze to give me one last chance to object.

I look at him with an overzealous leer.

"Go!" he shouts.

I begin jabbing my arms as if I'm shadow boxing. Aquila stands still, allowing me to send a bevy of shots her way, without the slightest attempt to return fire. I don't know whether she is toying with me or testing me. I don't bother waiting for her to change her strategy. After she crosses her arms and uses the patches of dirt around her as an impromptu shield, I send my next missile of soil hurling toward her from the rear. I think I've got her, but she bends a knee and ducks my shot just before it's able to graze her back.

I wait for her to return fire, but she doesn't. Yeah. She's definitely toying with me. She'll learn. I raise my hands to signal ten more pieces. Then I swipe my arms forward and send all of them swirling in a furious wave toward her.

"Not bad for a beginner." She giggles, dodging every single one of my shots. "My turn!"

Dozens of clods zip into a vertical line in front of her chest. I clutch my fists and get into a pose similar to a character's in an arcade fighting game. She shifts her head and squints, then moves her hands underneath her ammunition before she sends each one firing like they're shot from a machine gun.

My eyes broaden. Heart jumps in my chest, as I somersault out of the way. You'd think we were playing with live bullets. As my head rolls over the earth, Aquila comes back into view for an instant. I stretch out my hand and send one of her shots rotating back toward her.

Her gaze continues to fixate on me. She doesn't see it. What a move! I can't help but be impressed with myself for this one. I have my triumphant, one-to-zero fist pump ready, until I see Aquila jump. Only, I can't truly classify this as a jump. It starts off like one, but her body coils. My jaw drops. I have never seen any-thing like it. It's as if she is unaffected by gravity, and is walking on an invisible wall for a split second.

Her thin frame spins through the air. Her arm moves into a scooping formation. There is an awestruck gawk painted across my face as my shot cycles around her waist and begins hurling back at me.

Smack. Smack. Smack. Dirt flutters into my nostrils.

Damn it! I've already lost. I forgot to play defense… but how could I have possibly been prepared for what she's just done.

As my chest rests against the ground, my mouth spreads wide in sheer amazement.

Did Aquila just fly?

CHAPTER 17

"YOU NEED TO TEACH YOUR BOY SOME DEFENSE,
Aries." Aquila cackles from across the dirt circle.

"Yeah, yeah," he grunts. "You good, kid?"

I rise to my feet and wipe the dirt from my face and
hair. Aries stands above me, dusting off my shoulders,
but I brush by him.

"How'd you do that?"

"What? Fly?" Aquila replies, as if I've asked something irrational.

"Uhh…yeah! You guys can freakin' fly?"

"Duh." She laughs. "How the hell do you think we
got you here?"

"We don't ride around in busted sedans, bro," Aries
says.

"You have to teach me." My smile is giddy like a
child at Christmas.

I've always dreamed of flying, ever since I hovered my first cricket into the air. But I'd never thought it would actually be possible.

"No can do." Aries shakes his locks in disdain, wearing a parental scowl. "Not until you move that crate, homeboy."

"But I picked up Dirt War pretty fast without moving the crate."

"Dirt War is about instincts. To fly, you have to focus the kinetic energy around you."

"I can do th—"

"Nope. Gotta crawl before you run, kid. Now, go get some rest. You're back on the crates tomorrow."

I let out a frustrated grunt before tucking my hands into my pockets. I'm just barely able to see Aquila's tickled grin over Aries's shoulder as I trudge back toward the warehouse.

"Damn it!" I yell, as the crate in the distance drops.

I've been practicing all day, and I still haven't managed to move the stupid thing horizontally. I'd hoped that a refreshing night's rest would've given me the extra burst of energy needed to complete this annoying task. But after several unfruitful hours, all of the confidence I'd gained from learning Dirt War has been replaced with agitation.

I wipe my sweaty palms against my dusty jeans and make another attempt. The box raises higher than I've raised it before. But as it moves a few feet toward the next row, my arms begin to tremble, and a throbbing headache courses through my skull.

Clung! It lands sideways, but still not where it's supposed to be.

"Screw this." I kick the dirt and turn away.

The sun is beginning to set over the horizon. I turn to glance at the lights flickering from the grimy, warehouse windows. The enticing scent of beef stew is wafting from inside, and my stomach starts to rumble.

I know Aries means well, but I'm tired of this lesson. It reminds me of high school classes and learning the Pythagorean theorem and other overt, impractical nonsense I felt like I'd never apply in my adult life. I need to do things my own way. The stupid box will get moved. But right now, I want to expand my horizons. I want to see if I can fly.

I scan around to make sure no one is looking. If I'm going to try this, I'd better do it now. This shouldn't be too complicated. After all, Aquila talked about flying as if it was some neat sideshow trick. I just need to focus the kinetic energy around me. Simple.

My arms drift to my sides, and my palms become rigid, like rocket boosters are about to shoot out of them. I close my eyes and take a deep breath.

"Focus," I whisper. "Focus on the kinetic energy that's around me."

As soon as I exhale, the earth begins to shake under me, and my feet begin to leave the ground. A smile protrudes from my face as I feel the dusty air swirling around me. But my confident grin begins to dissipate barely a moment later. My arms start to tremble and a queasy feeling curdles through my stomach. I become lightheaded, like I've been spinning upside down and in circles. I open my eyes, but the feeling only worsens when colors and spots begin to dominate my vision.

My chest tightens, and my limbs grow numb. My head droops, and a flood of orange vomit spews from my mouth like a disgusting geyser. The world becomes a vacant blur. Before I know it, my back pounds against the ground, and everything fades away.

I awaken on my coarse, makeshift mattress in the loft. My body is still in pain. The last time I felt like this was in fifth grade, when I had the flu. I cringe and reach for my pounding forehead to feel a pack of ice spread across it. Aries is sitting beside me with a perturbed scowl, his face blanketed by the moonlit glow that pours through the warehouse windows.

"Next time, listen to me before you kill yourself."

"Sorry," I mumble, while cringing.

Talking, even barely above a whisper, only makes my headache grow.

"Aquila just made it look so easy."

"Yeah, well, you're not Quila," he growls, his brown eyes even more fierce than when I first saw him at that bank in Siler City. "Your body is a network of moving parts, dumb ass. You need to be able to fine-tune your power. If you can't focus on a hollow crate, how the hell are you going to move a body full of organs and bones?"

I stay silent and look away like a dejected puppy.

Aries stands. "I'd tell you to eat somethin', but I don't feel like cleaning up after you puke again."

As he storms to the other end of the loft, I catch the others staring back at me from the kitchen area with comedic grins. I turn and lay back down to hide my flushed cheeks. I've only been here for two days, and I've already disappointed the one Kinetic who was willing to guide me.

A kick against the mattress wakes me from a perfect slumber. My eyes flicker open, and Aries is standing above me, with the same perturbed scowl from the last time I saw him.

"Wake up." He scoffs.

I pull myself to an upward position and let out a massive yawn while stretching my limbs. Everything still feels numb, but at least the pain and queasiness in my stomach are gone.

"How you feelin'?" he says.

"Better. But—"

"Good. Let's go."

He darts toward the winding staircase. My eyes widen just enough to see his frame disappear into the dark warehouse's bottom floor. I glance at the other sleeping Predators before standing and grabbing my sullied hoodie from the floor. There is still a vomit stain on the bottom of it.

I scurry after Aries until we reach the railroad tracks. I stop to catch my breath and admire the scenery bathed by the waning moonlight. The air is stark and chilly. An eerie breeze whistles between the stacks of iron crates.

"Sorry," Aries says.

A glimmer of surprise enters my gaze as I slowly approach him. I can't imagine what he'd be apologizing for. I was the one who was arrogant and disobedient.

"I gotta stop trainin' you like I'm Pavo or Andromeda. All these lessons and steps—it ain't how we learned stuff."

He turns from the crates and faces me with a grimace. I take a deep breath and remove my hands from within my warm pockets.

"We learned from failure. And failure is the best teacher there is."

I nod, and a slight smile cascades across my face. Aries's brow hardens, which simmers my gratitude.

"So you know what you did wrong. Now fix it."

My gaze darts around. I want to ask questions, but I know they'll be met with a scoff and more agitation. So I just nod again.

"You can't just move the air under your feet." Aries rolls his eyes after analyzing my confusion. "You have to create a ball of energy around you."

I rub my coarse lips together and scan the ground. I take in his words like I'm being prepped for a final exam.

"The wind is your best friend."

He balls his fists and places his arms to his side. He slowly rises into the air like he's being lifted by an invisible parachute.

"Wind is constant kinetic energy, and we can manipulate it like it's our own."

A light shove against my chest knocks me back a few steps.

"Now you try," he says, while his body hovers several feet above the ground. "Create a bubble of kinetic energy around you. Don't worry about moving your body."

"Okay." I close my eyes.

"No! Don't close your eyes. See all of your surroundings. You don't need to trick yourself into it."

I nod again. I can't imagine how much the gesture must annoy him at this point. I follow his instructions and do my best to mimic his mannerisms. A deep sigh billows from my lips, and I focus my gaze. I mentally recite everything he's just said. *Remember, the air is my friend.*

I feel a calming breeze flow into my skin and through my clothes. I embrace each gust that comes my way. My heartbeat steadies, and I stretch out my arms the way I did when I was deflecting dirt clods. Slowly, my feet drift from the ground. No queasy sensation. No lightheadedness. I look down and can't help but smile at the gravel several feet beneath me.

"There ya go." Aries snickers.

It doesn't even feel like I'm floating. My body feels leveled, as if gravity no longer matters. There is no wind fluttering against my chest, but I can still sense the air wafting in my periphery like swirling waves.

"Higher." Aries rises several more feet.

I clench my fists and smile. My arms move to my side, and I drift further upward.

"Higher!" he says again.

I effortlessly rise. Then I rise again. And again. Before I know it, I am staring at the top of the warehouse roof and the exact spot where Perseus dangled me from a chair a few days ago.

Aries flies toward me and taps my shoulder, wearing a proud smirk.

"Not bad. Now, why the hell haven't you moved that crate?"

My grin fades when he points toward the sideways, steel box.

"I...I don't know."

"Yeah you do." He folds his arms as he rotates around me and waits for my reply.

"I...I start to get scared. I guess I'm afraid that I'll drop it."

"So what? Worst case scenario—ya drop it, everyone hears, we laugh at yo ass, then you get back to it."

I can't help but shrug. He's absolutely right, and the notion instantly feels ridiculous.

"Now, move the damn box."

He swipes his arm at the air, sending the sideways crate snapping back into perfect position. After a deep breath, I jerk my head to the side and reach out my hand. Everything around the box becomes a vacant blur, like I'm focusing a microscope. My eyebrows curl, and my teeth grind. I can sense every corner and rusted edge of the massive object, but I imagine that it's nothing more than one of my moving boxes full of clothes.

Clung! The crate plops onto another pile. It happens so quickly, so effortlessly, that I can barely replay the event in my head. I even glance at Aries to make sure he didn't just do it for me.

"See that." He chuckles. "And you did it all while still maintainin' the kinetic energy around your body."

My eyes widen, and I scan my stationary frame. I did it. Not only did I do it, but it came so naturally, like I was a kid learning how to stand for the first time. A grin pours from my lips, but the sensation disappears as quickly as it came, when Aries floats beside me with a sly smirk.

"Now, move all of 'em."

"What do you mean, *all of 'em*?" I scoff.

"I didn't stutter."

His body drifts backward, and his index finger stretches toward the rows of massive steel crates. They seem to spread across the length of a football field. I'd never counted them before, but there are six columns with four crates in each pile. I can feel a lump forming in my throat as I examine every inch of them.

"What the hell you waitin' for!"

My palms become sweaty, and my eyelids flicker like I've just gotten dirt in them. I hold out my arm, but it isn't nearly as firm and focused as it was before.

"Stop bein' afraid! Ya know what Auriga used to tell us? He'd say, *Fear is a self-inflicted wound before you've even started the fight.*"

I take a deep breath and hold out both hands. I turn my apprehensive grimace into an intense snarl as my gaze blares toward the field of metal containers.

"Focus on your goal." His voice echoes through the air when my arms start to tremble. "Your goal ain't in those crates. Your goal is to shed your limitations. Your goal is to recognize your own strength. Your goal is to become a true Predator."

My face begins to ache. I can feel my nose becoming rigid, and my teeth starting to grind. I peer at the boxes and imagine them being a pile of dirt clods, but they still don't budge. Frustration is beginning to settle in, and I know Aries can sense it.

"Use your emotion! Use that anger to fuel you."

Another deep breath. I focus even harder. My lips begin to wriggle, and my skin grows cold. Veins protrude from my aching brow. I feel my body starting to descend, so I put one hand down to steady myself in the air.

"Your goal is fighting Psyriin. Your goal is finding your mother!"

My face relaxes. There is still a deep scowl, but the fury coursing through my body no longer feels like a burden. It feels like...adrenaline. I picture each metal crate as the Psyriin tank-bus that separated me from my mother and chased me through that empty shopping center. I imagine that these crates are the only obstacle standing between me reuniting with her. I let a blistering scream into the night air. The crates burst from the ground like popcorn popping from a cast-iron skillet.

Clung! Clung! Clung! One by one, the crates rain down and shake the earth. Dust shoots as high as our dangling feet, but my deep scowl still hasn't gone away. My arms wade by my waist, with fists curled. My chest pounds.

"Wow." Aries grunts as the final crate falls from the sky and bangs against another. "I didn't really expect you to lift all of 'em."

The sounds of subtle applause comes from below. We both shift our gazes downward to the trio of action-figure-sized frames peering up from the ground.

"I think you're ready, kid!" Perseus shouts, with a hearty grin.

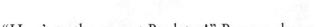

"Here's to the newest Predator!" Perseus cheers.

We all stand in a circle, clinking thumb-sized glasses together, before pouring the liquid down our throats. The small portion smells like rubbing alcohol and tastes like cold castor oil as soon as it touches my tongue.

"Ugh." I smack my lips.

"Looks like our boy is a rookie at the sauce, too." Aquila grins while slapping my shoulder.

I try to force a smile through my frown while the last disgusting remnants trickle down my throat. A warm and relaxed sensation follows that almost makes the bitter flavor worth it. *Almost.*

Perseus, Lupus, and Aries walk over to the plate of cheese and crackers laid out in the kitchen. Aquila remains standing beside me with a smug grin spread across her face. My cheeks grow rosy red as I try my best to ignore her rugged beauty.

"So how's your first Halloween party?" She stares deep into my eyes.

I'd almost forgotten about the holiday, and it only reminds me that I've been away from Mom for five agonizing days. But I have to admit, being around the Predators right now is calming my anxiety more than when I was at the Safe House with Leo, Ara, Pavo, and Lyra.

"Good," I reply, as suavely as I can muster. "I've never really had a group of friends before. But you guys...you guys feel like kindred spirits, ya know?"

She winks.

"So..." I mumble, trying to continue the conversation so she doesn't walk away. "The other day, you called Pavo and the others, the Phantoms?"

"Oh, yeah." She chuckles. "Because they're always going ghost when things get tough. Then they reappear right when you don't want 'em there."

An unbridled laugh billows from my jaws. Even though Pavo, Leo, and Ara rescued me from Psyriin, I have to admit the name suits them, after how unwilling they were to try to find the Charon.

For the rest of the evening, we all laugh, joke, toy with our powers, and dance to music blaring throughout the hollow warehouse. I've never been to a party before. I don't count the ones Mom threw when I was a child, because it was just the two of us. I imagine this is what a real party is supposed to feel like. There is a calmness and jubilance to the atmosphere. A welcomed escape from the chaos that surrounds each of our lives.

It's funny seeing the Predators in a drunken haze. Aquila shares dreams of all of them living together on an island, where no one can harm them once we've defeated Psyriin. I snicker when Aries quips about how ridiculous her idea sounds, and she responds by making his drink spill all over his chest.

Perseus rambles about the good ole days, when all twelve Clairvoyants were together, learning about their extraordinary powers. The passion in his voice makes me wish I'd come out of one of those tubes myself. There's even a hint of callous affection when he goes into a rant about how frustrated it made him that Pavo and Leo *let the family go to shit*. It reminds me of how I felt every time Mom decided to move us. I wonder if Perseus understands what I do now. Both Pavo and my mother might not have always made the best decisions, but their hearts were in the right place.

Throughout the night, one thing becomes clear—the Predators love Auriga. They each manage to make a snide comment about every other member of the Clairvoyants, except for him.

"*Leo is a self-righteous Boy Scout.*"

"*Carina was a bitch.*"

"*Lacerta was a cry baby.*"

But never a disparaging word about Auriga. To them, he is more than a mentor. He's the reason for their passion. He's what guides their every move, and their conviction to rescue him seems even greater than my longing to reunite with Mom.

Maybe it's that gross beverage settling into my system, but I've never felt so open around anyone. I talk to them for several hours, into the late night. It's amazing how soothing it feels to converse with them, considering how vicious they'd seemed over the past few days. I tell them all about Dee and the flash drive, and how I'd hoped it had contained valuable information. I give them the full rundown of everything leading up to meeting them, and they hang onto every word.

Eventually, I get around to asking them about the intricate tattoos on their left arms. Being so close to them now, I'm able to fully admire the immaculate detail of each one. They look like murals done by a world-renowned artist. Lupus apparently did all of them, including his own. It's something he is modest about, but he should be proud. I inquire about getting one for myself. I want something just as bold, like a tiger leaping through fire, or a venomous snake lunging from a swamp.

Lupus says he'll get around to it. The tone of his reply doesn't make me feel as excited as I was when I asked. He seems reluctant. And despite the few conversations we have throughout the night, I never get the feeling that he truly likes that I'm here. He's been outnumbered by Kinetics for years. So that there's another one in the group shouldn't bother him. He is clearly as valuable a member of the Predators as the others. So why does it feel like he's threatened by me?

"Listen up!" Perseus barks, through his smile, while using his powers to lower the music. "Tonight is not just a night celebrating the rookie earning his wings."

They all look to me, and I smile. Lupus's gaze is the only one that doesn't look as giddy. His smile is much more somber, like a child who isn't excited to learn his parents are having another baby, but has to appear enthused, nonetheless.

"While Rion was training, Lupus and I came up with a plan to find the Charon."

Exhilaration blasts through my every pore, and my weary eyes become bulbous. Aries turns to Perseus with an uneasy gnarl across his brow, while Aquila becomes intrigued.

"In a few days," he says, like he's a coach trying to rally a team before a big game, "we're gonna break into a television station."

My chest begins to thump. I glance at the others to see if their apprehension has blossomed like mine, but they each look focused on his every word. I don't know why I'm surprised. It's almost like I'd forgotten about the bank robbery.

Perseus continues to speak, but my tense thoughts wander, and I only catch the gist. He lays out the details of his plan to force Nastacia Arkright out of the shadows. He talks about how no one should get hurt if everything goes accordingly. He is adamant that Psyriin will give us Auriga and my mother, for fear that we'll expose our existence to the world, or harm hostages if our demands aren't met.

My stomach starts to churn. Why am I so nervous? Aries has taught me everything I need to know. And unlike the Phantoms, the Predators will have my back. Maybe it's the thought of engaging with Nastacia Arkright and her minions again. Perseus is confident in his plan. But what if something goes wrong? Empty metal crates aren't enemies with guns. Will I be able to take a life if necessary, when two days ago, I couldn't even kill one captured Psyriin soldier?

I feel all the Predators staring at me. I shudder from my vacant stupor and try to shake the nervous glimmer from my eyes.

"Everyone in?" Perseus grunts, as if he's asked this question already.

"Yeah." I nod. "Let's do it."

I can feel my conscience tugging at my skull. Perseus takes a large swig of that disgusting, clear liquid straight from the thin unlabeled bottle it came from. He smacks his lips and gives an exuberant smile. Aquila clasps her hands together, and her piercing gaze wanders toward the roof. Longing is evident in those spectacular pupils of hers.

I glance over at Aries. He breathes heavily, with his arms coiled together. As his apprehensive glare bombards mine, his words from the other night begin to chime in my head.

You ain't a killer, bro. But bes' believe, if you're gonna find this mom of yours…if you're gonna face Arkright and Psyriin… you're gonna have to become one.

CHAPTER 18

ON AIR

CONTROL YOUR BREATHING. CONTROL YOUR *breathing...*

I have to keep reminding myself over and over again, as the fierce winds pound my face and my eyes water. It's been over a week since Mom and I separated. I just learned to float a few days ago. Now, here I am, soaring through the air with the other Predators. We've been flying for a half-hour, just high enough to look like buzzards to any possible onlookers. I've managed to keep up just fine, aside from a few times where my body wobbled and I had to refocus to maintain balance. Aries keeps looking back at me with a concerned scowl. I can tell he is ready to lunge after me, should I pass out and plunge to the ground.

Every so often, I also catch Lupus glaring at me with his usual grimace. I tell myself he is only agitated because he's being pulled through the air by Perseus. He looks like a child who is embarrassed to still be using a car seat.

A cluster of buildings come into view. There's a large antenna protruding from the skyline, and I know we've just about reached our destination.

Perseus is the first to descend. My heart begins to rattle as we each follow closely. The others land on the roof, just a few feet away from the steel tower. Their feet touch the ground so casually, it's as if they were all aided by an invisible parachute. My landing is far less graceful. My feet skid against the rooftop, and I have to steady myself to keep from ramming against the edge of the building. I notice Aquila chuckling at me as I exhale and collect myself.

"Okay," Perseus says. "Let's do this."

He flicks his wrist, and the padlock on a rusty door flings across the vacant rooftop. We've rehearsed this operation several times, but I still feel nervous. I follow from the back of the group, taking deep breaths as the sunlight disappears behind the creaking door. We march down a long stairwell until we've reached the third of five floors. Perseus moves to the side, and Lupus takes the lead. My fingers twitch with anticipation as the Reader Clairvoyant closes his eyes and clutches the silver doorknob.

"The main studio is through here," he whispers. "Only one security guard on this floor."

"Remember. Secure the room." Perseus peers into each of our focused scowls. "We can't have anyone calling the police."

I ball my fists and give a confident nod. Part of me is excited. I've never done anything like this before. I know Mom would be angered by what we're about to do, but her safety is my only concern. If this is the quickest way to her, then it's what has to be done.

The door flies open. Perseus sets his sights on the lone security guard standing at the edge of the room, near a set of elevators. The guard reaches for his pistol, but it rips from the holster and zips into Perseus's hand before he can even yell freeze. Perseus flicks his other wrist, and the guard goes thundering into the crisp metal elevator doors, creating a massive dent, and knocking him out cold.

Aries and Aquila enter the hall. Three women at a nearby desk stand to their feet with terrified eyes. They aren't even able to let out a yelp before being flung into the walls and knocked unconscious. So much for no one getting hurt. But I suppose a gigantic knot on their heads is better than a bullet.

"Zip ties." Perseus huffs while twiddling the fingers on his outstretched hand.

Lupus frantically retrieves a pack of the plastic strands from his pockets, and hands one over to everyone but me. I stand against the door, my fingers twitching as the others gather the bodies and tie up their wrists.

I hear a pair of hurried footsteps. I glance at the others to see if they've heard the same, but no one moves from their task. My eyes widen. I turn my head just in time to catch another tall, burly security officer come from around the opposite corner of the hall.

"Stop right there!" he growls, as he brandishes his gun into firing position.

The words have barely left his lips, when I dip my body low and fling my arms out to subdue him.

Bang! The gun goes off just as the officer's body smashes against the wall.

My eyes close as I wince. The adrenaline rushing through my veins is the only thing keeping me from looking down to see if I've been hit. Once I realize I don't feel any pain, I open my eyes and gawk at the bullet hole in the wall, merely inches from my face.

"What the hell!" Perseus screams.

I stand to my feet and turn to Aries looking back at me, his hand outstretched. Once again, he's stopped someone from being shot. I give him a thankful nod before watching Perseus stomp over to Lupus. A vicious scowl blares from his face as he snatches Lupus up by the collar of his shirt.

"Thought you said there was only one security guard?"

"I-I'm sorry," Lupus replies. "He wasn't supposed to be there. The guard I read didn't know—"

"Well, get your head out of your ass!" Perseus tosses Lupus aside. "We can't afford screw-ups like that."

Lupus straightens his wrinkled shirt and takes a deep breath, while Perseus trots over to me.

"You okay, Rion?"

"Yeah." I nod, with a deep sigh.

"Secure those elevators!" he yells toward Aquila, barely a moment after planting two calming taps against my shoulder.

After a stern nod, Aquila turns and rips the doors straight off the elevators to reveal the empty cavern inside. Aries moves to her side to assist. I observe them shifting their arms to telekinetically twist the steel ropes that pull the elevator from each floor.

"We don't have much time now," Perseus barks, while passing another irate snarl toward Lupus. "Let's move."

We sprint down a long corridor until we've reached a pair of double doors. To our left is another entrance marked *Production Room*. We wait by the double doors while Aries rips the production room door from its hinges. Startled faces gawk at us from inside. Three men with headsets sit in front of a long desk filled with monitors and intricate equipment. Aries flings the men from their seats and ties them up, making sure to leave only one of them conscious. Lupus strides over to the frightened employee and clutches his sweat-filled brow.

Perseus enters the news studio on the opposite side of a thin sheet of glass. There is a male and a female anchor, a pair of cameramen, and a few other staff members, each looking on with confused gnarls when the Kinetic Clairvoyant strolls in.

"What's going on?" The male anchor stands, on the other side of a news desk.

Perseus just smiles and shifts his palm upward. Every civilian in the room rises to the ceiling and begins to scream.

"Everyone, chill!" Perseus yells. "We just have a quick message to send. Then we'll be out of your hair."

I stand in the doorway, my restless gaze peering back and forth between the studio and the vacant hallway. I keep expecting a SWAT team to burst through the walls and kill us all before we can flick a wrist.

"Anytime now," Perseus grunts toward Lupus.

"Hold on a second!"

Lupus finally drops his hostage's wriggling skull from his grasp, and pulls forth some duct tape to place over the man's mouth. Aries, Aquila, and I stand to the side as Lupus places a headset over his stringy, black hair. He sits in a seat at the center of the desk. I gawk in amazement as the Reader begins flipping switches and moving knobs like he invented every piece of equipment in the room. I'm not the only one impressed. Both Aquila and Aries glare at him with smirks as he tinkers away.

"I need someone to move the cameras," he says, over his shoulder.

Aquila shrugs and scurries past me before resurfacing on the other side of the glass.

"Okay." Lupus sighs as he pushes a knob upward. "You're live in five...four...three...two..."

A bright red sign with the words *On Air* blinks above me. Lupus points, and Aquila shifts every camera at once. Perseus responds with his most sinister grin.

"Ladies and gentlemen, your local news team will be back in just a moment to bring you your daily dose of high school sports, local homicides, and puppy footage. But for now, my name is Perseus. And I am here to deliver a message to Nastacia Arkright."

I feel my chest thumping as I gaze at Perseus's unyielding demeanor. He paces around the studio desk like a principal laying down the law to a group of cowering students. I can tell he's been waiting for this moment for a while. He's relishing in his chance to look like a terrifying force.

I glance over at Aries, who leans against the wall with his arms crossed. Deep breaths flow from his tightened lips.

"Arkright...you've stolen from me and my family." Perseus takes a seat behind the desk and props his feet up. "You have an hour to meet us here. Alone!"

I look up at the massive clock hanging from the wall. It's 7:00 a.m.

"If you fail to show, or if any police interfere..." A conniving smile spreads across Perseus's scarred face as he glances up at the hostages. "Well..." He laughs. "Let's just say today's weather forecast will get very interesting."

The crimson glow of the On Air sign disappears from over my shoulder.

"We've lost the feed!" Lupus is frantically pressing buttons and pulling switches.

"Good. That means she got our message," Perseus leaps from the desk and paces over toward the glass. "Now...we wait."

The words have barely echoed against the glass, when we all turn our attention to the sound of footsteps clamoring down the hall.

"Looks like the rent-a-cops from the other floors didn't get the memo." Aries huffs.

He jerks his head toward me, then exits through the doorway. I quickly follow, with my fists balled like I'm about to engage in a street fight. As soon as we turn the corner, we see four security guards sprinting at us.

"Take their weapons," Aries says, his gaze blaring forward.

My face turns to a sneer. I whip out my hands and watch the startled scowls of the guards as their pistols zing toward me. When the task is complete, Aries sends one of the fallen elevator doors hammering against their backs. Lupus comes trotting between us as soon as their frames huddle against the floor.

"That's all of them." He peers into the eyes of the last conscious guard.

"You sure this time?" Aquila snidely says, as she and Perseus calmly come up behind us.

"I'm sure." Lupus rolls his eyes.

I sit in one of the producers' chairs, with my feet propped up against the desk. The clock reads 7:45. I can't stop glancing up at it. The last half-hour has felt like an eternity. But I can only imagine what those innocent people dangling in the next room must be feeling. Every so often, I hear their tearful pleading, and it makes me wince.

The other Predators don't seem to be bothered, except maybe Aries. He continues to lean against the wall, his eyes closed, and face coated with an alert scowl. Lupus sits next to me, with his head rested against his folded arms. Aquila and Perseus have managed to pass the time with some mindless banter. Their conversations range from what food they'll eat later, to which hostage will pee themselves first.

Their resolve is staggering. I start to wonder just how many heists and violent escapades they've embarked on since leaving Pavo and the Phantoms. This entire experience seems mundane to them. Even carrying on casual conversation while telepathically dangling a dozen people from the ceiling seems like a nonchalant task to Perseus and Aquila.

"She's here!" Lupus glares at the security footage in the corner. "She's alone."

We both stand, with tense grimaces. Perseus just cracks a smug smile from the opposite side of the thin glass. I look over to Aries. He has barely budged, but his eyes have crept open. He looks perturbed, as if he's been woken up from a wondrous nap. He kicks himself from the wall and cracks his neck before strolling into the hallway with his arms firmly crossed.

"Showtime." Perseus turns to Aquila's equally anxious smile. "Watch our guests, will ya."

She nods and sits on the edge of the news desk. I give one more unnerved glance at the dangling hostages from behind the glass. I can't help but feel sorry for each of them as I wonder what might be going through their minds. They must think of us as terrorists. I have to tell myself that what we are doing is warranted. That the actions of Psyriin have forced our hand. We aren't looking for power or financial gain. We just want our family back. We just want to be left alone.

"Rion!" Perseus barks from the hallway. "You comin' or not?"

I scurry after him. Aries is told to stay behind. His job is to pull us up the severely damaged elevator once we've made contact with Arkright. He gives me a calming glance before we disappear into the stairwell. It's as if he is just as nervous about being separated from me, as I am from him.

Our trip downward is eerily silent. I can't help but feel awkward moving alongside the Predators without Aries watching over me. We march while the tension of what is to come seems to course between each of our breaths. Lupus is the first to break the silence when he mentions that all of the other workers in the building have fled. Perseus barely reacts. I can tell that after

Lupus's earlier mishap, he isn't inclined to fully accept anything the Reader says.

We exit the stairwell, and I freeze the moment we turn the corner. Nastacia Arkright comes into view with a relaxed, yet focused, grimace plastered on her porcelain face. She stands firmly in the doorway, wearing the same black bodysuit I'd first seen her in. There is no gun at her waist, and her hands rest behind her back.

Perseus steps forward in the center of the lobby. He swipes his hand to telekinetically latch the front doors shut. Arkright doesn't even flinch.

"Miss Arkright," he says, like he's doing his best impression of a James Bond villain.

She gives a soft grunt before nudging her head to the side to examine me. My brow curls as she scans my body up and down, like the kids used to do on my first day at a new school. I return her gesture with a scowl, as if I'm trying to look as tough as Perseus.

"She's unarmed," Lupus says, his eyes squeezed shut in concentration. "But there are soldiers surrounding the building."

Perseus responds to his words with a grimace. His scathing dark pupils glare into hers as we await an explanation.

"They're just here for the extraction and debriefing of the hostages," she says, in a soothing tone, as her gaze snaps toward Lupus.

He turns and nods toward Perseus to indicate that her words are truthful.

"I've met your demands. Now, let's get on with this."

Perseus responds to her with a smirk. He turns to his side, holding out his hands to guide her toward the elevator like a hotel bellhop. Her thick boots thump against the linoleum floor as she strides to the edge of the lobby. Perseus spreads his arms, and the steel elevator doors open.

I am the last to step inside. Perseus gives a heavy knock against the walls, and we begin to ascend before the doors can even close. I seem to be the only one distracted by the echoing grind of colliding metal. Lupus and Perseus stand calmly to each side of Arkright, with heavy snarls. But the Psyriin general doesn't appear to be intimidated in the least bit.

The piercing sound of the elevator coming to a halt causes me to wince and clutch my ears. Aries's outstretched arms come into view. The callous sneer he gives Nastacia Arkright is the most heinous I've ever seen him look.

"Right this way, ma'am." Perseus brushes by me and strides toward the television studio.

I follow closely at the rear. My hands begin to twitch by my side, and an anxious lump forms in my throat.

"Ahhh...the Queen Bee is finally here." Aquila wears a devilish smile as she tilts her head to the ceiling. "Congratulations, folks. You all get to go home now."

A grumble carves through Arkright's calm demeanor. She gazes upward and watches the host of civilians flutter to the floor like autumn leaves. They stampede toward the exit the moment their bodies thump to the floor. When the last one is gone, Aries steps in front of the doors and latches them shut.

"Okay." Perseus sighs as he leans against the desk. "Let's chat."

A chair behind one of the cameras whirls across the room and undercuts the unsuspecting Psyriin general. An agitated grunt billows from her ruby-red lips as Perseus telekinetically pulls her uncomfortably seated frame in front of us.

"So," Perseus growls, replacing his smirk with a callous grimace. "Where's the Charon?"

CHAPTER 19

THE DEAL

NASTACIA ARKRIGHT WIGGLES HER POSTERIOR into a comfortable position before folding her legs and clasping her hands together. I find myself becoming increasingly annoyed by her unbothered mannerisms, and I can sense the same sentiments in the rest of the Predators. Sure, none of us expected a Psyriin general to show fear, but this casual demeanor on display feels much more like a show of disrespect than a show of resolve.

I stare into her sinister smirk. It doesn't take a Reader Clairvoyant to know the thoughts swimming through her mind. She believes we are beneath her. And she wants us to know it.

"The Charon is here," she finally says, her piercing gaze fixated forward. "About a block east, to be exact."

Perseus leans against the news desk. He passes a glance to Lupus for confirmation, and the Reader responds with a nod.

"So that's your play, huh?" Arkright wears a devilish grin. "Get me alone, and try to extract secrets by sticking me in front of your walking lie detector. Is that it?"

My eyes widen. I look up and see everyone else staring at her with embarrassed scowls.

"Well, let me save you some time…" Her casual, yet stern, glare scans each one of us. "The Psionic Research and Intervention Initiative is a covert, globally funded organization run by Felix Bard. You'll never find him, because even I don't know where he is."

Our gazes dart toward Lupus. His cringe is all the affirmation we need.

"We know all about the four strains of Clairvoyants, and your abilities. We believe you are a threat to humanity. A fact that this very circumstance no doubt reaffirms. Our mission is to see each and every one of your kind dead, or in custody. And rest assured, we have the resources to accomplish this goal."

She nudges her head to the side, just enough to catch me in her glower. An exuberant smirk reappears. She is toying with us. It makes me want to send her dainty frame hammering into a wall. I can tell by their grimaces that the other Predators have more violent things in mind. Despite our obvious agitation, she casually carries on, like some sort of tour guide ferrying sightseers through a museum.

"And yes. We have the prophetic asset you call Auriga."

Perseus's nose trembles. He finally pushes from the desk and stands. I can hear his intense breaths swirling through the air with each of Arkright's heinous words.

"I'd say he's alive and well, but the latter would be a lie."

Her mocking tone makes Aquila and Perseus's fists stiffen, and the veins protrude around their intricate tattoos. My teeth begin to grind. I've never seen or met Auriga, but hearing him referred to as an *asset* makes my blood boil. It's as if we are objects to Psyriin. Not human beings.

"We've been working to induce his visions through heightened stress. Well...*torture*, to be specific. It's been a relatively unfruitful operation that has constantly left us one step behind." Arkright's wicked glare darts back to me. "Until a few weeks ago...when he predicted that a woman was hiding out in a small town in Missouri. A woman who worked in the same lab that created the Clairvoyants."

My heart freezes, and my mouth droops as I catch the dumbfounded looks from the other Predators.

Memories come flooding back. The locked closet full of papers, the random phone calls, Mom suddenly making us move again, the lifetime of secrets…it all makes more sense now.

"The asset didn't mention anything about a fourth Kinetic." She raises a brow. "But sometimes, cereal comes with a prize inside."

"Enough!" Aries huffs as he shakes the chair from beneath her.

Arkright barely stumbles when the chair flies across the studio. She stands to her feet without the slightest difficulty, and brushes a few specks of dust off of her black bodysuit.

"You're going to give Auriga and the woman to us, now!" Aries moves into her view.

Perseus looks on with an uneasy glower. There is a calculating glimmer in his eyes.

"We don't have the woman," Arkright replies.

Relief washes over me. They haven't gotten to Mom! Wherever she is…hopefully, she's safe. I feel like letting a celebratory grin protrude across my face, but I have no time to revel in the news. The sinister look in Arkright's eyes lets me know something devious will spew from her lips next.

"And we're not going to give you Auriga."

My gaze shifts to Perseus. He and Aquila step toward
Arkright with stout chests and heavy breaths. Lupus
moves next, to box her in, but Arkright merely crosses
her arms and continues in the same brash tone.

"You had the leverage to get me here, and nothing
more. My men have been instructed to destroy the
Charon if I don't walk out of this building. Or if
anyone else approaches it."

Perseus and Aquila take a step back. Anxiety seems
to leak from their dampened brows as they glance at
Lupus for a desperate sign that she may be bluffing.
His eyes are wider than coals, and his lips are rigid.

Nastacia Arkright hasn't lied since she stepped foot
into this building. She has come prepared for this
meeting, even calculating for the possibility of her own
death. She knows that Psyriin will replace her with
someone just as cold and unrelenting. But there's no
replacing Auriga.

Perseus appears to be searching his mind for a coun-
termove. His intense frustration seems to build when
he realizes that he has no reply. Arkright starts to pace
around in a circle. She gives intimate eye contact to
each one of us before her gaze settles on my scowl.

"But it's your lucky day. Because I'm willing to make
a deal."

My heart starts to thump. She takes one step toward me and turns back to Perseus.

"We'll trade you Auriga," she points at my chest, "for him."

"What!" Aries inches closer. "What do you want with him?"

"That's none of your concern."

"Like hell it isn't."

I look directly into Perseus's eyes. They are cold and conniving. I'm waiting for him to denounce her request. But with each hardened breath, I know he is more than considering the deal.

"You've known him for, what? A few days?" Arkright says. "What does he mean to you? Is he more important than your mentor?"

"Shut the hell up," Aries growls.

"Cool it, Aries." Aquila moves beside Perseus.

Aries's dark eyebrows begin to tremble. He glares at Perseus, who turns to meet him with forewarning ferocity. I want to say something. Want to remind them of that incredible night of camaraderie we shared. Want them to admit defeat so we can regroup and think of another plan. More than anything, I want them to know that I am still a Predator. I'm still committed to saving Auriga, even if my mother isn't aboard the Charon.

Before I can utter a single word, Arkright moves in again.

"You can leave now, and lick your wounds. Or you can use the only bargaining chip you have."

Sorrow begins to settle across my face. I try to fight it, but it only grows stronger once my gaze drifts to Aquila. She scans the ground, and begins to nod. I turn to Perseus. The stern, unwavering look in his eyes tells me all I need to know. I don't need to be Prophetic, or a Reader, to predict his next words.

"Sorry, Rion."

"You're not taking him anywhere!" Aries snarls as he moves his tattooed arm in front of my chest.

"What the hell are you doing, Aries?" Perseus sneers.

I scan the room to examine everyone's faces. Aquila steps forward with her fists coiled. Nastacia Arkright has her arms crossed as she still carries a calculated smirk. Lupus looks on with a nervous gawk from behind her.

"Are you kidding me!" Aquila shouts. "You'd protect this kid over Auriga?"

"He's one of us," Aries says.

"No. Auriga is one of us. Don't you get it? This kid has been hiding info from us. He's full of so many secrets that they'd rather have him than a Prophetic."

"Everyone, shut up!" Perseus shouts.

An offended grumble billows from Aries's snarl
before he and Perseus enter into a silent stare-down.
Perspiration is building on my brow with every second
that passes. Should I speak out? What do I even say?

"You won't kill the kid, will you?" Perseus says, in
a remorseful tone.

His gaze is still glued to Aries, but it only takes a
moment for me to realize he's talking to Arkright.

"Not if he cooperates." She inches closer between
the two predators while staring at me.

I take a slow step backward, like I'm preparing to
sneak away...until I feel Aquila's scathing gaze blaring
back at me.

"Place these on his face," Arkright says.

We each watch in confusion as she reaches into
a small pocket concealed along the left thigh of her
catsuit. She pulls forth three disks the size of silver
dollars, and returns her sly glare toward Perseus. His
perturbed gaze shifts to Lupus, like he wants to go over
and scold the Reader for not mentioning the objects
sooner.

"They will sedate him. Once that's done, I will
instruct my men to leave Auriga downstairs."

Perseus takes a deep breath after Lupus sends him
a doleful nod to confirm her words. I'm desperately
hoping that he'll look my way instead. Maybe, if he

sees my puppy-dog sulk, it'll convince him to rethink his next move.

"Look, Rion. It's nothing personal." His gaze finally shifts to my drenched brow. "You're a good kid. But ask yourself. If it were one of us—if they had your mother, and you had a chance to get her back by giving me up—what would you do?"

My gaze drifts downward. Mom encapsulates my thoughts. Her smile. Her voice. Her cooking. I've been without her for just over a week, and it has been agony. The Predators have been without their father figure for years.

My fear subsides, and is replaced by an uncanny sense of guilt. Perseus is right. I wouldn't even hesitate, unless it were Aries on the negotiating table. The rest of them aren't my friends. A few days of training and partying doesn't make me a Predator. My heart sinks. My head rises. Perseus huffs and nods when our gazes meet.

"Exactly." His palm unfurls toward Arkright.

"No!" Aries shouts.

He flings his arm toward Nastacia Arkright's chest. We all watch in astonishment as her body jolts across the room and slams against the wall in the blink of an eye. The three disks flutter from her grasp and bounce along the floor like loose change.

"Rion, run!"

I turn for the studio exit, but before I've even taken two steps, I feel my feet drifting from the floor. I whip my head around to Aquila springing forward with a blistering brow. With one swift swipe of her tattooed arm, she sends my frame pounding against the floor.

I rise, trying to ignore my aching back. Aries moves in front of me once more. He and Aquila share an intense stare, and objects begin to hover around us. Everything from chairs to loose pens and staplers flutter through the air like they're caught in a tornado.

Perseus flings his arm forth. Anger doesn't begin to describe the ferocious look in his eyes. His teeth chatter and his nose twitches. His peach skin turns to a fiery red as the three disks zip from the corner of the room until they are hovering over his shoulder.

Lupus is standing to the side with a terrified look on his face, like he's surrounded by a pack of hungry wolves. He has taken his focus off of Nastacia Arkright. I plant my gaze on her, just in time to see her pull a marble-sized object from a hidden patch on her sleeve. She peers directly at me before she chucks the sphere at the floor.

Bang! The searing sound is accompanied by a blinding white light that encompasses the entire room. I cover my head and squeeze my eyes shut . All of the hovering objects collide against the floor. When the chorus of clutter has finished, I peek through my arms to observe my surroundings.

Lupus is cowering on the floor, but the other Predators still stand. Their irate faces become visible as their arms drop from their once shielded eyes. We each take a moment to scan the entirety of the studio. As we all come to the same realization, the tension begins to climb.

Nastacia Arkright is gone.

I stand, bringing my arms into position like a poorly trained boxer. My heart is beating a mile a minute. It feels like I've just sprinted around a racetrack. I try to calm myself and hone my senses. I have to be ready for whatever the Predators might do next.

"Damn you, Aries!" Aquila shrieks.

"You really think Auriga would want us to do this!" he replies.

Aquila turns to Perseus as he steps forward with his arms folded. My glower is still focused on the disks that spin over his shoulder like buzzing wasps.

"She couldn't have gotten far," Aquila says to him. "We can still make the trade."

"Ain't gonna be no damn trade!" Aries shouts, at the top of his lungs.

Perseus passes a disgusted look over at Lupus, who is just beginning to pick himself up from the floor.

"Find Arkright!" He huffs before returning his fiery stare to Aries.

Lupus doesn't hesitate. He sneers at me before sprinting for the hallway. As soon as he has disappeared, Aquila telekinetically rips the nearest chair into pieces and positions each large chunk beside her. Aries begins to hover a few feet to my right. We share a quick nod and prepare ourselves.

Adrenaline and reflexes kick in. I fling my body backward, just in time to avoid all three disks from colliding with my face. One of the objects comes just inches from my cheek. It doesn't even hit the ground before Aries sends it flying toward Perseus. He uses part of the broken chair as an impromptu shield before bringing all three disks back over his shoulder, along with dozens of sharp pens.

Aquila and Perseus move into strategic positions at each other's side, and every ounce of debris flies through the air like bullets. I'm barely able to distinguish the disks from the pens and shards of chair that zoom toward me. It's like Dirt War times ten. But unlike my training, I have a teammate this time.

Every time I think I'm going to be clipped by one of the disks, Aries flings something in my path to block it. It's remarkable how well we play off of one another. We move in a rhythmic beat—Aries deflects, I counter. It amazes me how quickly I'm able to send each of my opponents' ammo zipping back in their direction. Perseus and Aquila seem to be getting more infuriated with each failed attempt to place the disks on my face.

Perseus drifts toward the ceiling. My chest sinks when he shatters glass from the nearest camera to fill the atmosphere with tiny shards. Aries rises even higher, just as Perseus sends the shards swirling through the room like paper planes. When I think I've pinpointed their trajectory, Aquila shifts them.

"Aargh!" I scream, as a stinging pain pierces my leg.

Aries adjusted the path of nearly every shard, but one jagged piece has managed to clip me. I can feel the wet sensation of blood trickling down my jeans, but I refuse to look down. There is no time for pain. There is only the next attack.

My arms move in a slew of jabbing motions, and every piece of debris around me begins to slice through the air. Perseus counters with an uppercut, sending each shard of glass careening into the wall behind him, except for one. I can't help but be startled by the sound of Aquila screaming in agony as the last shard slices her cheek.

She grasps the right side of her face as the blood gushes through her fingers. Her upper lip twitches, and her clenched teeth chatter. The look she gives me makes my body grow cold. Whatever attraction I might've felt toward her, whatever adoration she might have had for me, disappears with each drop of crimson goo that drips from her ebony skin.

Despite our injuries, the action refuses to cease. Aries has already launched another shattered chair at Perseus. He dodges and sends parts spiraling at both of our heads. My eyes turn into saucers. My heart is pumping so fast it seems like the massive wooden chunks are hurling toward me in slow motion. I plant my aching foot into the floor and jab my left elbow out. The wooden husk whips around my frame and into the wall, just before it can make contact with my head.

Aries deflects every shot away from his body with ease, but he loses his focus in his haste to find something to hurl back. He hasn't noticed the hefty chair leg being directed away from him by Aquila…and toward me.

Aries was supposed to defend me. It was my job to attack. But there isn't even a second for me to go back on the offensive. Instead of staying in the fight, I cross my arms to brace for the rapidly approaching impact. It thunders against my body so hard it knocks every

ounce of breath from my chest. I slide against the floor
for what seems like an eternity. As I huddle against the
linoleum and writhe in agony, disappointment creeps
through my mind.

I could've dodged it or deflected it. I know I could've.
But instead, human instinct had kicked in. There's a
reason the Predators called me a rookie. I was foolish
to think that I could face them after a few days of
training.

I'm sorry, Aries. Sorry I wasn't a better teammate.
Sorry I let you and your training down.

A series of excruciating coughs force their way up.
Blood spouts from my mouth, and my vision blurs.
Even in my hazy view, I still catch the sinister snarls
of Aquila and Perseus as they corner Aries.

I try to get up, but my body remains sore and rigid.
I can feel my extremities just enough to know that
they're still attached. My fuzzy vision catches Aries
dolefully nodding at me. I can't tell whether he's disgusted, or simply just afraid for me.

"Sorry, bruh."

At least, that's what I think he says. My senses are
so distorted that there appear to be three Aries deject-
edly shaking their heads.

My cheek scrapes against the cold floor, but I can
still see Perseus lining up the disks in front of him. I try
once more to get up. Summon every ounce of strength

I have to at least hover my body into their air. But it's no use. I maybe move an inch before I clump back down to the floor, and another wave of throbbing pain courses through me.

I feel the cool metal disks slap against my forehead and each of my cheeks. A warm sensation courses through my face like I've just stuck my head in an oven. I give my last bit of strength to glance up. Aries begins to rapidly ascend, with an animalistic gnarl plastered on his wriggling face as he lets out an earth-shattering howl. He reaches out with his fingers spread.

The entire building begins to shake. The roof begins to rattle and crack, causing Perseus and Aquila's eyes to widen. Every object they'd been hovering drops to the floor. They both swoop into the corner and hold out their arms to create mental shields they hope will protect them from the falling debris.

Everything begins to slip away as the ceiling crumbles. Enormous hunks pound into the floor, creating a barrier that surrounds me. Aries's sorrowful grimace is the last thing I see before my last thread of consciousness wanes.

CHAPTER 20

PRISONERS

ALL I SEE IS BRIGHT SUNLIGHT WHEN I AWAKEN.
There's still a throbbing sensation coursing through
every inch of my body. I feel just as limp and lifeless
as I did before I passed out, but at least I'm alive.

My vision starts to clear up, and the mountain of
massive concrete chunks come into view. The entire
building has been leveled, and I can barely make out
the pieces of the news studio scattered amongst the
wreckage. It seems like a miracle that I'm alive, until
I realize that Aries must have strategically collapsed
the building around me to keep me safe.

I begin scanning everything around me, in search of
Aries, or even the other Predators. I don't see anything.
Not a body, not a limb, not even splattered blood. I
attempt to push my body from the cracked piece of
floor, but I don't budge.

"Well, that was something."

My senses barely capture the sinister voice from behind me. The sound of multiple footsteps clumping through the debris echoes in my ears. I take a deep breath and pray that it isn't who I think it is.

"So much for your human lie detector," Nastacia Arkright says, as her black boots step inches from my aching brow. "Give a Reader something interesting to look at, and they'll ignore all the tiny, important details that aren't on the page."

I slide my head upward and scowl at her. I can just barely make out her sly smirk through the piercing beam of sunlight.

"I never anticipated that you would be here. And I certainly didn't think that one of them would actually fight for you. Guess it was just my lucky day."

I scream out in agony as two soldiers grab me by the arms and lift me to my knees. I want to spit a big wad of blood onto her unscathed black bodysuit, but I can barely move my lips. It's as if my mind is clinging to its last shred of consciousness.

"Take him away!"

A tear trickles down my cheek. My head drifts to the ground as the armored soldiers drag me away. The sunlight begins to fade. A massive hovering ship appears in the distance, just as my eyes shut.

Beep. Beep. Beep.

The sound wakes me up to the sight of blackened metal walls. I look around. There are no windows or doors, only the metal slab I'm lying against.

My body jolts upward. A strange numbness in each limb. I'm still in the same murky pants and shoes from the TV studio, but my chest is bare. There's a plastic patch stuck to the left side of my chest. I try to peel it off, but the edges cling to me like they've been welded to my skin. The number 81 glows red at the center of the patch. A red line glides beneath the number and peaks in the center, like the vital sign machines I've seen in hospitals.

"Glad to see you're finally awake."

The voice startles me, and I whip my head around to the man standing at the edge of the room. I don't even bother to examine him before swinging my fist with every ounce of strength I have. Instead of sending the stranger careening into the steel walls, the frame wriggles and shakes like a glitch in a computer game. My eyes widen as the pixels squirm back into position, and the figure takes another step forward.

"You can stop trying to use your powers," the man says, in a calming voice. "We've long prepared for every strain of Clairvoyant prisoner."

My arms droop, and a defeated grunt billows from my sore jaws. The figure approaches me with his arms folded behind his back. He is wearing a suit similar to the Psyriin soldiers, but with far less armor. His hair has been trimmed close to his scalp, like a fresh Army recruit. His pale face looks worn, like old leather, and his brown beard is speckled with untamed strands of gray. A pair of thick, graying eyebrows tilt into a stern frown above his hollow brown eyes.

There is no scent to him, and no sound is created by his footsteps. He must be appearing via some sort of hologram, but my eyes can't tell that a real-life man isn't standing in front of me.

"Who...who are you?" I say, in a scraggly voice.

I don't even know why I ask. There's only one person this could be.

"My name is Felix Bard. I'm the head of the Psionic Research and Intervention Initiative. Or Psyriin, as you all like to call us."

I look away and examine the room again. I'm desperately trying to find some sort of secret doorway or latch—any sign of how they got me in here. All I notice is a pair of thin slits carved into the ceiling. It's some sort of air vent, but one could barely slide a sheet of paper through them, much less any fingers.

"I've never cared too much for the name *Psyriin*." Bard paces around the room.

It's as if he knows I'm looking for a way out, but couldn't care less.

"In Greek mythology, Sirens posed as beautiful women in order to lead ships to their doom. But there's nothing beautiful about our organization. And there's certainly more nuance to our objectives."

"You hunt people! People like my mother and Auriga, who just want to be left alone."

My voice thunders against the metal surroundings. Bard waits a few seconds for the echo to cease, before he nods and glances at the floor.

"True. And I certainly don't blame any of you for fighting for your survival. Such is the right of all sentient beings."

His soothing, deep voice makes my skin wriggle and my lips tremble. I see now, where Nastacia Arkright gets her unyielding fortitude from.

"But we represent that same right for the billions of non-Clairvoyant beings that live on this earth. How does one live in a world where there are beings who can curve bullets and level buildings with the mere thought? How does one govern when someone can enter the body of a world leader. Or even do something as simple as read your mind to steal your bank account information?"

My body starts to shiver. My enraged sneer is now a pathetic grimace. I can feel the water welling in my eyes.

"The truth is, the world simply isn't ready for your existence." Bard lets out a deep sigh.

I glare into his listless eyes, unable to tell if he's truly remorseful, or if it's just some cruel façade meant to torment me.

"Sometimes, in conflict, there is no right, wrong, good or evil. Only opposing perspectives that are both fair. So while I don't blame you for considering us your enemy...I'm afraid we are no more evil than a person who kills a wasp for wandering into their home."

Tears start to flood down my face. I'm not sure I've ever cried this hard. I can barely look Felix Bard in his digitally rendered pupils.

"Are you going to kill me?" I blubber.

He glances down at the ground and turns away.

"Clairvoyants are unnatural. They were created in a lab by rogue scientists trying to play God. That's why you and your mother are so important. It isn't just that she holds the only information about how Clairvoyants were created. If she truly birthed you...if your

kind is somehow the next stage in human evolution...
the human race deserves to understand how."

He turns to glare into my eyes once again. His once
apathetic demeanor is gone. Replaced by the searing
look of determination that normally graces Nastacia
Arkright's harsh brow.

"We must uncover this mystery, by any means necessary."

A yellow gas begins to seep from the ceiling and
cloud the room. I close my eyes and weep. All this
time, I feared that Mom would be tortured by these
people. Now, I have to prepare myself for the inevitable pain to come.

"Welcome aboard the Charon, Mister Grean."

With a whiz, the hologram disappears. My back
clumps to the cold, coarse bed. My squeals echo
through the brutal silence as the grimy mist billows
into my lungs and sends me into a daze.

I wake up to more black steel walls surrounding me
on each side. This room is even smaller than the one
where I encountered Felix Bard. My arms and legs
have been clamped to a frigid slab. I am covered in an
uncomfortable set of gray scrubs that feel like paper

against my coarse skin. A single lamp blares above me and bathes the room in piercing white light.

"Hello, Rion," says Nastacia Arkright's hellishly calm voice, from behind.

I growl as she moves into my view and takes a seat at a chair near my feet. She has an electronic pen and tablet in her hand, and is dressed in a dark pantsuit. It's the first time she doesn't look ready for battle.

I try to use my power to knock the pen and pad from her grasp. Unsurprisingly, nothing of the sort happens. Instead, the image of her body just wriggles like the holographic likeness of Felix Bard. She responds with a grin.

Is anyone in this prison actually here? It makes sense, the more I think about it. The Charon is meant to be a holding for all Clairvoyants. It wouldn't be smart to have actual people roaming around if a Reader, like Leo, or an Aural, like Ara, were held captive.

"I'm going to ask you some questions," Arkright says. "It would behoove you to be truthful in your responses."

My gaze drifts to the ceiling ,and a dejected sigh echoes from my chapped lips.

"We'll start with something simple. What's your full name?"

"Rion James Grean," I mumble, still glaring at the bright ceiling.

"Interesting. Why did your mother give you that name?"

"I don't know."

"Hmm." She jots down some notes. "Your first name…it has a distinctive spelling. Like the constellation Orion, without the O."

My listless gaze finally wilts toward her artificial glower. I'd realized this a long time ago, but I had never put any real thought into it, until now.

"The original Clairvoyants were given designations on their wrists in the form of constellations to identify them. Is that why your mother named you after Orion? So that you had a connection to them in some way?"

"Don't know. Never asked."

Her supple lips scrunch. She shakes her head before making more notes.

"What did you and your mother usually talk about?"

I give a deep sigh and stay silent. Arkright doesn't seem bothered. She crosses one leg over the other before the tip of her black stiletto begins to move in a tapping motion. I roll my eyes. There's no point in not answering her questions. Being silent won't get me out of here any faster.

"We talked about my day, usually. Listened to music. Watched TV. Nothing out of the ordinary."

"Did she ever talk about her job or her past?"

"No."

"And your father. Did she ever mention you having one?"

"She said I had one," I reply, with agitation. "But she never talked about him."

She squints, and adds more notes.

"I imagine that was frustrating for you," she says, in a calm tone, like she's some sort of therapist.

"Very."

"Did you ever try to get answers from her?"

"A few times."

"And what happened?"

A groan resonates from my cheeks. I think back to every time Mom uttered the words, *Your father is gone,* and I become even more annoyed.

"She never told me anything. Once, she mentioned that she might not even know who my father is."

"Hmm. And did you believe her?"

"No."

"Why not?"

"Because I know when she's lying."

Arkright nods. Several seconds of eerie quietness looms over the hollow room as she adds to her computer tablet. She places her fingertips to her lips, and her eyes thin.

"Did she ever mention that there were others like you?"

"Never."

I expect an immediate response, but Arkright sits still and taps a finger against her chin. She begins vacantly gazing around the room, like she's looking for her next question.

"What did she say to you before you separated?"

I take a brief moment to remember that day. I picture Mom shoving me from the car and speeding off. I thoroughly remember her look of heightened distress, sprinkled with a dash of hope.

"She told me to trust her. And that she loved me."

My eyes begin to well with tears. I slow my breathing and harden my jaw to keep a droplet from sliding down my face. I don't want to give Arkright the satisfaction of seeing me that vulnerable ever again.

"And where do you think she is now?"

"I don't know. She never gave me any clues."

"Do you think she is trying to find you?"

"I don't know," I growl.

I can sense her frustration rising through her twitching red lips. What did she expect? Did she and Felix Bard really think I had any knowledge of her whereabouts? Why would I have been with the Predators, if I knew where she might be?

"Last question," she mutters, after a deep sigh. "Did you ever stumble upon any information that might've involved her research with the Clairvoyants?"

That stupid flash drive begins to flutter through my mind. Should I tell her? Would she know I was lying if I didn't?

"I thought I did. There was a flash drive that fell out of her bag one day."

Arkright's eyes widen. She unfolds her legs and leans forward, like a reporter about to get the scoop of a lifetime.

"But it didn't have anything on it," I say, trying to fight my smirk.

Seeing Arkright's disappointed reaction makes me glad I told her. She grunts and stands to her feet, tucking the tablet under her arm and straightening her suit jacket.

"That's enough for today," she murmurs.

I give her one more sneer, before that disgusting yellow gas begins to flood the room from every corner.

With no clocks or windows, it becomes harder and harder to keep track of when one day ends and another begins. Every so often, I wake up to a plate of disgusting gruel that I shove down my throat. It smells like oil, and tastes like paste, but I am so hungry and weak that I scarf it down like a junkyard dog. Even the water they serve me tastes like it was scooped from a dingy toilet.

One morning, I try to use my powers to locate a doorway but I am met by a jolt of electricity that bursts from the walls and singes my body. I'm never able to locate a camera, but I know that somehow they are always watching me.

I have a few more sessions with Nastacia Arkright's holographic ghost. She asks me about my abilities and jots down all of the information I give her about their manifestation. I don't tell her about the metal crates. Don't want her to know how strong I can be.

She asks about the Clairvoyants that I've met, but I only give her intimate details about the locations of the Predators. Her casual reactions let me know how much she understands the uselessness of this information. All of the other Clairvoyants would be foolish to remain where I found them. They've all likely relocated by now, and I can tell that she is growing weary of the lack of helpful information I'm providing.

Every time I'm tossed back into my cell, the sound of curdling screams wakes me from my uncomfortable sleep. It must be Auriga, being tortured for visions, while I lay helplessly in my steel cube. His cries of agony last much longer than my interview sessions. I can't help but feel grateful that I'm not going through nearly as much trauma. Once the sounds have stopped, I'm eventually able to doze off into a nightmarish slumber.

I am awakened by the sound of screeching metal. My eyes open to the tray of gruel sliding through a shallow slit and along the floor. I think about using my abilities to keep the tiny slot from closing, but I don't have the strength to suffer through another volt of electricity.

My sore frame droops over the edge of my cold, metal cot, and I reach down to grab the tray. I am disgusted by its moldy appearance, but the rumbling in my stomach guides my hands toward it anyway. The last time I ate it, I kept my eyes closed and held my breath so I could ignore the taste. Now, I no longer care. I'm going to be here a while. Might as well get used to the stuff.

I take a massive scoop into my palm and glare at the gross, lumpy texture. Lord only knows what they're feeding me. I don't even chew as I shove it into my mouth and let out a whimper. Once it's down, I give a dejected sigh and prepare myself for the next unpleasant serving. I reach into the tin bowl for the next scoop, but something in its silver surface catches my eye. Beneath the smeared residue, there seem to be scratches. An intrigued gnarl covers my brow, as I nudge some of the greasy substance to the edge of the bowl.

There's no question I'm tired and weak. But not so much that I can't tell these are intentional markings, and not mere scratches. The letters U, C, and A are the first to appear. I shovel another glob of gruel to the side. There are more letters.

For a moment, I think to pour out the rest of the gruel to get a clear image of what's beneath. But I quickly remember that I'm probably being watched. Instead, I tilt the bowl to the sky and pour the remaining sludge down my throat. Once the last grotesque bit is gone, I stare into the bottom of the bowl.

The message is as clear as day. My eyes widen, and my heart begins to thump faster than it has since I arrived in this prison. I can't let them know. Whoever is watching—Bard, Arkright—they can't know what I see.

I stand and take a deep breath. I look up, as if I know the hidden camera is blaring straight at my drenched brow. With a tightening of my fist, the cup withers into a rigid ball the size of a marble.

The yellow gas starts to pour into the room from every corner, but it doesn't matter now. I've read the message. And as the mist fills my lungs, the letters flutter through my mind.

U CAN CRASH IT.

CHAPTER 21

U CAN CRASH IT

NASTACIA ARKRIGHT'S HOLOGRAPHIC FRAME stands over me, with her hands tucked behind her back. For the first time since I've been aboard the Charon, she isn't dressed like a CEO. Instead, she is back in her black bodysuit. There is a searing grimace on her face as she glares down at my shackled frame.

"Last night," she says, in a seething tone, "you saw something in that bowl, didn't you?"

I remain still and look away from her to stare, into the dingy iron walls. She responds to my silence with a disgruntled sigh before a volt of electricity blasts through the metal slab against my back. My fists clench, and my bare toes curl as I squeal in agony.

It lasts for several excruciating seconds. When it is finally over, she moves toward my feet.

"What was in the bowl!"

"A delicious dinner."

Another shock comes, this time longer and more agonizing than the first. I feel my heart rattle against my chest, and it feels like my lungs are going to cave in.

"It was a message from Auriga! Wasn't it?"

My face trembles, and my extremities start to feel numb, but I remain silent. I send the largest wad of spit I can fathom, flying through her digitized chest. Her nose starts to twitch through my blurred gaze.

"I get it. You think he's your ally?" She moves over my shoulder and stares into my reddened eyes as a devious grin curls her rosy lips. "You think that because you're a Kinetic, he sees you like he sees the others. But you are nothing to him."

I snarl at her as the feeling slowly begins to come back to my body. I'm not sure how many more shocks I can take before I pass out. Or worse.

"He's been in our custody for years, and has never given us any information that led to the capture of the other Clairvoyants. And yet he didn't hesitate to give away your mother's location."

My breaths start to settle, and my coarse lips tremble. She's just trying to get in my head. She is taunting me. Even if it's true, Auriga must've had a good reason.

"Whatever message he gave you was just a ploy to help him escape."

The crude writing etched into the tin bowl begins to resonate through my aching skull.

U CAN CRASH IT.

Was it an instruction? Has Auriga already foreseen our escape? Or did he have a vision of himself escaping, while I die attempting to crash the Charon?

I want to block out the thought that he would sacrifice me. Could he really be that cruel? This is the same man that the Predators looked up to. Should I trust his message?

I close my eyes. Think about Pavo. He was so gentle and fatherly in the short time I spent with him. Could he have been stringing me along, too? Maybe he'd foreseen it all, and him leading me to the Predators was a ploy to get me aboard the Charon so I could free his old friend.

But Aries comes to mind next. He believed in Auriga, too. He fought for me. Maybe even gave his life for me. I can still remember him quoting Auriga before I moved the metal crates.

"Fear is a self-inflicted wound before you've even started the fight."

My eyes open wide. Arkright's holographic face looms over me as she gives her most heinous snarl.

"So I'll ask you one more time. What...was in...the bowl?"

I don't care anymore. I don't care about the allegiances of the other Clairvoyants. Don't care if they used me as a pawn. All I know is that I don't want to spend the rest of my life eating sludge in a windowless prison. I'd rather give everything I have to escape, than live another day knowing I may never see my mother again.

I lean my head over to Arkright and fasten a smirk across my face as I begin to hone my senses.

"You shouldn't have brought me here," I whisper.

I shut my eyes so tight it feels like my sockets might bleed. I think about the metal crates. Think about my surroundings. I remember what Aries said about channeling the kinetic energy around me.

A warm sensation covers my back. I know another deafening jolt of electricity is imminent, but it doesn't matter. Everything around me is darkness. Everything around me is mine, because I want it to be.

My eyes blare open. Arkright has a look of astonishment as she takes a step back and places her hand to her ear.

"Code seven!" she shouts.

Her image disappears, and a thunderous scream billows from my jaws.

The jolt of electricity comes, but instead of shocking me, the volts begin to shoot out and singe the walls. The entire room looks like the inside of a microwave that someone has stuck a metal fork into.

I don't stop screaming. Anger and instinct are controlling me now.

Use the emotion, Aries's voice says, in my head.

The shackles around my wrists and ankles snap. I hover into the air and watch the lighting storm around me.

An alarm sounds, and red lights begin to flare as I float several feet from the floor, with arms spread wide. My veins protrude from every ounce of brittle skin. My screams overtake the howl of the blaring sirens. The yellow gas starts to pour into the room from all corners. I flip my wrists, spread my fingers, and grind my teeth. The clouds of gas begin to flutter toward my palms like my limbs are a vacuum. In a matter of seconds, the room is clear, and gaseous balls swirl above my hands.

I no longer feel my limbs. The pain of all of the electrocutions, and the weariness of days without proper nourishment, threaten to settle in. But I refuse to let it. I hold the aching sensations at bay, giving everything I have. If I can lift a field of iron shipping containers, I can crash this damn ship.

I shut my eyes once more, and everything around me starts to rumble. I can faintly hear the sound of snapping wires and tiny explosions in the atmosphere. It's working, but I can't stop now.

Gravity settles in, and the room tilts. I hold out my arms and send the clouds of gas dissipating through the tiny cracks in the walls. I can sense the entirety of the structure. Can envision the wings and the empty cockpit. Can feel the sputtering engines and grinding steel. The Charon is mine now.

The walls begin to shift. Massive guns slide from each corner and point at me.

Idiots. Do they really think they can shoot me down?

The weapons charge. The sides begin to glow and bathe the room in a harsh, orange tint. I wait as I continue to guide the ship downward. My gaze is focused forward like I'm steering the vehicle from the cockpit.

The guns fire. I smile. Nothing touches me. Without even the slightest loss of focus, I have guided each deadly laser into another gun. I demolish them all after one shot. Fire and metal billow through the room to mix with the remnants of the yellow haze. Everything swirls around me like I am in the eye of a hurricane.

My limbs start to tremble, and my head starts to feel dreary. The lightheadedness makes everything feel

like a dream, but I can't pass out now. I can crash it!
I have to crash it.

I feel my grip on reality loosening. Doesn't seem to
be any feeling left in my body. This is it. It's now or
never.

My grunts echo through the atmosphere of smoke,
fire, and broken metal. I throw my hand out like I'm
trying to chuck a football a hundred yards. I lose the
telekinetic grip on my body, and my back slams against
what used to be the left wall, but now seems like the
floor. I can hear the sound of the structure blasting
through the air.

"I love you, Mom," I murmur, as my vision begins
to waver.

I use the last ounce of strength I have to keep my
chest from being impaled on a piece of jagged metal.
Even with every sensation having left my body, the pain
of the ship thundering to earth hammers through me
like a million car crashes.

"Rion!" a voice calls, as my body trembles against
warm steel.

My eyes creak open, and the sight of the ferocious
wreckage leaves me in awe. It looks like a war zone,

with massive flames shooting to the sky, and deafening explosions shaking the earth every few seconds. To my left, I can barely make out what used to be one of the Charon's wings. It has been snapped in two like it was made of Styrofoam. I try to lift myself from the metal pile that surrounds me, but my arms feel limp and lifeless.

"Rion!" the unfamiliar voice calls again.

I scan my surroundings in a daze. I try desperately to locate the voice's origins, but nothing comes through the thick clouds of fire and smoke. There are no toppled buildings or screaming pedestrians. We've crash landed in a field. The only structure seems to be a dilapidated barn in the distance. I think I'm lucky at first, but it only seems logical for the Charon to travel over unpopulated areas. Auriga must've known this, too.

Auriga! It has to be him calling out to me. Does he see me? Is he running toward me? Or is he just trying to let me know that he is still alive?

"Auriga!" I shout, praying that a Psyriin soldier doesn't find me instead.

"Rion!" he replies, with a stiff laugh. "You did it. Son of a gun, you did it."

I can't help but chuckle. The aching pain that I feel in my chest makes me wish I hadn't. My brain feels as if it's bouncing in my head, like my skull is a trampoline.

"We have to get out of here!" he yells. "We don't have much time!"

I can hear him groaning and grunting, like he's trying to wriggle free.

He's right. It's a miracle Nastacia Arkright's goons haven't come storming in to scoop us up already. I've survived the crash. But if I don't move, I'll be dead. Or worse—right back in another Psyriin prison.

I am just conscious enough to breathe in the thick soot, and hear Auriga's cries. I abandon the notion of trying to pull myself up, but I am strong enough to move the bits of iron wall blanketed around me. I jolt my hand up and let out a loud grunt. It should be a simple task, but now it seems like the smallest exertion of my powers is like pushing a car in neutral. After a few agonizing seconds, the steel slabs move and I am finally free.

I clamber over a rough surface of dirt and metal shards. I can faintly feel the pricks of broken wall and singed wires against my skin. I crawl like my life depends on it. Because frankly, it does.

I feel like an Army man scurrying through a fox hole. Reminds me of the old war movies I used to watch with Mom. It's awkward, but effective. Before I know it, I'm several yards clear of most of the wreckage. The size and girth of the demolished Charon amazes me.

It looks like I blew up an entire junkyard. Did I really crash this thing?

"Rion!" Auriga screams.

Sparks fly, and another explosion detonates.

I have to get up!

The more I think about the task, the more difficult it will be. So I force myself away from steel slabs, continuing to crawl like an infant, through callous shards. I extend both hands and use my telekinesis to push myself upward. My intense screams echo into the night air as my legs come to a kneeling position, and my fists rest against the warm mixture of gravel and dead grass.

"I'm coming, Auriga!"

I break into the goofiest run ever. I must look like a drunk person stumbling through a parking lot. But at least I haven't fallen on my face.

"Auriga!"

"I'm here!" he yelps.

A ghostly white hand goes up. I stagger over several heaps of searing hot metal until I've finally reached him.

No one ever found the time to describe him to me, but I always pictured Auriga much differently. I always thought he'd look similar to Pavo, like an off-duty mall Santa. Or a creepy elder leaning from a rocking chair with a cane, and telling kids to get off of his lawn. But Auriga looks young, even though his pale skin is so worn it seems like it might peel with the slightest breeze. The only hair on his head comes from his thick, dark eyebrows. He has a definitive jawline, like something you might find on the stereotypical drawing of a vampire. His eyes are beady and sharp, and his irises are so dark that they blend with his hazy, blackened pupils.

I exert enough energy to stay standing, while I fling pieces of the Charon from the area. My spine feels like it's going to pop out of place when I bend down to pull Auriga's emaciated frame from the dirt. As he wraps his lanky arms around my shoulder, our chests graze, and I feel the warm dampness of his gray, scrublike attire. Blood covers his clothes. Looks like he just painted a red wall with his abdomen.

His gaze meets mine. I'm expecting an agonized grimace, but Auriga just meets my stare with a hearty grin.

"Let's move," he grunts, ignoring my obvious stupor.

I glance around to make sure no one is watching or charging toward us. My heart hasn't stopped thumping since we crashed. After several excruciating minutes, we reach the worn-down barn. When I'd first noticed it, the withered auburn structure looked like it was only a few yards away. But the trek here felt like we'd dragged on for miles.

An explosion roars behind us, just as I push my weary fist against the barn door. It's the loudest eruption yet. I turn to peek at the wreckage. The charred metal and broken glass look like a ripped-open baked potato. Hard to imagine that this was all one vehicle.

My feet grind as I limp across the dusty floor, with Auriga draped over me. We hobble to a thick bed of hay laying in the corner, and flop down. Compared to the steel slab I'd been sleeping on in the Charon cell, the prickly surface feels like a bed of feathers. We are barely there for a second, when Auriga starts to crack up laughing.

He takes a big whiff.

"Ahh. You smell that?" He laughs with his eyes closed.

I take a moment to breathe in the rank aroma of mildew and feces, and it makes me gag.

"That's the smell of freedom."

I roll my eyes and rest my aching head.

"It's funny. I knew it would work. I saw it work. And yet I can't believe it did!"

A somber grimace protrudes through my brow as Nastacia Arkright's words come climbing back into my thoughts. I saved him, but this is still the man who gave up Mom's location to Psyriin. This is still the man who caused all of this.

I turn to him with my frown as intense as I can fathom. His haughty grin slowly disappears.

"Why'd you do it?" I murmur.

His tongue glides along his chapped lips as if he's been dreading this moment.

"Why'd you give them our location?"

Auriga responds with a deep sigh. His weary eyes glance off into the rigid wooden ceiling, like the answers are somehow above us.

"I'd love to tell you that it was all some divine master plan, Rion. But the truth is, you're looking at a tired old man."

My scowl starts to unfurl into something resembling a frustrated pout. His tone is the most defeated one I've ever heard.

"When I gave myself up to save the others, I thought the soldiers would just kill me. But I was wrong. I—we—had no idea how strong Psyriin was. Their knowledge. Their preparation. It's like they know us better than we know ourselves."

My gaze droops to the floor. I notice his hand trembling against the blood-splattered stain on his chest.

"I spent the last few years terrified. Just hoping I could do enough to keep my family safe."

When he says this, my heart sinks. Clearly he is referring to the other Clairvoyants, and not me and Mom.

"And then, one day…"

His eyes begin to water. Mine do the same.

"I had a vision of your mother."

His doleful stare is fixated at the doorway, and the sight of the flaming debris in the distance. My dampened gaze darts upward, refusing to look his way.

"I saw her rummaging through all sorts of files about us. I'd never seen her before, but I knew there had to be some connection. And I thought that if I gave Psyriin this, it might just buy me a little more time to survive."

My heart begins to rip. I can't fight my look of disgust as my eyes well with tears. Auriga scrunches his lips and nods. He takes a deep breath, and his gaze drifts to the cold hay bedding beneath us.

"It didn't matter to me that she had a son. For what it's worth, I didn't know you were a Kinetic. In my desperation, I never even considered it, even though I knew that Prophetic visions always involve Clairvoyants."

"It shouldn't have mattered if I was a Clairvoyant or not!" My lips tremble.

I can barely see his withered face through the accumulating droplets in my eyes.

"You're right. And not a day went by where I didn't regret my decision."

I try to fight my snarl.

He finally turns to me, and attempts to crack a warm smile.

"Psyriin...they can't be negotiated with. They don't compromise. I learned that the hard way."

A tear drifts from my face, but I toss it away before it can hit the grimy floorboards.

"When did you know what I was?"

"A few days ago, when I had the vision of you crashing the ship. I refused to tell Arkright about it, so they gave me more hell than anything I'd been through before."

A gentle sigh cascades through my sore chest, and my anger starts to subside.

"If I had been there another day," he says, "I'd probably be dead."

I drag my hand over my damp scalp. How can I be mad at Auriga? Who knows what lengths I would've gone to in order to prolong my survival if I'd been in that heinous prison for years.

"But I believe your mother is safe," he says, through a sniffle. "And I believe it is no mistake that fate has brought you here."

I glare at him with a grimace. There is a look of unyielding determination in his eyes as he cracks a warm smile.

The sound of propellers cuts through the air. I turn to peer through the doorway, just in time to spot several large helicopter-like ships approaching the front of the destroyed Charon. It's Psyriin. They have finally found us.

"As my old friend Pavo used to say..." Auriga huffs as he fights the pain in his chest to lean upward. "When you can see the future, you fully grasp that everything happens for a reason."

CHAPTER 22

HOW VISIONS WORK

"WE NEED TO MOVE!" I SHOUT.

I turn and telekinetically rip a hole in the back of the barn, letting the stale night air pour in. The sounds of the helicopters overtake the atmosphere, and the wind grows more swift by the second.

I stagger over to Auriga. His lighthearted demeanor has begun to wilt as the pain in his body grows more intense. With one hand clutched under each of his armpits, I attempt to scoop up his lanky frame. I've barely moved him an inch from the floor when he lets out an agonizing howl that makes me cease. My brow curls, like I'm the one bleeding from my chest.

I glance outside. All three helicopters are now clearly visible through the doorway, dousing the cluster of flames with their powerful gusts. One of them remains hovering just barely inside of my view, while the other two start to descend.

"How bad is it?" I say, as my anxious grimace meets Auriga.

"Well," he winces, "it ain't a flesh wound, son."

My teeth begin to chatter as my head whips back and forth between the rapidly landing copters and Auriga's injured body.

"Did Pavo ever tell you how visions work?" Auriga squirms against the floor in a feeble attempt to sit up straight.

"What?"

"That sixth sense where Prophetics concurrently see their own future. Ya know…the visions that thankfully don't take a damn seizure."

He chuckles with one eye creaked open and the other bound shut. He must be going into shock. I shake my head. Now is not the time for rambling.

"Auriga, we need to—"

"They're beautiful, really. It's like my life becomes one of those choose-your-own-adventure novels."

I try to ignore him as I kneel down to make another attempt at bringing him to his feet. Auriga jolts out his hand to stop me.

"Leave, Rion."

My skin grows cold. His eyes are now as red as the wooden floorboards, but I can't take my gawking stare off of his dejected, yet buoyant smile.

A switch goes off inside my aching head. He's experiencing a concurrent vision at this very instant! He knows I can escape successfully without him. And now, he's commanding me to do so.

An anxious tingle shoots down my spine as the night I decided to leave the Phantom Safe House comes to mind. I remember what Pavo told me about how these visions work. I still have a choice, and Auriga knows the outcome, regardless of what I decide to do.

"What happens to you if I leave?" I say, in a tone full of sorrow.

He holds his fist to his coarse lips as a few rough coughs sputter from his lungs. Droplets of blood scamper from his mouth with each blistering hack.

"The same thing that'll happen if you stay," he finally manages to muster, between wheezes.

A gnarl comes across my face. I look out at the hole I've created in the back of the barn. Empty fields of green grass, and a cluster of trees spread in the distance. The wind is much calmer on this side. It seems to call to me as it whistles through the jagged wood.

I turn back to the barn's front door as the helicopters land amidst the charred pieces of the Charon. Psyriin soldiers start to pour out of each one like water from a bucket that's sprung a leak. Must be dozens of them.

"Keep pressure on your chest." I huff as I stare at Auriga.

I snatch his wilted wrists and place them over the center of the drenched red stain on his shirt. He gives a deep sigh, but there's still a grin on his lips as his eyes shut.

I step through the doorway with my fists clenched. What am I doing? Freedom is in the other direction. They won't look for me. If Auriga dies, they wouldn't even know how to find me. I could look for Mom. I can escape from all of this.

I fling out my arms. Pieces of the Charon's broken wing zing through the air until they are pointed over each of my shoulders like gigantic knives. I get myself into the perfect stance for a Dirt War. It seems like there are hundreds of Psyriin soldiers, each clad in the same blackened armor that shimmers against the stray flames and moonlight. A bright beam of light blasts from the helicopter, which still hovers in the air. I place my hands over my brow as it blares toward me.

"Rion!" Nastacia Arkright's unmistakably harsh tone clamors through a loudspeaker.

My face molds into a snarl as I try and see through the blistering white beam.

"Stand down!"

Her voice echoes through the night air while her minions strategically spread into position. Once they've stopped their frenetic movements, the soldiers brandish their long, rifle-like weapons and point them at me.

"This won't end well," she says. "You don't have to die today!"

If not today, when? A few days from now, in another hellish Psyriin prison? Perhaps a few weeks, when Nastacia Arkright finds me on the run and puts a bullet through my unsuspecting brain? No. I've had enough. I was never going to leave. Auriga had to have known this. Even if I could get away, I'd live a life of fear, constantly looking over my shoulder for Felix Bard and the black-suited henchmen of the Psionic Research and Intervention Initiative.

I'm part of this war, whether I like it or not. I may not be a Predator, or one of Pavo's Phantoms, but I am a Clairvoyant. That makes Psyriin my enemy. They're the reason my mother is on the run. If I'm going to die, I'm going to do it on my own terms. And I am most certainly going to take as many of them with me as possible.

I close my eyes and cross my arms into an X. I sense the weaponized pieces of wreckage above me begin to shift. One looms over my frame and shields me from the heinous helicopter spotlight, while the other forms a barrier over most of my chest. Let's see how well these jerks can shoot.

"Have it your way," Arkright growls.

I'm ready. I can barely feel my extremities, and my heartbeat is now a vacant murmur. I'm prepared to send a wave of kinetic energy that will send Psyriin soldiers flying through the air like fireworks. I know I won't get them all. I know Arkright's helicopter will send a barrage of gunfire as soon as I've moved. But they better not miss.

I take a deep breath and think of Mom, knowing that this might be my last time to do so. I imagine she'd be proud of me. I know I got my fighting spirit from her.

My fingers twitch. The glow of their weapons makes the atmosphere brighten with an eerie blue radiance. I prepare to swing my arms. I have to remember not to use all of my energy so I can be ready for a counter-move in case I survive their first onslaught.

"Grenade!" one of the Psyriin soldiers screams.

Boom!

It happens so swiftly that my perfect stance turns into an awkwardly attentive pose. My eyes widen and my jaw drops. The blast shoots into the sky. Most of the Psyriin soldiers flutter through the air like popcorn. The ones that aren't hit dive for the ground.

I shake from my confused daze and shift back into my fighter's stance. There's no time to figure out how one of them accidentally set off a grenade. I have to take this fortuitous time to act. I'm about to send my arms into a jabbing motion, when each helicopter rises. A missile appears from the side of each copter, just as the unharmed Psyriin soldiers start to rise to their feet and prepare to fire. If I focus, I can deflect the missiles and still shield myself. It won't be as easy as a Dirt War, but it's the only play I have.

I grind my feet into the soft dirt beneath me. Each helicopter places its spotlight on me. Here goes nothing...

As if I'm dreaming, one of the Psyriin soldiers starts shooting the others. I try to fight my unhinged confusion so I can stay ready for the oncoming missiles, but it's no use. I can't believe what I am seeing.

A Psyriin soldier shoots down five of his allies, until he's shot from behind. The body of my unexpected helper doesn't even hit the ground before the soldier that kills him starts to blast away at more of his compatriots. Once he is gunned down, a new soldier starts to betray the rest. Within seconds, more than half of the surviving soldiers have been dispatched.

"Fire now!" Arkright screams.

The discourse in her tone makes it seem like she is just as shocked by the events as I am.

The other helicopters heed her command, and the missiles come firing toward me. I thought I would be ready. Knew I was going to be ready. But the missiles are coming faster than I'd expected. Smoke scatters behind each one as they whistle through the air at breakneck speed. Was the grenade and the Psyriin soldiers turning on each other just a ploy to distract me? If it was, it worked.

My mind is flustered. I want to shift each missile and perhaps send at least one hurling back toward its sender, but my arms just fold. I turn the remains of the Charon into a massive barricade and prepare for the inevitable.

As soon as I've braced for the terrifying impact, I hear a burst of wind blaring from behind me. It comes so fast that I barely have time to turn toward it. No way! It can't be. I must be hallucinating.

A person flying in from the sky. But not just any person. Aries!

He swoops in with a fierce look on his perspiring brow, his golden dreadlocks bouncing when he lands. He doesn't even waste time to look my way. His arms swipe through the air like he's a seasoned martial artist.

I stand in awe as each missile spirals upward moments before they can collide with my makeshift shield.

Aries finally turns to me. I can read the thoughts echoing from his intense scowl. He needs protection!

I send a piece of the Charon's wing in front of him, just as the gigantic bullets begin firing from two of the helicopters. We both grit our teeth and cringe as the ammunition rattles into our shields. Some of the bullets hammer the ground in front of us, sending heaps of dirt into the air.

"Rion!" Aries shouts, amidst the chaos. "I'm comin' over to you."

I nod and hold out an arm, while the other remains up, with a fist. As the endless rain of bullets continues to scour our surroundings, Aries executes the most athletic summersault I've ever witnessed. He looks like an Olympic gymnast, perfectly tucking his head and folding his legs. By the time he's back upright, he is on the other side of me.

He is barely to his feet when he makes three swift aerial punches. The bulking helicopters have no time to react. The missiles are heading straight for them, even faster than when they were first fired.

I finally take a minute to look up and watch. The highest copter jolts upward to dodge the attack. A focused gnarl spreads across my weary face. There is

no way I'm going to let this one get away. I drop my
shield and look at the cockpit, as if I'm glaring right
into Nastacia Arkright's devilish sneer. I spread my
fingertips and twist my wrists. It's like I have the last
missile on a string. It makes a sharp upward turn, just
in time.

Pow! The sound of contact blasts through the atmosphere like a thousand grenades. The wind grows
wild, and a gust blares toward us with the strength
of a tornado. Metallic debris shoots through the air,
sending us diving to the ground. I foolishly cover my
head, as if my hands and arms are strong enough to
withstand chunks of spiraling, jagged iron.

Aries remains focused. He stands and telekinetically
brings more large shards of the Charon hovering over
each of our bodies. A piece of flaming propeller stabs
the ground just a few inches to my left. I shudder at
the terrifying *thud!*

Just as the noise stops echoing through the night
air, a new sound enters my senses. It's the unmistakable hum of an engine, and tires rumbling against dirt.

With each passing second, this entire experience feels
more like a dream. I look up and see a blue minivan
screeching to a halt several yards to our right. A
minivan? Yes, a minivan. Dried mud is caked along
its edges, like it's just finished driving through miles

of muck. The windows are tinted. The driver's side window rolls down, and Leo pops his scowl out.

"C'mon! Let's go," he shouts.

Leo is the last person I expected to see, and I remember how much I loathe him. And yet I've never been happier to see anyone else rolling up in a blue minivan.

I stumble to my feet as the clumps of flaming helicopters start to collide with the already demolished Charon. Somehow I expect to see Nastacia Arkright flipping through the air with absurdly large guns hulked over each shoulder. But no one comes from the wreckage. The entire field is littered with Psyriin minions screaming in agony as their hides burn and their broken bones ache. Makes my stomach churn.

"Mama's Boy!" Leo calls again, in a far more agitated tone.

He even honks the van's horn as if he's knee-deep in city traffic.

"We have to get Auriga!" I yell back at Leo, as I point toward the barn.

"Well move your ass!"

Aries and I go sprinting for the barn door. Adrenaline seems to be the only thing moving my aching limbs.

When we enter, Auriga is still huddled over the haystack. His eyes are closed. He doesn't appear to be

breathing, but his hand is still resting over his bloodied clothes, where I left it.

Aries grabs Auriga's shoulders and nudges his head
down. I grab his feet, and we begin waddling toward
the exit, until something in the doorway startles me.
I almost drop Auriga, but I maintain just enough of a
grasp to only warrant a grimace from Aries.

A Psyriin soldier is standing in front of us. His armor
is riddled with scrapes and blood stains. His dark visor
has been sullied by large quantities of soot.

"What are you waiting for?" the soldier snaps, in a
raspy voice as he places his weapon to his side. "Let's
get out of here!"

The soldier's body clumps to the floor like a wet sack
after the words have screeched from his helmet. My
eyes widen, and my frame grows rigid.

"It's Ara, genius," Aries says.

Of course. I can't help but feel dumb for not realizing
it. The entire ordeal comes rushing back to me like I'm
rewinding a movie to an intriguing part I'd missed. The
grenade. The soldiers offing each other, one by one. It
was all Ara. She was doing the same thing she'd done
when she masqueraded as the fifth soldier.

I shake from my confused stupor, and Aries and I
trot toward the minivan. Leo glares at the wreckage
with his hands clasped against the steering wheel. The

side door slides open, and Ara—the real Ara—leans over the backseat. Her sparkling gaze blares toward us as she waves for us to move faster.

We finally reach the vehicle and load Auriga's limp body inside. Shocked and impressed wouldn't be enough to describe my feelings. I had seen Aries topple a building and deflect Perseus and Aquila's attacks with ease. But the intensity and will in his eyes when he shifted those missiles was something beyond sorcery. It's hard to imagine that type of skill existed.

And Ara. The focus and precision it must have taken for her to shoot several Psyriin soldiers, then shift into another's body before she was killed, was nothing short of miraculous.

I turn to scan the huddled bodies of every Psyriin minion, just as I leap into the van and the doors glide to a close. The engine rumbles, the tires screech, and Leo whips the wheel to his left. Aries, Ara, and I each hold on to whatever piece of the vehicle interior we can find. It's as if Leo is driving a dune buggy. I hear the thump of his boots as they shift from break to gas, and in seconds we are speeding away.

My face is in a gawking stupor, and my body wriggles with each bump in the road. Ara sits in front of me, with Auriga's sweaty head resting in her lap. She lovingly rubs his scalp and smiles at his closed eyelids, a nurturing gleam in her glistening stare.

I look beside me at Aries. His somber grimace is fixated on the passing trees. His tattooed arm rests against the door, and his fingertips twiddle.

"You came back for me?" I mumble.

He turns to me and laughs.

"Yeah. And you sure as hell owe me."

"But...how-how'd you find me?"

Aries nods and pokes his lips in dissatisfaction. Ara's gaze shoots upward, and a grumble skirts from Leo's jaws. I listlessly look around, waiting for one of them to reply. Ara takes a deep breath and finally answers.

"Pavo had a vision. He saw the Charon crashing, and gave us the location."

A warm smile cascades across my face. For years, Pavo had been unable to conjure a vision about the Charon's whereabouts. Yet, just when I needed him more than ever, the old man came through.

My thankful cheeriness dissolves as I notice none of their demeanors have changed. I catch Leo glaring from the rearview mirror.

"It wasn't easy, Mama's Boy." He grunts. "It came with a price."

My heart seems to come to a halt. My body feels cold and rigid. I turn my widened gaze over to Aries. He continues to peer downward with the biggest look of dejection and remorse I've ever witnessed on his usually brash visage.

"Bob Marley here came to our backup safe house." Leo scoffs, shifting his blue eyes to glare at Aries through his crisp glasses.

"Should've changed the locks, playboy," Aries says, harshness oozing through his tone.

Looks like I'm not the only one who isn't too fond of the Reader Clairvoyant.

"He told us what happened," Ara says, her eyes swarming with sorrow. "And he convinced Pavo to let us try to induce a vision."

I lean back in the soft seat cushions and clasp the edges. I think about Auriga, and I glance over at his immobile, bleeding frame. The sounds of his agonizing screams echoing through the Charon walls come roaring back. I imagine the pain and suffering Psyriin put him through to induce his visions.

The rest of the ride is filled with silence. All I can think about is Pavo wailing in the night, like Auriga.

His teeth rattling as he endured whatever torture they needed to put him through.

What did they have to do? Shock him? Burn him? Stab his skin over and over again? Submerge him in water until he felt a drowning sensation? How long did he have to endure the pain before he had the right vision?

Picturing it all makes me cringe. And for the first time since being rescued, I wish they hadn't come back for me.

CHAPTER 23
PROMISE AND PROPHECY

I AWAKEN TO CRIMSON WALLS AND THE SCENT of fresh linens. After my time aboard the Charon, this hotel room feels like a palace, and I can't remember having such a replenishing slumber. A cat's tail flickers in front of my face as I rise from the supple bedsheets. My head nudges down at Lyra rubbing her face against my side. I reach out and let my hand glide against her soft fur. She responds with a soothing purr.

"If I didn't know better, I'd say someone has a crush on you," Ara says.

She's grinning from the doorway when I look up. I smile and hold out my arms for Lyra to nuzzle her way to my chin.

"She always was one for younger boys." Ara says as she crosses her arms and steps forward.

"If you ever get out of this cat, I'm all yours, Lyra."

I lean in and plant a gentle kiss between those somewhat feline eyes. I know cats can't smile, but I swear Lyra grins back at me before she leaps from the bed, trots between Ara's legs, and exits through the doorway.

The mood changes right after Lyra scampers out of the room. I sit up and move to the edge of the bed. Ara keeps a slight smile, but her head lowers and she starts to bite her bottom lip.

"How long? How long was I on that ship?"

I almost don't want her to tell me. I've been dreading asking this question from the moment we'd driven from the Charon's wreckage.

"Just over three weeks," she replies. "Happy belated Thanksgiving."

Chills shoot down my spine. Every minute I'd spent between those hellish metal walls feels like a blur. I shake my head and scan the room in disbelief. Three weeks in a prison, being tortured and fed gruel…and still no sign of Mom.

"I'm so sorry, Rion. We should've helped you from the start."

Maybe it's instinct. Or perhaps it's the innate sensation of knowing I am finally free that triggers me to leap from the bed and rush toward her. I wrap my arms around her thin waist and collapse my chin over her shoulder. She doesn't hesitate to embrace me, and I feel her tiny arms fold over me.

"It's okay," she whispers, as tears begin to billow down my face.

We hold each other tight. Eventually, I feel the trickle of moisture down my neck, and I know she is crying too. We sob for what feels like hours. Some of them are tears of joy. Joy in believing that we are somewhat safe, and having finally brought Auriga home. But most of it is pain. Each stream of tears that floods down our faces seems to relinquish all of the stress and agony that has encompassed this entire journey.

When the crying is over, and we've both wiped the residue from our faces, I finally exhale.

"Is Leo back?" I say.

The recollection of last night comes roaring back. We had driven to a hotel in a small town just outside of Knoxville, Tennessee. We were staying in a master suite. Ara had rented out an entire floor after using her abilities to inhabit the attendant at the front desk. Once we were secure, Leo took off to dispose of the minivan and find as much medical equipment as possible.

"Yeah. He actually came back with a pretty sweet SUV." Ara gives a gentle smirk.

"He probably jacked one with a *How's my driving* sticker. Or one that says, *My kid is an honor student.*"

We both share a laugh, before the somber realization settles back in.

"So how's Pavo?" I murmur.

Ara gives a deep sigh.

"Still weak. But he'll be fine, with time."

A deep knot forms in my chest, like something has
been shoved down my throat. Ara's gaze drifts to the
crimson carpet. We both know my next question, but
it's as if neither of us wants to speak.

"And...Auriga?"

Her entire demeanor seems to wilt into a pathetic
sulk.

"Not good. He...lost a lot of blood."

Moisture starts to matriculate in her eyes again. It
seems that even this grave response is sugarcoating
the situation.

"Hey." Leo taps his knuckles against the doorframe.

His eyes look weary, and his skin is more pale than
usual.

"Auriga wants us."

The dejection in his voice makes my chest sink. Ara
and I both give a somber nod and follow him down
the hallway. Each step I take makes my heart grow
heavier and heavier.

We enter into what Leo has somehow turned into a
makeshift hospital room. Machines hum and beep all

around us. An IV protrudes from Auriga's arm as he lays vacantly against the bed, with Pavo on one side, and Aries on the other, with a solemn grimace. Pavo is in a wheelchair, with his hands clutched over Auriga's wrist. If he didn't still have his bushy hair and full, scraggly beard, his faded skin would make me think he's someone with a terminal illness.

Lyra is the last to scamper in. She leaps onto the bed before curling into a ball at Auriga's side.

"There they are," Auriga manages to whisper.

My eyes begin to water as I gaze at his emaciated face.

"What's up, partner." I move to the edge of the bed.

He gives a deep sigh before a few hellish coughs rip from his lungs. He tries desperately to lift his head, but Aries steps in and places his hand over his old mentor's chest to calm him.

"I'm glad you all are here." Auriga slowly scans the room, with a gleam in his reddened eyes. "I wish the others were here, too, but..."

I notice Aries slightly turning away like a pup who has disobeyed his master, but wishes desperately for forgiveness. It's strange to see him like this.

"They say you can't choose your family. So I'm grateful the good Lord saw fit to connect us. I wouldn't change anything, even if I saw it all coming."

Leo presses his fingertips underneath his glasses and between his watering eyes. Ara has already begun to sob, and slides her hand to intertwine with his.

"I want you all to promise me that no matter what happens, no matter what decisions you all decide to make, that you will love each other unconditionally. Because you are a family."

My lips begin to tremble, and a tear trickles down my cheek. I wipe it away as if a single drop might embarrass me. Auriga turns his head to face me. The gesture seems to take all of his strength to accomplish.

"All we have is each other," he mutters, before his eyes glide shut.

Pavo reaches out to hold his hand tight. I pace over to him and place my fingertips on his shoulder. He responds to my gesture with a light smile. Before I know it, we have formed a connected circle around Auriga. Ara has one hand in mine, and the other clutched in Leo's grasp. Leo has an arm around Aries's shoulders. Physically, they couldn't be any more different. But at this moment, they look like siblings. Long lost siblings who, despite their differences, will never stop loving each other. I never thought I'd see Aries cry. I can tell it isn't something that comes natural to him.

We stand in this circle for what seems like forever. We weep in silence, never letting go of one another.

The beeps of the heart monitor grow more and more faint. Aries turns and covers his face on Leo's shoulder.

By morning, Auriga has passed away in his sleep.

A heavy yawn escapes my cheeks. My arms rest against the edge of the hotel suite's balcony. I gaze out into the silent rooftops of the unsuspecting cityscape, and marvel at the orange glow of the evening sunset. Pavo sits in his wheelchair beside me. He has a light smile on his wrinkled face, and his hands are resting in his lap. I'm still surprised Leo will let me near him.

I glance through the window to look into the living room. Ara is hunched over on the other end of the couch, in a deep sleep. Lyra is curled in her lap in an equally deep slumber. My gaze drifts to the closed door across the room. I know Aries is inside, even though I haven't seen him since Auriga died two days ago. I can't imagine what must be going through his mind after watching the mentor he'd spent years trying to rescue, die hours after the goal had been accomplished.

"Did you know?" I turn my somber gaze to Pavo. "Did you know what would happen when you sent me to the Predators?"

His eyes flutter, and a long sigh spills from his bearded jaw.

"I knew there was no way you were going to stay with us. But I also knew that if I let you go out on your own, you probably would've wound up on the Charon sooner."

I let a smile peak across my face. I couldn't imagine what it would've been like to be a prisoner of Psyriin without Aries's training.

"All I saw was the bank robbery. So I took a leap of faith."

"Well, you didn't have to do it," I reply. "You didn't have to try to rescue me either. You guys didn't ask for any of this."

Pavo's pale cheeks puff as he lets out a hearty laugh, and his gaze meets mine.

"I'm afraid you got a crash course in Clairvoyant life. But we were born into this war, Rion."

I give a solemn nod. His soothing gaze makes me feel at ease as the cool air begins to waft between us.

"Besides, inducing the vision was my choice. My only regret is not making it sooner."

I reach out my hand to pat his shoulder. The gesture makes my smile dissipate. His once robust body still looks frail, and I can feel the bone through his brittle skin.

"In fact," he sighs, "once I've recovered, I'm going to do it again."

My eyes widen, and I retract my hand. I glare at Pavo with a grave scowl. He stares back at me with a resolute smirk.

"I'm going to do whatever it takes to reunite with the other Clairvoyants and find your mother."

My mouth widens. I want to reply, but I don't know what to say. Should I thank him? Should I tell him that he shouldn't? I stand in a vacant daze. I'm about to respond, when the balcony door slides open and Leo steps out.

"Dinner time, Pop." He smiles.

"Ooo...stew!" Pavo grins, as he claps in excitement, like a child.

Leo and I share an adverse glance before he rolls Pavo inside. The old prophet gives me a subtle wink, and the door glides shut.

I turn and continue to stare blankly at the scenery. I'm hellishly exhausted, but I still feel on edge, so the last thing I want to do is sleep. I'd spent the last few late nights scanning every television channel to see if there was any coverage of the Charon's crash. There isn't the slightest inclination, and I start to wonder what Felix Bard must be doing right about now.

The door glides open again, and my gaze meets with Aries. We both share a look of surprise as he steps into the open, evening air.

"What's up?" I say.

"What up, bro. You doin' aight?"

"I'm good. Physically, I feel better. But mentally..."

"Yeah, I hear ya." He huffs as he turns to stare at the sunset. "My bad, dude. Didn't know anyone else was out here."

I notice the unlit cigarette clutched between his fingertips. After all I've been through the last few days and weeks, the last thing that would bother me is a little cigarette smoke. Besides, I could always use my telekinesis to shield my senses if I got too discomforted.

I smile and give him an inviting shrug. We share a few quiet minutes as Aries puffs away.

"Thanks again, by the way," I say, to break the silence.

He turns to me with his usual hearty smirk.

"Not just for rescuing me, but for everything. The training. Fighting for me when no one else would."

He takes another hefty puff, and chuckles.

"Chill, bruh. Don't get all sentimental on me. After all, you're the one that freed Auriga."

My head bows, and we both turn to gaze at the sunset. He finishes his cigarette and flings it over the balcony before he turns to me again.

"I'd rather have him die here, with family, than in some Psyriin prison."

I wish his words gave me comfort. Somehow I can't help but feel like there's more I could've done to ensure Auriga's survival. As the disappointment starts to seep in, I feel Aries's fist jab against my shoulder. I look over to him, and a grin is plastered across his face.

"And you. You actually crashed the Charon! You're a wild dude."

We both laugh. I shake my head as if what I did was second nature and not some monumental feat.

"C'mon," I reply. "I watched you level a building and deflect missiles. You're the baddest Kinetic walkin' right now."

"True, true." He boisterously shrugs. "But I didn't pick this stuff up a month ago. Truth is, I probably learned as much from you as you did from me."

He stares off into the distance, with a fervent smile. He looks calm and gratified, like he is at peace for the first time in ages.

"This whole time, some of us were raisin' hell, while the others were cowerin' in a corner. Never crossed any of our minds that we needed to be both Predator and Phantom."

I crack a gentle smile. For the first time since encountering the Clairvoyants, I truly feel proud.

"You woke us all up. So thank you, bro."

The balcony door rushes open. We both turn to Ara's frantic scowl. I didn't even realize she was awake, but the look on her face makes our hearty grins vanish.

"Guys!" She's clutching the doorway.

Lyra comes running out and rambles through our feet, like she wants to tell us something, too.

"It's Pavo!"

My head jolts to Aries. His face has molded to the same intensified grimace as mine. We give each other a nod before marching back into the hotel room and slamming the door behind us. My heart jumps the second we've stepped into the living room. Pavo's wheelchair has been knocked on its side, and he is writhing on the floor. Leo is hunched over him with a deep scowl.

"What's wrong with him?" I yammer.

Aries darts to Pavo. He and Leo each grab the old prophet's wriggling body and scurry toward the couch.

"He's havin' a vision!" Aries says.

This is a vision? This looks terrifying.

Pavo's eyes have rolled into the back of his head, and saliva is spewing from his lips. His arms and legs are flailing. Aries and Leo have to evade to avoid being clocked in the face. If this is an unprovoked vision, I can only imagine how gut-wrenching it must be to see one that has been induced.

I stand beside Ara and Lyra, with my fingertips twitching at my side. Aries and Leo hold Pavo's limbs to keep the thrashing to a minimum.

"Does he need water or something?" I'm completely dumbfounded, and frozen.

"We just need to wait it out!" Leo barks, his gaze focused on Pavo's sweaty brow.

"Ahhhhhh!" Pavo screams.

His voice echoes through the room and makes Ara jerk backward. My eyelids barely move as I gaze at his protruding chest.

"Predators! Tyler! Psyriin!" Pavo hollers. "Predators! Tyler! Psyriin!"

Leo and Aries look up at each other with unnerved grimaces as they hold him down.

After a few more writhing minutes, Pavo's convulsions begin to simmer. His eyes close. A gasp escapes his chest, and the thrashing finally ends.

"Yo, grab a towel!" Aries snatches one of the tiny pillows from the couch to place underneath Pavo's head.

Ara turns to oblige, but before she can even take a step forward, I've already used my abilities to send one of the decorative kitchen towels fluttering into Aries's hands. Leo relinquishes Pavo's feet and leans back as Aries dabs his drenched forehead. I can only see the shimmer of his glasses, but I can tell Leo is staring off toward the walls.

"Predators. Tyler. Psyriin," Pavo whispers, before he enters a deep sleep.

He's barely been silent for a second when I run both of my hands through my damp, nappy curls.

"Oh, my God! Are they always like that?" My eyes are so wide that my sockets ache.

"We need to get out of here," Leo whispers, as he stands, with a frantic gaze.

"What does it mean?" Ara says.

"Who the hell is Tyler?" Aries murmurs, his brow in a confused gnarl.

He leans against the couch, with his hand running through the bleached blond hairs on his chin.

"You think it's another new Clairvoyant?" Ara says.

"Who cares!" Leo shouts. "We need to get our things and get back to the Safe House, ASAP. Pavo can explain on the way."

Aries rolls his eyes. Leo continues to yammer, but my thoughts have already begun to decipher the meaning of Pavo's frenetic words. The realization strikes my memories.

"Oh, no," I whisper.

Leo silences, and his scowl darts in my direction.

"What?" he grunts, as he paces up to me. "Do you know something?"

"I...I'm not sure."

"If you know who Tyler is, you better spit it out," he growls.

"I don't think it's a person," I reply, as I scan the vacant floor.

The room grows eerily silent.

"It's my old school. The one in Missouri. Tyler High."

Leo glares into my pupils through his thick lenses. I can hear his breaths becoming harsher by the second.

"Why would Psyriin and the Predators be at your school?" Ara moves to my side.

"Maybe they're tryin' to bait you," Aries says. "Your friend is there, right? What was her name? Bree?"

He finally stands, and meets us in the center of the room. My skin feels brittle, and my head starts to ache as Dee comes to mind.

"Dee," I groan, slapping my forehead for telling the Predators about her.

Aries takes a deep breath and folds his arms.

"Perseus probably doesn't know you got captured." Aries grunts. "So he thinks Psyriin still has Auriga, and is still after you. Maybe their plan is to lure you in and try the trade again."

"Good," Leo says. "So we just don't go."

"You saw Pavo," Ara says. "That clearly wasn't a pleasant vision."

"Whatever the Predators get themselves into is their problem now."

I notice Aries in my periphery, glaring at Leo with an unforgiving grimace.

"Are you listening to yourself?" Ara huffs. "What were Auriga's last words? We're all family. Predators included."

"Except they are family hellbent on getting themselves killed." Leo spreads his arms. "And after what we just pulled helping Mama's Boy, Psyriin is going to make us priority number one."

I roll my eyes. I want to give Leo a telekinetic uppercut.

"Innocent people could get hurt," Ara says.

"I have to save my friend!"

My shout quiets the room for a brief moment, and they each shift their stares to my intense brow.

"You guys don't have to come with me."

"Like hell we don't." Aries grunts out a laugh.

"What is with you Kinetics?" Leo shrugs. "It's like you always want to jump right back into the fire before you've even cooled off."

A groan resonates from the other side of the room. We each turn as Pavo attempts to sit up on the couch. Leo is the first to scamper over to him, and places his hands against the old prophet's back.

"Easy, Pop," he whispers. "Easy."

Pavo's eyes flutter, like he's entering light after days of darkness. Ara runs over to the kitchen and pours him a glass of water.

"Turn on the TV," he mutters.

He takes the beverage into his trembling hands, and brings it to his coarse lips. Aries zips the remote into his hand from across the room, and turns the television on.

"Channel Two," Pavo says.

We each stand around the massive flat screen with eager attentiveness as the image comes into view. It's a breaking news report. The anchor—an older Asian woman—has a somber, terrified look on her face as she speaks.

"The video went viral about an hour ago. We warn you, viewer discretion is advised."

Her image is replaced by an unrecognizable man sitting in a darkened room. His eyes and mouth are covered by white handkerchiefs. His wrists and ankles have been bound to the chair. Reminds me of the fifth soldier in the interrogation room. But none of us are prepared for what we see next. I can feel the gasps billowing from each of our jaws as Perseus and Aquila enter the screen.

"This message is for Nastacia Arkright and Psyriin," Perseus growls.

The ferocity in his voice is matched by the fiery gleam in his eyes.

"We're done playing games. You want to make a deal…let's make a deal."

I turn my discomfited glare toward Aries. Our gazes meet, and the anxiety seems to billow from our every pore.

"Meet us at the kid's school," Perseus continues. "Eight o'clock. Don't be late."

I peer at the digital clock displayed at the bottom of the screen. That's only an hour away.

"If you're late, then there will be more than one person's blood on your hands."

Perseus moves to the side. Aquila looms over the bound man's head, with her palm outstretched. She glares at the camera, like she's looking directly at me. Then she flicks her wrist.

Snap!

"Oh, my God!" Ara clasps her hands over her mouth.

The footage cuts just as it happens. My chest starts to thump as I turn to everyone else. Leo's astonished face trembles, and Aries has a look of culpable disgust. He turns the TV off and tosses the remote aside like he wishes he'd never turned it on.

"I was right," he growls, with his head bowed.

"We have to stop them." A deep sigh flutters from my lips.

"The Predators *and* Psyriin would both turn on us." Leo is frantically shaking his head. "We'd be walking into a war zone." He stares off at the walls while clutching Pavo's shoulders.

I step into his view, making sure his gaze meets my stern grimace.

"We have the drop on 'em," I say. "They don't know I'm with you guys. If anything, they'd only expect Aries to be with me."

"I can't read any of their minds, genius." Leo scoffs.

"And I've never been able to project into other Clairvoyants." Ara gives a dejected sigh. "Rion, we'd be useless in a fight against Persey and Aquila."

"Then get the hostages out!"

All of their somber glares fixate on me. I run my hands across my face before slapping them against my waist. I can't do this without them. I have to convince them to help me.

"Look, I can't let my friend, and other innocent people, get hurt because of me. I'll let Perseus give me up before that happens."

Aries steps in front of me and grasps my shoulders. The look of ardent resolve echoes through his eyes, and I know that no matter what happens, he'll be by my side. He turns to Leo like he's about to deliver the grandest speech imaginable. But before he can utter a word, Pavo lowers the empty glass from his face and speaks.

"You're wrong." His weary gaze passes between each of us. "They don't want to trade you, Rion. They're going to try to trade something else."

A confused gnarl cascades across my face. We each step forward in eager anticipation.

"Their plan is to trade something more valuable than any of us."

My eyes widen, and I fold my arms. Lyra nuzzles between Pavo's lap. It's as if she doesn't want him to give the bad news. He runs his hands between her ears and shakes his head before his remorseful stare darts into mine.

"Information is what they're going to trade. Information from a flash drive."

CHAPTER 24

BACK TO SCHOOL

"THE FLASH DRIVE." ARIES CLOSES HIS EYES, AND
his head drifts to the floor.

"Why did I tell them about the stupid flash drive?"
I cover my face and pace across the room.

"Flash drive?" Leo groans. "What flash drive?"

"It was his mother's." Aries places his hands on his
hips and shakes his head like we've already taken a
loss.

"Why did your mother have a flash drive with information about Clairvoyants?" Ara says.

I don't respond. I cover my mouth with both hands.
All I can think about is how I wish my special abilities were time travel instead of telekinesis. Why did
I have to tell those dangerous psychopaths about the
flash drive?

"Arkright found out from Auriga that his mother had info on us," Aries says. "Pretty sure she worked in the facility we came from."

I send a harsh look his way. I want him to shut up. He doesn't even notice me, and continues on, like he isn't throwing me under the bus.

"It's why Psyriin came after them in the first place."

Leo's face grows fiery red. He gazes around the room in utter amazement and irritation.

"And at what point did you plan on sharing this pertinent information with us, Mama's Boy?"

"I gave it to my friend because there was nothing on it." I spread my hands.

Then my eyes grow wide as the folder labeled *FB* jolts into my head like I'm seeing it for the first time on the library computer monitor.

"What?" Leo says.

"There was a folder labeled *FB*. I think it stands for Felix Bard."

Ara and Leo let out hellish groans and begin pacing around the room as if my blunder is unforgivable.

"But I checked it. Everything was deleted."

"Yeah, but nothing's ever really deleted," Aries says. "The right tech genius could uncover lost files with time."

I slowly turn and give him my most annoyed snarl.

"Or...someone who's explored the mind of a tech genius." Ara lets out a deep sigh.

"I've seen Lupus comb through computer manuals like they were Dr. Seuss books." Aries watches me slap my palm against my forehead. "He could uncover those files in a second."

"Great! Just great." Leo gives a sarcastic chuckle. "You happy, Mama's Boy? Not only can you move things with your mind, but you also have the inherent ability to constantly screw all of us."

"Stop it!" Pavo says, before I can even open my mouth to send Leo my most heinous obscenities. "All of you, just stop."

Water starts to collect in his reddened eyes, and it causes all of our anger to disperse. Silence fills the room as he glances at each of us in disappointment.

"Anger and fear. It's a disease in this world that has infected us, the Predators, and Psyriin."

We each stare at him with lowered brows, like young children being reprimanded by a parent.

"The Predators are angry because our lives have been taken from us. And they should be. Psyriin is afraid of us because of what we can do. And they should be."

Pavo's lips tremble as he clutches Lyra between his arms. She purrs and stands on her hind legs to lick away a stray tear, just as it streams down his cheek.

"But we can be more than anger and fear. We have to be more."

Our gazes drift to the floor, all of us too embarrassed to even look at him.

"If we are ever going to coexist with this world, we must rise above anger and fear."

Leo is the first to look up at his mentor, with an apologetic gleam in his gaze.

"I'm sorry, Leo," Pavo says, as their gazes meet, and he cracks a gentle smile. "I'm sorry for making you believe that we could run from this."

The rest of our heads rise. We step closer, forming a semi-circle around the couch. Pavo looks up with newly blossomed ferocity.

"The time for running is over."

"That's what the hell I'm talkin' about, Big P!" Aries wears a confident snarl.

Before anyone can say another word, he jabs my shoulder and marches for the doorway. I smile and pass a thankful nod to Pavo before jogging after Aries. He and I exit the hotel room and rush up the stairwell. We don't stop to look back as we head for the roof.

"All that stuff Pavo said was nice and all." Aries keeps his focused gnarl fixated forward. "But if you and I are gonna do this, we're gonna need a lil' bit of anger. You feel me?"

"Hey," I shrug, "we got a score to settle, right?"

"My boy!"

Our fists pound together as our footsteps echo against the stone walls. We reach the rooftop door, and the evening air rushes against our faces.

"Wait!"

We turn around. Leo is stomping behind us with a scowl.

"You geniuses want to come up with a plan first?" He steps through the screeching door.

"Oh, my bad, fearless leader." Aries scoffs and rolls his eyes. "Yo, Rion, let's waste more time while Fred from *Scooby Doo* comes up with an elaborate scheme for us."

"Hey, scale it back, Goldilocks."

Leo steps inches away from Aries's face. Their fiery glares meet. For a moment, I'm sure one of them is going to throw a long-awaited punch right into the other's face.

"Both of you, shut up!" Ara shouts.

Our heads each dart to the doorway, just as she comes stomping through, with Lyra clutched between her arms. Her strict demeanor looks foreign to me, but no less intimidating. She drops Lyra to her feet and moves between Aries and Leo.

"For God's sake, Auriga has been gone for two days, and you're already back at each other's throats." She points her finger an inch away from Leo's gawk.

"I know you're the oldest, but maybe we'd be more inclined to listen to you if you'd stop talking down to all of us like we're your offspring."

Aries chuckles, but his boyish grin disappears when Ara snaps her scowl his way.

"And you! Everything can't be solved by blowing something up. You're not a Predator anymore so stop acting on every dumbass impulse that creeps into your head. Leo is right. We need a plan."

I stay silent and just stare in awe. It's marvelous to behold. At this point, I wouldn't be surprised if Ara grabbed them by their ears and started twisting.

"After you idiots marched out, Pavo said that the Predators are going to be holding hostages in the school gymnasium. So, this is what we're gonna do." She crosses her arms and glares at each of us. "Rion...you and Aries are gonna fly us out to the school. Once we find your friend, Leo will locate the flash drive and retrieve it. I'll evacuate the hostages. You and Aries will have to keep Persey and Aquila out of our way."

"What about Psyriin?" I say.

"If they show up, I'll handle them." Ara releases a deep breath.

Aries and I give firm nods, while Leo keeps glaring at his feet.

"Oh, and we'll need to bring Lyra," she says.

We each look down at the adorable little feline, who is glaring back from below. It almost looks like she's smirking.

"Pavo was clear that we'll need Lyra."

We take turns glaring at one another and nodding. I can feel my heartbeat rattling as adrenaline starts to spread through my limbs. Despite my anxiety, a warm smile cascades across my face.

"The hell are you smiling for?" Leo says.

"Nothing," I reply, just as we break from our huddle. "It's just...this feels right."

Ara laughs, and the others look at me like I'm an idiot.

"I never had siblings, but if I could choose—"

"Hey, Mama's Boy. Save it for the after-party, okay?"

We all snicker and nod. Even Leo grins. I always thought it would feel awkward seeing him look at me like I'm not some repulsive alien. But his smile actually seems genuine.

"Aight, then." Aries shrugs. "Try not to move while I'm pullin' you."

"Oh, hell no!" Leo scoffs as his head shakes, and his smile disappears. "I'm not letting you pull us through the air. How do I know you and Mama's Boy won't drop us if you sneeze or somethin'?"

We each share an awkward stare. I can tell by Ara's nervous look that even though she made the suggestion, she isn't too keen on the idea herself. I just learned how to fly a month ago, so my vacant stupor makes it clear that I'm not exactly confident either.

"Fine, Leo." Aries groans while turning his back to us. "Hop on then, champ."

Ara and I try to fight our laughter. Leo shakes his head in disgust, but reluctantly trots over to Aries. As we move to the edge of the roof, Lyra leaps into my chest. I wrap my arms around her like she is precious cargo. I can't help but snicker when I notice Leo staring off at the sky and shifting to position himself on Aries's back. He looks like an oversized child getting a piggyback ride.

"Geez, dude. How much do you weigh?"

"Shut up!" Leo sneers. "Maybe if you'd stop smoking, and lift something with your arms instead of your mind once in a while..."

They bicker for a few seconds, before my attention shifts. I feel Ara wrapping her arms around my shoulders and folding her hands under my neck. It makes my cheeks grow rosy red, and my heart starts to flutter with butterflies.

"Umm...let me know if you're uncomfortable," I say, as her warm cheek nearly grazes mine.

"I'll be fine." She giggles. "Just...ya know...don't go too fast."

"I got ya." I wink.

Her soothing scent wafts into my nostrils. I have to look away from her sparkling gaze and warm smile to refocus. After Aries and I share a deep breath and one last conferring stare, we launch into the air.

The large dome of the Tyler High School gym appears over a patch of trees. The glow of lights blares through the night air as we begin to descend. Cars spread for almost a mile, covering the parking lot, the surrounding grassy fields, and the sides of vacant streets.

"Why are there so many cars here!" Aries shouts.

"Must be a basketball night." My face gnarls to combat the gusts of wind smacking against it. "Basketball is a big deal here."

"Just means more hostages." Leo grunts, the uneasiness blaring through his fogged bifocals.

"There's got to be at least a thousand people here," Ara says, as we start to descend.

I do my best to make my landing smooth. My feet slide against the dirt like a paper airplane coming to rest. I can't help but let out a deep sigh once we've come to a halt. Lyra wastes no time in leaping from my grasp.

"Nice flying." Ara winks.

I try not to blush.

A moment later, Aries comes clamoring to the ground like a baseball player sliding to home plate. He remains upright, but Leo flops to the ground with a *thud*.

"Really?" Leo huffs as he stands to his feet, and wipes the twigs and dirt from his clothes.

"My bad, bro." Aries laughs.

Leo gives him the middle finger before brushing by him and moving to the forefront. We watch with annoyed grimaces as he scans the scenery like some leader of a military team. Once he's finally done, we scamper from the tiny forest. We head to a long wing that protrudes from the gym and connects it to the school's main building.

The gym is only a few yards away, but there's an eerie silence coming from the area. With this many people here, cheers should be thumping into the atmosphere. We should at least hear the sound of a basketball hammering against polished wood. Either it's a timeout and Tyler High's varsity team is getting uncharacteristically demolished by their opponent. Or the Predators have already arrived.

"You think they're here?" Aries whispers.

"Shhh," Leo says.

Aries rolls his eyes.

We wait against a pair of double doors until Leo turns our way with his eyes bound shut.

"They entered the gym a few minutes ago and knocked out the security guards. People are panicking."

"What are we waitin' for?" Aries places his palm over the door.

"No, wait!" Leo says. "They've chained the doors shut on the inside."

"So I'll just break 'em off."

"And risk them knowing someone's here?" Leo growls.

His familiar agitated scowl reappears and blares toward Aries.

"Then what do we do?"

They start to bicker again, and I get annoyed. We're wasting time. Every second might be placing Dee's life in more and more danger.

"Hey, guys," Ara whispers.

They ignore her and continue their spat, as if they're the only two people that matter.

"Hey!" she growls.

This time, their voices cease, and they turn to meet her perturbed sneer.

"I think Lyra found another way in."

We turn our attention to the side of the gym. Lyra is standing in the grass, with the moonlight reflecting from her glistening eyes. Once she knows she has all of our attention, she meows and scampers around the corner. We each share a dumbfounded stare before sprinting after her.

"Oh, my God!" Aries says, as soon as Lyra slows down.

No one reprimands him, not even Leo. It only takes a second for us to comprehend the reason for his outburst. Lyra has led us to a rusted, steel doorway resting between a pair of dumpsters near the back of the gym. The grotesque odor almost makes me hurl, but Lyra doesn't seem to be bothered. While the rest of us fight the urge to gag, she waits like we're about to hand her a treat.

"Good job, Lyra," Ara whispers, as she struggles through a squint of discomfort. "Now one of you, please open this door."

We each feverishly nod. Leo smacks Aries's back, as if another minute of the odor might cause him to faint. Aries moves past the dumpsters, and to the corroded entrance. His eyes are watering as he does his best to focus on the chains that bind the door handles. The metal snaps in two, and he flings the door open.

"Hey." Ara clutches her nose as we start to head inside. "I'll keep a watch for Psyriin by the bus lot, and send Lyra in if they come."

"Got it." Leo exhales. "Be safe."

"You, too." She smiles before she and Lyra disappear around the corner.

The door slams shut, but the rank scent of the dumpsters has barely dissipated when a new, musty smell wafts into our senses. We've entered into some grimy storage area adjacent to the gym. Despite the disgusted grimaces we share, we don't waste time acknowledging it. We scramble past the dusty shelves and displaced janitorial equipment, until we've reached a doorway on the other side. Leo approaches it first. He closes his eyes again, and hovers his hand over the knob.

"They've moved everyone to one side of the gym," he says. "We have to hurry."

The door creaks open, and we enter a dimly lit hallway draped with trophy cases and banners. On our right are a pair of double doors, and the brightly lit interior of the gymnasium. We can't see any people through the glass window in the gym doors, but I can already make out Perseus's callous shouts. The hall splits into two adjacent corridors on the opposite side. I recognize this area. The classroom where Dee and I had sociology isn't too far from here.

Aries and I are about to storm toward the gym entrance, but Leo holds out his arms, as if to tell us to wait. We stand to each side while he closes his eyes once more. He lets out a deep sigh.

"What's the hold up now?" Aries whispers.

"Shut up," Leo says. "I'm trying to locate the girl."

My eyes widen. As much as I loathe Leo some-times—well, most of the time—I can't help but marvel at his power. Lupus failed to calculate how many secu-rity guards were in the TV station, but Leo seems confident in his ability to sift through the minds of hundreds of people in a matter of seconds. He truly is a master Reader Clairvoyant, and I'm thankful to have him on my side.

"What the hell?" A frantic snarl blares across Leo's face.

"What?" Aries says.

"She's not in there."

"No way. Look harder!"

"How many girls named Danielle, with an emo-tional connection to Rion, do you think there are?"

"Why would Pavo send us here if she isn't here?" I spread my arms in frustration.

"Big P never said she was here." Aries scowls. "He said the flash drive was here."

"So how the hell are we going to find it if she isn't here?" I say.

I can feel my brow starting to perspire. The sounds of Perseus's yells grow more vacant, and I can almost

make out what he's saying. Did he just tell the cowering audience to tell him where Dee was?

"Rion?"

The soft, yet confused tone echoes through the silent
halls and sends each of our frantic gazes twirling in
the opposite direction. My heart starts to pound. My
eyes enlarge. It's Dee. She's now standing right in front
of us, with a confused frown.

"Dee?"

She scans me up and down, like I'm some sort of
ghost. I can feel Leo and Aries glaring back at me from
my periphery, as I gawk into Dee's gigantic pupils. She
almost looks unrecognizable. Her dark brown skin
still has the same effervescent glow that it had the last
time I saw her, but her hair has been woven into thick
braids and pulled back into a ponytail. There's a blue
paw print painted on her left cheek, and she's wearing
a bulky Tyler High Tigers sweatshirt. I never imagined
she'd have this much school spirit.

"What are you doing out here?" I hustle toward her.

"Ummm..." she sarcastically grunts, while peering
around my shoulder at Aries and Leo. "I was in the
bathroom."

"Why didn't you use the one in the gym?"

"I didn't wanna poop around hundreds of...wait."
She scoffs.

Her face curls. She appears angry as she shakes her head at me.

"Why am I answering your questions? I still go to this school. What are you doing here? I thought you moved away?"

I sift through my thoughts. I want to tell her everything. Want to apologize for how I left things. But I remind myself to stay focused.

"It's a long, looong story. Right now, I need you to tell me where the flash drive is. Ya know, the one I left with you?"

Her gaze drifts from side to side, like she is contemplating. After a few quiet seconds, she looks like she's ready to respond.

"No need." Leo strides forward. "It's in her locker. I know the combination."

Dee's eyes blossom, and her lips protrude. I can't tell if she's shocked, horrified, or offended as she watches Leo jog by us and toward the left hallway.

"Ummm...who the hell is he. And why does he know my locker combination?"

Her hands flutter through the air with each word, before crossing over her chest. The way she cocks her head and waits for a response with a perturbed, yet feisty, scowl reminds me of my mother.

"I...it...there's just..."

Every time I stutter, her lips pout even more, and her grimace hardens.

"Look. I'm sorry about everything, Dee," I finally muster. "But we need to get you to safety."

"Safety!" She grunts. "Why do you need to get me to—"

My brow curls in confusion. Her demeanor has shifted from enraged to uneasy. Her gaze has drifted away from me and darted just above my shoulder. I whip my head around to Aries, who looks just as dumbfounded as I do.

I realize what has caught Dee's fretful gaze. Aries turns to follow our glares. As soon as he does, we catch the full view of Aquila and Perseus snarling back at all of us.

Aquila's palm jolts forward, bringing Dee's frame zipping toward the gym, like she's a piece of lint being sucked into a whirlpool. Her curdling screams reverberate against the stone walls. I ball my fists to retaliate, but before either Aries or I can act, Perseus has already made a move.

The banners rip from the walls, and the trophy cases shatter. Aries and I go spiraling down the hall with one forceful blast of kinetic energy. Our bodies tumble against the linoleum floors, but we manage to stop ourselves just before our backs hammer into the wall.

As soon as I look up, I am startled by a swarm of broken glass hurdling toward us. I put my arms up to brace for the sharp pain, but Aries is prepared. He shifts his arms into an X, and each hostile shard stops in the air, mere inches from our faces.

The gym doors swing open like a tornado has just forced through. Dee's body slams to a halt, midair. She tries to cry out, but all we hear are squeals. Perseus and Aquila each give a devious smile and turn the corner, with Dee floating behind. Aries and I share a glance before we take off, like rockets are strapped to our sneakers.

CHAPTER 25

STANDOFF

ARIES AND I EXPLODE THROUGH THE DOORWAY and halt near the center of the gym. Perseus and Aquila arrogantly grin from the giant tiger logo at midcourt, while Dee dangles above them. Lupus stands behind them with a vacant scowl plastered on his youthful brow. I peer to the other end of the gym and see the unconscious frames of two security guards sprawled out beside a massive pile of cell phones.

The hostages in the bleachers turn toward us with terrified grimaces. Their trembling gasps echo against the ceiling and make my heart rattle. They're all huddled together like the roof is about to cave in. I recognize my old sociology teacher, Mr. Keenan, and a few other former classmates, who stare at me in astonished confusion.

"Ladies and gentleman!" Perseus shouts, with a sinister smirk. "We have some guests."

Aries and I ball our fists. Neither of us seems to know what to do, so we just stand there in readied fight stances, listening to Perseus prattle on.

"Your very own former Tiger, Mister Rion Grean, has joined us."

I can feel every gaze blaring my way, and my forehead starts to flood with sweat.

"And this traitor's name is Aries."

The two Kinetics look at one another. Perseus's smirk is replaced by a snarl. I can feel his mind recounting our skirmish at the TV station, as his beady, black eyes become narrow.

"The flash drive is in her locker," Lupus says, as both Aquila and Perseus continue to fixate their grimaces on us. "But Leo is already headed that way."

"Leo?" Perseus scoffs. "You actually brought that Boy Scout?"

He turns to Lupus, who responds with a frustrated frown and a reaffirming nod. Aquila just shakes her head in disgust when his annoyed scowl meets hers.

"Quila, go get that drive."

"No!" Aries growls.

He clenches his fists even tighter, slamming the doors behind us, which sends a *thud!* echoing against the hollow atmosphere.

"Really?" Perseus grunts, as he rolls his eyes.

More frantic gasps ring out. Five more bodies jerk from the audience and hover to join Dee above the Predators. Several people amongst the multitude start to weep, and I can hear many of them calling out the names of some of the students who have been taken.

One of them is Alex, the blonde girl who used to sit alone in the cafeteria, eating chicken sandwiches and French fries each day. I peer beside her and see Brendan, the boy with the boot on his leg. I can picture my first day, when I helped him get on the school bus. I'd never managed to hold a conversation with either of them, yet seeing their petrified bodies floating beside Dee makes me even more furious.

"You know how easy it would be to kill them, right?" Perseus says. "Like crushing a pile of dry leaves."

My breaths become harsh and heavy. Aries starts to shake his head, as if Perseus mocking him with hostages makes him want to lash out even more. For a moment, I think he might make a move, because there's still some Predator in him. To my relief, he remains calm. His eyes briefly shut, and his lips begin to mumble, as if he's communing with Auriga's spirit for guidance.

Perseus lets out a devious chuckle.

"Go!" he shouts at Aquila.

She gives one last conniving sneer before sprinting around us and racing toward the hall.

The squeals of the dangling hostages continue to ricochet through the gymnasium. Dee is trying her best to face me through her tearful frown. I want to tell her it'll be okay. I want to believe it myself.

"You don't have to do this," Aries says, while we each stand with tightened fists.

Perseus just laughs. The petrified audience is looking back and forth between them, like they're watching an intense tennis match.

"C'mon, Aries. All of the blood you've spilled over the years, and *now* you have a soft spot for the common folk? And because of what? This runt?"

Perseus doesn't even look my way when he says it. He's barely glanced at me since we stormed in. I don't know if it's because my very presence disgusts him, or if he is just trying to prove to himself that I'm not significant enough to be a threat.

"Auriga wouldn't want this." Aries's tone becomes more calming and brotherly.

Perseus's haughty grin disappears, and an offended grimace replaces it. He turns to Lupus, whose nose begins to crinkle, like he's trying to mimic the fierce wolf tattooed on his bare arm.

"You don't get to tell us what Auriga would want!" Perseus points at Aries. "You sold him out for a kid you'd just met."

My heart begins to rattle, and my gaze droops to the empty corner of the gymnasium. I'm afraid to look over at Aries, for fear that he might be heeding Perseus's every word. I know he made the right decision, but I hope he doesn't regret it.

Something behind him catches my eye and causes me to do a double take. Is that? Yes! It's Lyra. She is creeping underneath the opposing hoop like a ninja.

I glance at the terrified crowd. None of them have noticed her. Who knows how she got in undetected, but I've never been happier to see the furry little Clairvoyant.

What is she doing, exactly? Has Psyriin arrived? Did Ara send her back to warn us?

I have to shake from my astonished daze. I can't let the Predators turn around and notice her.

"You chose the kid over us!" Perseus continues to yell, his fist thundering against his chest like he doesn't care if he bruises it. "The ones you grew up with. The ones who fought with you and for you. Your real family."

Aries's stern gaze begins to curl. He sees Lyra, too. But Perseus is staring directly at him. If he doesn't say something quickly, the Predators are sure to notice his attention waning.

"Auriga is dead!" I say, when I notice their shifting stares.

Perseus's snarl jerks toward me.

"What did you say?" he grumbles, his lips barely parting.

Lupus's eyes grow wide, and his crossed arms begin to unfurl.

"It's true," Aries says, realizing my attempt to stall.

The Predators snap their grimaces back over to him. I keep Lyra in the outskirts of my vision as she leaps onto the edge of the empty, opposing bleachers. She moves up as high as she can before placing her catlike gleam on a small red box at the corner of the wall. The fire alarm.

"Rion was captured by Arkright," Aries says, in his most somber tone, while the Predators attentively glare. "He helped Auriga escape the Charon."

Perseus and Lupus's eyes grow weary and red. Their chests start to inflate, and their limbs begin to tremble. Aries stares at each of them. I can tell that his words are shattering whatever emotional shield his two former allies have left.

"But...Auriga didn't make it. He died from injuries, two days ago."

A tear seems to trickle down each of their cheeks simultaneously. The Predators clearly had no idea. The thought that they'd never see Auriga again appears to rip through their hearts like a dagger. I almost feel sorry for them, until I look up at Dee and the other terrified students still floating in the air.

Perseus stands in silence, and I notice the hovering hostages beginning to descend. He is losing his mental hold on them with every agonizing thought of Auriga's death.

I glance at Lyra as she wiggles her bottom like she is preparing to jump. I prepare myself. I have to time this perfectly.

"Did...did he suffer?" Lupus murmurs.

Wheeeeeeeeeeeeeee!

The piercing sound echoes through the gymnasium like an ambulance has just driven across the court. Everyone else winces and covers their ears, but I take the moment to act. As soon as Perseus and Lupus cower, I reach out my arms and send Dee and the other five students hurling back over to the rest of the audience. They crash into a few people, but it's the safest landing I can give them.

Perseus's scowl shoots toward me, and his hands drop from his head. Before he can make a move, Aries swings his fist in an upward motion, sending both Predators spiraling in the other direction. It's almost like they are characters in a video game, who have been assaulted with a finishing uppercut. Their cartoonish flutter through the air comes to a *thud!* on the opposite end of the gym.

"Everybody, get out of here, now!" I scream, as I telekinetically fling the doors open.

The massive swarm of people start to clamor for the exit, shrieking and stumbling over everything and everyone. Aries keeps his hands up, ready to send another furious wave of kinetic energy the moment our opponents stand. My vision, however, has drifted to Dee, who looks back at me with a widened, fretful stare.

"Hurry!" I shout.

She sorrowfully nods, and after helping a few teachers scoop up the fallen students, she bolts for the exit, just before the searing alarm ceases.

Aries and I get back into our readied, Dirt War stances as we focus our intense grimaces forward. Lupus continues to lay idle against the floor, but Perseus stands with the most heinous glare I've ever seen.

"You dirty liars!" he screams.

"Find Quila," Aries says to me, as he and Perseus's fiery gazes meet.

"But—"

"I got this, Rion. Don't let her get that flash drive!"

I give a loud grunt, but I oblige. I turn and kneel, lowering my fingers to the floor like a track runner preparing for an Olympic sprint. It only takes an instant to hone my energy before I burst toward the gym doors.

A *blast!* blares from behind me, just as I skirt down the hallway. It's as if Aries and Perseus have both shot cannons at each other. I wonder about Aries's safety, but I don't look back. I know he can handle himself, and that my priority is protecting Leo and securing the flash drive before Psyriin arrives.

I race down the corridor until I've reached Dee's locker. The door has been slung open, and all of her books and papers are scattered along the floor. I scan the hallway. No one else is here. I continue to soar down every hallway, hoping to find Leo. But there is nothing.

The school busses! That's where Ara was waiting. That's where Leo likely would've taken the flash drive once he'd found it. That's where I'll find Aquila.

I shoot through the air again. I move even faster than before, my fist outstretched like some sort of superhero. I burst through the doors leading to the front parking lot, and a bevy of screams flood my ears. The last few hostages are still scrambling for their vehicles. Those who have managed to get in their cars are driving over hills and grass, ignoring any rules of the road to escape.

Meeeeeeeow! Lyra's call echoes through the night air. She's standing at the edge of the parking lot. I swear she's like a tiny angel, appearing whenever one of us needs her.

There is a frenzied look in her eyes, and I can tell she wants me to follow, so I sprint her way. When I'm close, she turns and scampers off, leading me to where there's sure to be trouble.

We weave through the last group of frightened civilians scuttling to safety. It's difficult to keep up with Lyra's swift, feline maneuvers. It would be much easier to follow her while flying, but I can't risk the remaining civilians being distracted any further.

When we finally reach the bus lot, only one of the yellow vehicles remains. My heart jumps through my chest when the two figures come into view beside it. Aquila is standing with her tattooed arm raised. Her hand is outstretched in a vicious clawing gesture, and Leo is suspended several yards above her. His face is turning purple, and his hands are wrapped around his neck like he's being choked.

He looks my way. There's an apologetic gleam in his watering eyes before they flutter and close. As my hurried footsteps halt, the flash drive rips from his pocket and lands in Aquila's palm. She stuffs it into the side of her tattered vest before turning her smirk toward us.

"Don't tell me it's just you and the cat?" She chuckles.

My scowl blares at Leo's limp frame colliding with the concrete. I hold out my hands to telekinetically pull him toward me until he is resting at my feet. Lyra whimpers when she prances over and nudges Leo's pale cheek.

I take my eyes off of Aquila for a brief moment to scan my surroundings. Where is Ara? Is she safe? Aquila just continues to hellishly grin. She cracks her knuckles and tilts her head to each side. I glance down at Leo, and his chest slightly moves.

"He's family, so I didn't kill him!" Aquila hollers from across the lot. "But I suggest you get him out of here before Psyriin comes and finishes the job."

My vicious gnarl snaps toward her, and her hearty smirk only widens. For a brief second, I wonder if I'm strong enough to beat her without Aries's help. But Auriga's words begin to swim in my mind. *Fear is a self-inflicted wound before you've even started the fight.*

I step forward with hardened fists. I can't be afraid. Whatever it takes, I have to retrieve that flash drive.

"Your plan isn't going to work!" I yell, as I continue to pace forward.

"Oh? And why is that?" She crosses her arms in amusement.

"Because Psyriin is setting you up. They don't have anything to trade you."

Aquila rolls her eyes and shakes her head. "Sounds like the Phantoms and their pathetic philosophies are starting to get to ya, kid."

"It won't work, because they don't have Auriga anymore."

Her face crinkles into a confused expression, and her arms unfurl. She stares into my eyes, waiting eagerly for an explanation.

"Auriga is dead."

My words might as well be an anchor hammering down on her chest. Her eyes grow red, and her lips begin to twitch. I take advantage of her vulnerability, subtly wiggling one of my fingers, and focusing my peripheral vision on the vest pocket where the flash drive is being held.

"You're lying," she mumbles.

"Psyriin took me after the TV station. Auriga helped me crash the Charon and escape. And then he died, with Pavo and us by his side."

Her face still looks angered in disbelief, but there is a deep pain coursing through her visage that is undeniable. She seems frozen in sorrow, her pearly pupils dancing around her sockets in deep recollection. Her breaths are heavy and loud.

Even through my glower, there is still disappointment. I never wanted to be the bearer of bad news to the Predators. Hell, I wanted to be a part of them. They aren't much different than I was—willing to go through whatever means necessary to find a loved one who was unfairly taken from them. They just lost their souls amidst their search, and had it not been for Aries and the Phantoms, I would've been just like them. It could've been me harming innocent bystanders in desperate hope to reconnect with Mom. It took weeks aboard the Charon, and being rescued, for me to realize that she'd rather I live a noble life than risk my instilled virtues to find her.

The flash drive finally spurts from her pocket, but Aquila snatches it in her grasp. Her despondent gaze shifts to mine. Even though she's only known of Auriga's death for a minute, her weary face seems like she's been in mourning for hours.

"This is your fault," she growls, as tears trickle down her cheeks.

I give a deep sigh. Here I was, thinking that the news might actually calm her and make her see the light, like Aries did. I feel naïve and foolish. There is no avoiding this fight.

Aquila lashes her arm out to the side, and the flash drive flies through the air. Even with street lights bathing the area in a white glow, I'm unable to follow the tiny object as it flutters into the distance. I barely have time to react before Aquila rushes toward me.

"It should've been you!"

I spin around her, just in time to keep her from jabbing my face. As soon as I'm facing her again, I don't hesitate to send a heavy dose of kinetic force thrashing into her chest. Her body zips across the lot and bangs against the bus, leaving a dent in the vehicle's yellow coating. A *thud!* echoes into the night. She's too vulnerable. I'd never land such a crude move on her if she were focused.

Aquila stumbles to her feet and wipes the mixture of saliva and stray blood from her lips. She glares at me with a vicious snarl. I feel like I've just awakened a sleeping giant.

She spreads her legs into a fighting stance. Holds out her arms and lets out a hefty grunt. A steel rim rips off of the back tire of the bus and flattens into a sharp disk. My eyes widen when she chucks her arm like a world-class pitcher throwing a fastball. The metal disk comes zipping toward me at breakneck speed. I leap into the air, twisting my body horizontally in the process. Aquila attempts to counter this move by turning the jagged, spinning rim on its side. It drifts inches from my chest before passing by.

Aquila's fist rushes downward, but I swipe my arm in midair, and send her kinetic force away from me. The asphalt cracks beneath us. I barely let my sneakers graze the fractured ground before I jump back into the air. I don't know how I saw it coming. Maybe it's Aries's training, or instinct, but somehow I'm already mentally equipped for Aquila to send another flattened bus rim slicing from behind me. It's like I'm being held up by strings that are pulling my body upward with every dodge.

Aquila moves her arms like she's practicing Tae Bo. I remain airborne for what feels like an eternity, twisting and turning to avoid the pair of disks that swim around me. I keep ducking and dodging, performing numerous aerial backflips. They'd make my jaw drop if I weren't the one doing them, but I'm not sure how much longer I can keep this up. I have to go on the offensive.

Only one move comes to mind. If it doesn't work, I'm pretty much screwed.

I do a midair pirouette, twisting my frame like a ballerina to avoid the swirling disks on each side of me. As soon as they've passed, I swipe my fist in a jabbing motion, and the back of the bus jerks toward Aquila.

She hops to her side to avoid contact, but I've done all I need to distract her.

I plant my feet and send one of the rims spiraling downward. It pierces the ground like a hot knife through butter, causing Aquila's gaze to jolt toward me. She telekinetically pulls the remaining rim like a yo-yo, and it comes swirling past my head, making a searing whistling noise. It spins in front of her, then zings back at me.

I'm ready. In fact, I am more than ready. It feels like I'm Auriga or Pavo, the way things play out exactly how I pictured them in my head.

I sprint toward her with a look of boastful focus, and watch as Aquila's eyes widen with shock. She flings the rim at my face, with a look of desperation on her brow. It's as if she's been playing a game of chess, and she is making her final move before her opponent says *checkmate.*

I'm not sure if I've ever been more in-tune with my abilities. It feels like the deadly disk is moving in slow motion. I wait patiently, knowing that I have no backup plan if this move fails.

The disk slips by my nose so close that the grimy metal surface bathes my skin in its warmth. I jump into the air again, moving my body horizontally as I ascend. My feet reach the side of the school bus, and

I begin running along it as if gravity never existed. I spread my hand outward to mentally grasp the projectile and hurl it back toward her. As soon as she begins to move her arms to counter my attack, I push myself from the school bus. My stomach churns in my chest as I summersault through the air, watching Aquila's frenetic glare go from upside down to right side up.

Before she can send the disk back at me—before my feet have even touched the ground—I have used my free hand to telekinetically rip the other rim from the concrete. Aquila tries to shield herself, but it is no use. One thick plate hammers against Aquila's back, while the other slams her chest. I watch her eyes widen as a thunderous gasp skirts from her jaws. Her body pounds against the ground in a *thud!*, and her eyes shut.

Maybe if she weren't blinded with vengeance, she would've been able to avoid it. But even that is doubtful. As I land with one knee to the ground, and a hand clutched against the warm asphalt for balance, I realize that it is one hell-of-a move. Even Perseus would be impressed.

I stand, and an astonished look spreads across my sweat-drenched face. I did it! I actually won. A smile manages to creep through, but it only lasts a second, before I feel the chilling winds beginning to rise.

My gaze drifts from Aquila to my surroundings. I glare past the streetlights and towering trees, until the starry night sky and crescent moon are in view. Goosebumps spread across my skin, and an anxious tingle goes down my spine. There in the distance, speckled amongst the stars, are helicopters.

Psyriin has finally arrived.

CHAPTER 26

THE REAL ENEMY

I CAN FAINTLY HEAR THE HUM OF PROPELLERS.
The Psyriin soldiers could arrive in minutes. I turn
and look at Leo's unconscious frame lying against the
concrete. Lyra is nuzzled against his chest, but she is
glaring back at me with a sorrowful frown.

There are still cars attempting to escape. They've
created a frantic clutter in the streets around the school,
and I fear that Dee might be among them. And where
is Ara? I keep scanning the horizon, hoping that she'll
pop up.

I swerve my frenetic gaze over to Aquila. In my haste
to defeat her, I'd never thought to ask about Ara. Had
she been choked, too? Is she lying unconscious somewhere around campus? Should I go look for her? Do
I even have time to?

Another loud crash echoes from the school. I whip my head to the gym's domed roof peeking through the trees. Aries must still be battling Perseus. I reach out and ball my fist, causing Leo's limp body to rise into the air. He looks like a ragdoll being lifted by a frail piece of string. I wiggle my fingers, and his head flickers back and forth like I'm planting a host of gentle slaps against his face. He still doesn't wake up.

The air is growing even colder, and the winds continue to rise. I can't stay here. I need to move. I keep my hand outstretched and glance at Lyra. She responds with a distressed purr before she scampers back toward the school. I follow her, sprinting, with Leo hovering over my shoulder. We advance to the gym's outside entrance before halting. I lay Leo against the cool grass and begin tapping his face, this time with my rigid palm.

"C'mon, Leo. Wake up!"

Lyra trots over and starts to lick his face like it's covered in ice cream. Again, he doesn't budge. The thunderous hum of an engine, and the sound of sirens, blare from behind us. I look up at the red and blue lights flickering against the stone walls of the gymnasium. Lyra is glaring back at me like she's waiting on me for the next order, but my body is stiff. I have no idea what to do.

I spin around and raise my hands to the air. A police car comes roaring up, just inches before concrete turns into brittle strands of grass. The flashing lights cause me to squeeze my eyes shut, so I can hardly make out the figure stepping from the driver's side door. A bulky, statuesque man draped in a navy-blue uniform comes sprinting forward. His chiseled features are barely visible until he's just a few feet from us.

"Officer." I pass frantic glances to the multitude of helicopters beginning to speckle the distant skyline. "I can explain—"

"Rion, it's me," the officer grumbles, through a raspy voice as he reaches us.

"Ara?"

The officer says nothing, and kneels to examine Leo's brow.

"Why are you always jumping into dudes?" I move to the other side of Leo's immobile frame.

"I wasn't exactly in a position to pick and choose," Officer Ara says.

It's so awkward to be talking to a white, middle-aged male policeman like he's the petite Asian girl I know.

"I was able to create a path for the hostages and keep the rest of the police at bay. What happened to Leo?"

"Aquila." I huff as we collectively lift the Reader Clairvoyant by his shoulders.

"And where is she?"

"The bus lot. She's unconscious."

Another *crash!* echoes from above us, causing our gazes to divert upward. We look on in distress as Aries's unmistakable frame darts along the school's roof. Perseus emerges from the gymnasium like a speeding bullet.

"Help me get him into the car!" Officer Ara says.

We lift Leo and shovel him into the backseat. Ara's actual body is leaning against the passenger's side door in a deep slumber.

"I have to help Aries," I say.

The sound of the approaching Psyriin helicopters nearly overtakes my voice. Ara peers back and forth between the top of the school and the skyline. I can see her real eyes through the officer's anxious scowl.

"Meet me at my old house!" I shout. "704 Milport Crossing."

Lyra hops into the backseat, and into Leo's lap. I slam the door and glare into the officer's eyes with a calm resolve.

"Okay." Officer Ara nods.

I sprint back into the grass and prepare to launch into the air, but Ara interrupts me.

"Rion!"

I turn to meet the officer's fierce stare.

"Kick Persey's ass."

"What happened to *we're all family?*" I give a wily grin.

"I didn't say kill him." Officer Ara smirks before hopping into the driver's seat.

Funny. Even though I'm not actually looking at Ara, I can still sense her voice and feel her mannerisms through her host. It's as if she's wearing a Halloween costume, and not inhabiting another person's body.

The cop car swerves around and races over the grass. I ball my fists and focus upward. Perseus comes into view. He raises his arms, and chunks of the gym's roof begin to hover above his head. I kneel down, placing my hands against the grass, while still keeping my laser-like vision plastered on the leader of the Predators. I feel the dirt and gravel begin to ascend around me. In an instant, I blast into the air like a missile.

Perseus is just about to heave his heavy projectile at Aries, when I catch his eye. He turns his startled look toward me, but I am too fast for him to react. I fling out my arms like I'm shooting an imaginary wave of fire into his chest. Perseus goes spiraling toward the ground. My feet slide against the stone pebbles speckled throughout the school's roof, and I sprint over to my wounded friend. Aries lifts himself to his feet before I can help him up.

"C'mon, bro!" I say. "I thought you had this."

Aries rolls his eyes and sneers.

"Shut up." He grunts out a laugh while clutching his ribs and coughing up stray droplets of blood. "Final boss is always easier with two players, anyway."

We share a smirk before flashing lights in the distance captures our attention. The first pair of Psyriin helicopters have reached the edge of the forest surrounding the campus, and are searching the grounds for any stray humans. We may have a few minutes before they find us.

The remaining empty cars scattered throughout the parking lot begin to rise into the air. Our startled gawks follow all ten vehicles as they swarm like leaves in the wind.

"That can't be good," Aries groans, while watching the cars fly above us.

Perseus lets out an earth-shattering screech as he ascends. Our gazes dart into his fiery stare, and we space ourselves out to get into fighting poses.

"I'm going to hand both of you traitors over to Psyriin in pieces!" Perseus growls, with his arms spread high.

The cars begin to spiral around him in a violent circle, and I feel my chest rattle.

"We got this, right?" I say to Aries. "They're just like dirt clods. Four-thousand-pound, metal, explosive dirt clods."

"Uhhh..." He's still glaring upward with widened eyes.

My face begins to twitch, but I take a deep breath to settle my thumping heart. Perseus is powerful. But just like Aquila, his head is muddled with anger and despair. We can beat him. We just have to use his rage against him.

"Hey!" I yell over to Aries, as an idea comes to mind.

His grimace meets my stare with an evident hint of nervousness.

"Cover me!"

Aries shrugs and nods as we turn and prepare ourselves for the inevitable onslaught. Perseus growls and flings his arms forward. The vehicles fire toward us from all directions as if he's trying to pin us down rather than outright smash us. Aries's scowl hardens with focus. He waits until the first car is merely feet away before he diverts it over to me. I leap into the air, flying inches from the car, and spin my body around it. Another car comes, but I send it fluttering over the edge of the roof. Aries sends the next vehicle hurling back at Perseus before he diverts the next one back toward me.

The roar of metal hammering against the rooftop cascades through the air. Sparks flare around us, bathing the atmosphere in a fiery orange glow. I count off every car as it hurls in each direction.

We continue on like we're playing a deadly game of dodgeball. Aries uses every ounce of his strength to keep the vehicles away from his wounded frame. With each car he re-routes, I dip and dodge around them, moving closer and closer to Perseus. I catch a glimpse of his infuriated scowl every time I move from car to car. He hasn't pinpointed my location. How can he? Aries is giving his all by sending enough return fire to keep Perseus's mind occupied.

When the second to last car passes, I make my move. I spin my body around a vehicle that is just below Perseus. His gaze snaps toward me, and he brings a banged-up sedan clamoring for my chest. My gaze sharpens. This is it. It's now or never.

I swirl my arms around, and the vehicle moves to its side seconds before colliding with my body. In the blink of an eye, I focus my fingertips and rip the front doors open on both sides. Adrenaline rushes through my body as I close my eyes.

If my timing had been off by a millisecond—if I had miscalculated a single move—my body would've been smacked from the sky like a mosquito. But my senses have never been sharper. Maybe it's the adrenaline. Maybe it's the heightened emotion. Whatever it is, it has not only saved my life, but given me the upper hand.

Perseus's nose curls. His coal-like pupils begin to explode through their sockets as he watches me swoop through the front of the vehicle like a dolphin jumping through a hoop. He curls his fists. Swings his arms across to divert another vehicle toward me, but he isn't quite fast enough. My feet have barely passed the car's doorframe, when I fling out my palm and send it flipping back around like a boomerang. Perseus sends another projectile hurtling at me, just a split second later.

Unlike the leader of the Predators, I am not alone in this battle. A tire nearly grazes my face, but Aries jolts the furious shot sideways. By the time it has skirted past my frame, I can already see Perseus's face molding to a sorrowful, desperate scowl. He moves his arms to brace himself, but he knows that it is of no use.

I tighten my fists. Widen my mouth. Curl my eyebrows. The kinetic force I deliver into Perseus's face might as well be a deafening punch from Muhammad Ali in his prime. Blood and saliva spew from his lips as a circular dent plasters across his cheek. Before his eyes can even open, his body smacks against the roof of the vehicle I'd flung toward him. I hover in the air with a heavy snarl as the car smashes against the rooftop, with Perseus's body wilted atop.

"Daammmmnnn!" Aries shouts, his fist covering his grin as he stares at Perseus's squirming frame.

I haven't even taken a moment to marvel at my attack. My glare has already turned to the helicopters speeding toward us.

I continue to float in the air, squinting toward the bus lot and scanning for Aquila. But she is nowhere to be found. As Aries flies to my side, my gaze drifts to Perseus lying against the car like a beanbag.

"Lupus is still in the gym." Aries grunts, as if the sense of urgency has finally hit him. "Where's everyone else?"

I don't respond. My heart starts rattling, and my stomach is churning like I've just eaten expired meat.

The helicopters have just reached the center of the parking lot. I look to the opposite horizon speckled with trees. I can sense Aries staring at my vacant stupor and anxiously waiting for me to reply. A deep sigh flows from my chest as Auriga's dying words begin to swim through my thoughts.

Promise me, I sense him whispering, in my head, *no matter what happens, you are family.*

"Ara took Leo and Lyra to safety. But we have to get the Predators." I turn back to Aries. "Go get Lupus. I'm gonna go find Aquila."

He looks back at me with a nervous twinge on his brow. We both understand the situation. If we don't leave now, we'll have to deal with Psyriin. Neither of us has the energy to confront them, but we know we can't leave the Predators behind.

Two vehicles folded over the school's rooftop begin to move. Both Aries and I gawk midair as we watch them go spiraling toward the helicopters like they're toys being flung by a belligerent child. The Psyriin helicopters bobble through the air to regain their control. They swing upward to dodge the attack, but Aries counters by making the two cars collide in front of them. A fierce inferno blankets the atmosphere, sending both helicopters spiraling in reverse.

My awestricken gaze peers through the mixture of fire and falling steel, until I'm able to barely make out the ground below. As two more cars rise into the air, I spot Aquila at the edge of the parking lot. Her tattooed arm is raised high, but the other is clutched around her left rib. She has one knee pressed against the concrete, while the other leg fights to keep balance.

Even at this distance, I'm able to make out the streams of blood billowing from her snarl. It's as if I can read her thoughts through her watering eyes when she looks at me. In the brief moment, I can feel the frustration and despair resonating from her ebony visage. Despite that I'd just injured her, she is giving every ounce of remaining strength to buy us more time. Whatever qualms the two of us had are like cinders wafting into the air. Aquila has finally realized who the real enemy is.

"Rion!" Aries shouts.

I whip my head around just in time to see another swarm of helicopters flying toward the gym, from over the sea of trees. My gaze briefly meets Aries's worrisome grimace before I swoop down to Perseus. I am prepared to scoop him up by his limp shoulders, but before I can, his palm jolts forth and he claws his fingers against my arm.

"Auriga," he murmurs, his eyes welling with tears. "Is he really gone?"

All I can muster is a sorrowful nod. My eyes widen when he struggles to lift his sore frame from the car's dented shell. It's as if the final ounces of animosity toward us have been knocked out of his system by my telekinetic punch to his jaw. He shoves me aside with his fists clenched, glaring toward the gym's cracked dome. A wad of spit and blood jolts from his lips and splashes against the rooftop.

"Let me and Quila handle them. You and Aries get outta here."

"But—"

"Go!" he growls, his fiery gaze boring into mine.

Vehicles continue to jolt through the sky to detract the helicopters to our right. Aries comes zipping downward, and lands in front of Perseus as if to block him from moving any further. They stare into each other's eyes, frustration and sorrow billowing from their faces. They seem frozen, as if they are locked into an intense conversation.

"I'm not leavin' you here, P." Aries huffs.

"Please," Perseus replies, his vicious snarl trying to mask his teary eyes. "Let us do this...for Auriga."

Aries's head bows in frustration. Perseus folds his arm across his heart, his fist remaining coiled. Aries copies the gesture, and slowly, their tattooed arms collide between them.

"Keep 'em safe," Perseus whispers.

"Predators," Aries dolefully nods. "Not prey."

Their arms droop back downward. Aries has barely moved aside when Perseus bursts into the air, toward the gym.

"Let's go, Rion." Aries lets out a reluctant sigh as he rests his hand on my shoulder.

I can feel the anguish billowing with each syllable. My lips drift into a discomfited pout. I attempt to shake away the memory of the Predators throwing me my first real party, and the warm embrace I received when I lifted the crates.

Why did they have to turn on us? We could've stopped Psyriin together if they'd just listened. Maybe Aquila and Perseus understand this even better than I do. They've finally realized how they'd allowed their anger to overrun them. Perhaps staying behind is their way of setting things right.

The helicopters above the parking lot begin to move back into formation as the smoke clears. I let out another heavy sigh before Aries and I turn and blast off toward the towering trees without looking back. My heart grows heavier with each second that the sound of explosions rains behind me.

Perseus and Aquila are strong, but each of us knows they are fighting a battle they won't win.

CHAPTER 27

THE AFTERMATH

A HEAVY SIGH FLOWS FROM MY CHEEKS AS ARIES and I turn and stare at the moonlit horizon. We can still see smoke billowing through the sky. Our feet gracefully land amidst the tall weeds of my old yard, when the front door of the house opens. Ara, now back in her dainty body, trots out with a look of fatigued relief. We jog over to meet her at the edge of the porch, and I lunge out to give her a warm embrace.

"You guys okay?" she says, as I relinquish her from my arms.

"We'll live," Aries replies.

A light smile forces through my tiresome cheeks. Ara stares deep into my eyes and rubs the center of my back. She knows the Predators are still on my mind. I can tell from her apologetic look that she also wishes they'd come flying in behind us.

We limp into the house. Candles are lit throughout, but there's still an eerie darkness seeping from every corner. We pass by the kitchen, and I glance at the patched hole in the wall. My chest tightens as Mom starts to creep back into my memories.

"How's Leo?" I say, trying to distract my own sorrowful thoughts.

"I've had better days." The Reader Clairvoyant huffs as he steps from the living room, rubbing the reddened skin along his neck. "Could definitely use a massage. But it could be worse."

He gives me a warm smile, and I return the gesture. Feels like the first time he's been delighted to see me.

Lyra comes trotting in by his feet. She scurries over and rubs her fur along the tips of my sullied jeans.

"Thanks, Rion." Leo winks. "You did good."

I humbly nod as we stand in the dimly lit hallway.

I did more than good. I defeated Aquila, one on one. I helped save countless lives, while managing to avoid Psyriin. And yet, it still feels like we're in the losing locker room right now.

"Yeah, well, I wish I could've gotten the flash drive."

"Wait!" Aries darts his aggravated grimace toward me. "You didn't get it?"

I turn to him with splayed arms. An annoyed grunt wafts through my jaws.

"Aquila tossed it in the woods somewhere, and I had to go help *you*. So sorry if I was a little preoccupied."

"You mean, this flash drive." Ara wears a sly grin.

Our eyes widen as we watch her tinker with the tiny crimson object between her fingers.

"How'd you find it!" I say, my smile wider than it has been in days.

"I didn't."

Her gaze drifts to the floor. Lyra lets out a soft purr. The crafty feline sits between us and looks up with a gleam in her pearly eyes. We each share a laugh.

"Lyra the MVP." Aries chuckles before kneeling down to scratch her furry chin.

He embraces her like a long-lost friend rather than a pet. For the first time, I can tell he misses the real Lyra as much as Ara does.

"Still think we should've stayed at the hotel?" I lean over toward Leo.

He shakes his head and attempts to fight his protruding grin.

"My neck and Aries's ribs might beg to differ. But all things considered, it was a successful mission, Mama's Boy."

We take a moment to catch our breaths. Ara, having snatched some crude medical supplies before ditching the police car, tends to Leo and Aries's wounds as best she can. As the night passes by, there are few words between us. No one actually suggests it, but we decide to get some rest before making the trek to meet Pavo.

Aries falls asleep immediately. You'd think he was lying on a bed of rose petals, and not a dusty beige carpet. After tonight, I'm sure any surface feels like a brand-new mattress to him.

Leo comes to rest on the couch soon after, with Lyra huddled on his chest. Ara and I sit against the living-room wall. It doesn't take long before she dozes off against my shoulder.

It feels like I'm awake for several more hours. I never thought I'd see this place again. Even though it was the shortest stay for me and Mom, I'm sure I'll remember this house more than any others.

I look around and think about all the days I'd failed to lift things during my afterschool practice sessions. I've come so far in such a short time. Mom would be proud.

Ding-dong!

The sound of the doorbell resonates through the walls of the apartment door. Leo and I wait in a hallway. Both of us are anxious. My heart is thumping as I stare at the golden numbers atop the doorway. Leo keeps peering down each corridor as if Psyriin soldiers could leap out at any minute.

"What if her parents are home?" I say.

"They aren't."

We hear the thump of footsteps, and I take a deep breath. The door gently creaks open, and Dee pokes her head from inside. An awkward grin cascades across my face as I wave like I'm some sort of Girl Scout selling cookies.

"*You* can come in," she says to me, with a sigh.

Her brow molds into a scowl as she glances at Leo before disappearing back inside.

"It's cool. I'll stay out here and keep watch. Don't be too long."

I nod and pat his shoulder before sliding through the front door that Dee has left cracked. A heavenly, clean scent fills my nostrils as soon as I step inside. Mom would love this place. It looks like a professional has been through to dust every countertop and shine every ounce of metal.

"Start talking," Dee says, as I follow her into the living room.

She plops down on the couch and crosses one leg over the other. She grabs a glass of what looks like wine, before placing her scowl on me.

"First things first." I sigh. "I'm sorry for how I left things."

Her eyes flutter. She takes a sip. I know her well enough to notice that she's pleased with my immediate apology, no matter how much she tries to hide it.

"You were an amazing friend. The first real one I'd ever had. You didn't deserve to be treated rudely."

She sucks her teeth and rolls her eyes. I pause and bite my lip. My knees bend, and I rock in place while anxiously waiting for a response.

"Well...you did save my life. And it looks like you got school canceled for a while. Which is good, 'cause all of my class notes were on that flash drive. Soooo...I guess we're cool."

A gentle smile billows across her chocolate-brown cheeks. I don't even try to conceal my sigh of relief. She nudges her head to signal me to take a seat, and I oblige. She takes another long gulp of her beverage as I attempt to get comfortable beside her.

"Now..." She smacks her lips. "What the hell is going on?"

I take a deep breath and begin. I tell her everything. I don't skip the slightest detail—from my separation from Mom, to my defeat of Perseus. She seems entertained by my story. The parts where I nearly die make her smile widen like she's hearing parts from a movie.

It feels like I talk for hours. But after glancing back at the kitchen clock, I realize it's only been twenty minutes. When I've finally finished my explanation, we move to her apartment balcony to watch the sun setting over the adjacent building.

"Wow," Dee murmurs. "So you're like a superhero?"

I laugh and rub my hands together to give them warmth over the cold winds.

"I'm serious! Saving lives, cool powers, super friends. All you're missing is the spandex, dude."

I let her get a few more hero jokes out of her system before I finally ask her what the town has been like since last week, when the Predators arrived. She explains that she, along with several students and faculty, had been interviewed by local police over the past few days. Even though they'd all sworn to violent telekinetics holding them hostage and engaging in an all-out war, the authorities refused to believe them without physical evidence. The Predators' viral video was the only reason they'd chalked the whole situation up to something hostile at all. The county police and media were framing the incident like a terrorist attack with assault weapons and explosives.

It didn't help that the only officer on the scene— the one inhabited by Ara—had no recollection of the ordeal. Much of the wreckage had been fixed before other police had arrived. This was, no doubt, Psyriin's doing. It figures they'd want to keep things under wraps. Especially now that they might have the Predators in custody.

"The media thinks we're crazy." Dee laughs. "We're like the new Roswell."

I chuckle, before I notice something moving in our periphery. We turn and see Leo walking into the living room, with his stern gaze focused on me.

"Didn't I tell him to wait outside?" Dee scoffs.

My head drifts, and I let out a heavy sigh. I knew this moment would come. Leo and I had discussed it over and over again. It was the only reason we'd returned after reconnecting with Pavo and moving to our new safe house. And yet I'm still dreading every passing second.

"Listen…"

Her gaze snaps to mine, and she gives me an apprehensive scowl.

"I didn't just come here to apologize and explain everything."

"You came to say goodbye." She huffs.

It's hard to look her in those big brown eyes. I try to fight the lump in my throat, but it bombards through, and I feel my eyes beginning to water.

"Psyriin probably has the Predators in their custody. Including the one who could read your mind."

I notice Dee's head starting to lower. She bites her lip, and I can sense her heartbeat starting to thump when I wistfully continue.

"We can't let them pick your brain."

We make eye contact. Every second of her silence is like agony.

"Dee, there's only one way to ensure that you have a normal life. That's why he's here."

She stares down at the wooden floorboards beneath us. Her head begins to nod. When she finally looks back at me, those huge, sparkling eyes have become as red as Leo's sore neck.

"I promise it won't hurt. He's just going to…make you forget. He has to do it to everyone else who was in that gym, too."

She lets out a long sigh. "Well, this sucks."

"It's not that bad." I grin. "You still have Alex, farmer boy, and that kid with the boot."

We both laugh. She wipes away a tear before the droplet can even fall from the corner of her eye.

"We'll be like the Island of Misfit Toys at prom." She giggles.

The sun finally sets, and the wind replaces our silence. I muster up the strength to look her right in the face. I've never fully noticed how pretty she is. Her braided hair is coiled like a beehive atop her head. Her clothes consist of a *Ninja Turtles* T-shirt and a pair of navy-blue leggings. She has never looked more adorable.

"Dee...I wish things could've been—"

She lunges up on her tippy toes, and our lips touch. My eyes widen. It lasts for a few seconds, and the entire gesture makes my body freeze. The closest thing I've ever had to a kiss was when Suzy Beamon planted one on my cheek in fifth grade. This one, I certainly don't mind.

When Dee finally leans back, I respond with a gawk. She looks proud and unrelenting, like she's wanted to do it for a while. I notice Leo in the corner of my eye, trying his best to withhold boyish laughter.

A hefty grin blankets my face. But inside, my heart is aching. I'd never looked at Dee like a girlfriend. But now...as I look at my reflection in her eyes, all of the feelings come rushing through at once. No one knows me better than she does. Not even Mom. No one ever made me laugh like Dee. No one knew how to brighten my day like her. It seems cruel for this to be the last moment we'll ever share.

"I may not get to remember you, Rion Grean." She wipes away the unrelenting tears flowing down her cheeks. "But you're damn sure gonna remember me."

CHAPTER 28

THE HIDDEN FILES

I GRIT MY TEETH AND CLASP THE SIDE OF THE bed. I've shut my eyes so tight that stray moisture is beginning to slide through. This whole thing was Aries's idea. It was supposed to get me out of my sulking mood after saying goodbye to Dee. But even after spending weeks in the Charon, I'd never imagined this moment would come with so much pain.

"Hold still," Aries barks, from my side as he jolts my wrist back into position. "I'm almost finished."

The burning pain continues to shoot up my arm. My heart is pounding. I'm giving every ounce of strength I have to not let embarrassing droplets billow down my cheek.

"Done." Aries pulls the needle from my skin.

My watery gaze flutters open, letting the bright light from the bedroom window rush in.

"You good, princess? Should I get you a lollipop?"

I flash him my middle finger before leaning forward to wriggle my sore limb. I bring my left arm into view and peer at the black dots freshly tattooed along my wrist. It looks good, and I can't help but feel happy that the pain wasn't in vain.

"I better not get an infection," I say to Aries, while staring at his work.

"Hey, I'm no Lupus. But I'm not some hack, either. Just don't ask me to do a full sleeve, 'cause your arm might end up lookin' like a four-year-old's coloring book."

As we share a laugh, the door creaks open. We turn just as Ara pokes her thin frame inside.

"Well, look at you!" She grins. "Looks like you're an official Clairvoyant now."

I continue to smile and stare at the constellation on my brown skin. I can't help but wonder what Mom would say if she knew I'd gotten a tattoo. She'd probably roll her eyes, but I have no doubt she'd be fine with this particular design.

"Orion?" Ara tilts her head to examine the modest design.

"Yeah." I smile. "The unfortunate nights of being interviewed by Arkright made me feel like my name was more than a coincidence."

Ara nods and comes over to rub my shoulder. Her soothing scent makes the pain subside.

"He's considered the greatest hunter in Greek mythology." She smirks. "It suits you."

Aries stands to his feet and begins to wrap my wrist in a white bandage. Lyra comes rushing in like a nosey child as soon as he's finished. She lets out a gentle purr before leaping into my lap. I stroke her warm, orange fur while she sniffs at my covered mark.

"I came to tell you guys that Leo is ready," Ara says.

My eyes widen. Excitement starts to replace any remaining twinges in my body. From the moment he'd finished spending days tracking down the Tyler High civilians to erase their memories, Leo had dedicated virtually all of his time to uncovering the deleted files from the flash drive. His intense focus had turned him into an even bigger curmudgeon than usual. But for once, I didn't mind. I appreciated his dedication over the last few weeks. It was as if he was more intrigued by the mission than I was. He'd refused to talk about it to anyone, even Pavo.

I manage to catch Aries's scoff as soon as Ara speaks. In his mind, the whole thing is dumb, and he's repeatedly told me not to get my hopes up. He's the only person in the house who doesn't expect some mind-blowing mystery to be uncovered. Pavo's vision had all but confirmed that there was something important lurking within that drive. But Aries is still skeptical.

We pace down the hall, our feet squeaking against the wooden floor. Our new safe house is a remote beach cabin along the Florida coast. Ara has managed to decorate enough for it to feel comforting. We each have our own room. Even the tiny laundry room has been made into a cozy space for Lyra. I can't wait for Mom to experience this. After all the years we'd spent running, it would be nice for her to get the extended family she'd always been afraid to have.

As soon as we reach the edge of the hall, Pavo comes rolling out of his room, in his wheelchair. I dart over behind him and push him forward. Once we've turned the corner, we see Leo hunched over the island counter in the center of the kitchen.

"Okay," he says, with a deep sigh once we are all circled around him. "I'll kill some of the intrigue. If you were expecting a picture of Rion's dad, or an in-depth journal about his mother's past...I'm afraid that flash drive contained nothing of the sort."

My head drifts to the polished counter surface. My own dejected reflection is peering back at me. Ara leans over and runs her soothing touch along my shoulder again. I respond to her gesture with a calm smile before placing my attention back on Leo.

"The files on the drive were encrypted. Took me a while to hack, even after I recovered them from deletion."

Each of our eyebrows comes to a perk. Even Aries looks intrigued.

"So what did you find?" I say.

Leo's gaze shifts toward mine.

"Rion..." He lets out another somber sigh. "Do you remember any other kids, growing up?"

My face gnarls in confusion. The others dart their gazes at me. I search my mind for a reply, as if Leo is asking me a loaded question.

"A few classmates here and there." I shrug. "But I didn't really have any friends until Dee."

Everyone looks back at Leo. He seems to be shaking his head as if this was the answer he was afraid to hear.

"Your mother ever mention any siblings or distant cousins?" He peers over the lenses of his glasses like he can read my mind and already knows the answer.

"No," I groan.

"What does this have to do with the flash drive?" Aries says.

For someone so skeptical about this, he certainly seems impatient.

Leo straightens his back and takes a deep breath. He runs a hand through his trimmed, dirty-blond hair, and folds his arms.

"The drive had basic files on all twelve known Clairvoyants before we were released from the lab. Our constellation designations aren't mentioned, but the physical descriptions and ages match each of us perfectly."

His unsettling tone makes my gaze start to drift. I'd already figured out that Mom knew about the others. But hearing Leo confirm it makes my stomach queasy. Even with her whereabouts unknown, I can't help but still be agitated that she'd withheld this information from me.

"But there's more..." Leo says.

My gaze shoots back to him, and my heart starts to rattle.

"There were three other Clairvoyant files listed."

Our eyes widen like the bright sun blaring through the living room window. Even Lyra's head perks up, like she's just as shocked by Leo's words as the rest of us.

"Fifteen in total." He scans each of our dumbfounded faces.

"So who are they?" Ara says.

"Rion's the fourth kinetic," Aries says, before Leo's mouth can open. "These other three cats must be a fourth of the other strains."

Leo shakes his head, but I'm the only one who seems to notice. He rolls his eyes in irritation as Ara and Aries continue to go back and forth.

"But if that's true, there should be sixteen," Ara replies. "Why wouldn't Rion be counted with the rest of us?"

"Hell, I don't know." Aries scoffs. "Maybe his mom deleted his file?"

"They aren't like any of us," Leo finally says. "And Rion is not described or mentioned anywhere on the drive."

The room goes silent again. I notice Pavo glaring at the floor and running his frail fingertips through his tangled beard.

"The files were separated into five folders that were originally inside the one labeled *FB*. The twelve of us were all grouped with our strain. These new three were grouped together. And none of their listed physical attributes matched Rion, or any Clairvoyant we know."

An uneasy stillness fills the room. I glance at Ara, Aries, and Pavo. I can tell that the same question is on each of our minds.

"The files don't list any of our abilities," Leo says, as if he's suddenly been gifted with the ability to read our thoughts. "So I have no idea what this fifth strain might be."

After another minute of anxious silence, we each turn to Pavo. Somehow we're hoping the old prophet has some insight that might make sense of it all. Once he notices our gawking stares, he turns to Leo with a resolute scowl.

"Was there anything else?" Pavo whispers.

"Yeah. There was one picture on the drive. I printed it out."

Leo pulls a photo from his pocket and rests it against the countertop. We each lean toward it like we're tourists at a zoo. My heart sinks as soon as I shift my gaze to dodge the glare reflecting from its surface.

Centered on the photo is my mother. But she isn't alone. Three kids surround her. There's a young girl, probably no older than ten. Her freckled skin is a light caramel brown, and she has curly auburn hair. Beside her are two teenage boys with dark hair. One is short, chubby, and looks of Filipino descent. The other is slender, with olive skin and bright, hazel eyes. A smile is blanketed on each of their faces. They are sitting on a tiny couch, and Mom seems to be holding the camera to take the photo.

My blood starts to boil. They all look like one happy family. In all of our years together, I'd never seen her this happy with anyone else before. Here I was, thinking that Mom was some loner. Instead, she's been lying to me my whole life, while she took *selfies* with other kids.

"I managed to track down the SUV Rion's mom was driving." Leo pushes his glasses closer up his face. "Police found the vehicle incinerated off the highway, about an hour away from where we found Rion."

A chill shoots down my spine. Horrible notions are creeping through my mind, but I refuse to let them dominate my thoughts.

"You don't think…" Ara murmurs.

"A body wasn't found," Leo says, "and we know Psyriin didn't catch her. From what I can tell, the car was definitely set on fire with everything still inside. I believe that after she dodged Psyriin, Rion's mother destroyed all of her files so the info couldn't fall into the wrong hands. These kids in the photo match the descriptions of the fifth strain. And I'm almost certain that up until now, Diana Grean is the only one who has known of their existence."

My brow begins to harden with frustration. I can't help but feel a bit foolish. Why didn't I do more sleuthing when I was in that closet at our old house? What secret information was in there? What else was my mother trying to conceal?

"As far as she knew, the flash drive was in that car with everything else." Leo huffs.

"You think she's with the fifth strain now?" Aries says.

"The trail goes cold. But I'm willing to bet she went to secure the other strain's safety."

My chest thumps as soon as the words echo from Leo's lips. Everything he says makes complete sense, but I don't want to believe it. I turn and storm from the kitchen. Ara calls out to me, but I ignore her and dart toward my room.

I slam the door shut with one telekinetic swipe. Questions start to flood my mind, and I stare at the wall as if Mom is glaring back. Where do I fit in? Do I fit in? If I wasn't created in that lab with the others, then who is my father? How could you just leave me, Mom? Was this fifth strain—this other family of yours—were they really worth abandoning me for?

Moonlight glistens against the clear water, and lights the night sky like a lantern. I stand at the edge of the beach and watch the gentle waves as they billow into the coast. It's nice to be here when most of the country is snowed in. I wiggle my toes between the soft, cool sand and embrace the warm air that wafts against my face. I wish I could sleep. But after everything I've been through, it seems fitting to stay awake at night.

I haven't spoken to the others since this morning. Christmas is just days away, but I feel anything but festive. Mom used to put up the tree around this time. We'd drink hot chocolate and watch old movies together. But right now, all I can think about is her creating memories with three other children, without me.

I hear footsteps brushing behind me. I don't turn to see who it is. I know it's Ara. Who else would come out from the cabin to meet me at this hour?

"You okay?" she says, as soon as she comes to my side.

Her black hair is unfurled over her shoulders, and her hands are tucked inside the same red, hooded sweatshirt she'd worn during our first ever late-night conversation.

"I don't know." I kick up a few grains of sand and glare off into the horizon. "I just...wish I had more answers, ya know?"

"Yeah. Kinda feels like the calm before the storm."

I give a deep sigh and remind myself that Psyriin is still out there, licking their wounds.

Ara is right. This is only the beginning. Somewhere, Felix Bard is plotting his next move to find us.

It doesn't worry me as much as it probably should. After everything I have accomplished—after every obstacle I've managed to overcome—what reason do I have to be afraid? I'm stronger than I could've ever imagined, and I also have Pavo, Aries, Ara, Leo, and Lyra by my side.

"Your mother didn't abandon you, Rion." Ara's hand grazes my arm.

At first, I think she's just saying whatever she thinks will make me feel better. But as my disheartened brow drifts upward, I sense the resolve in her smile.

"This fifth strain—whoever they are—they might've needed her more than you did. She knew how strong you were, even if you didn't see it in yourself. I know she's just as proud to have you as a son, as we are to have you as part of our family."

I gaze at the sparkling pink streams that swim through her pupils, and a smirk forces through my somber glower. I realize that no matter how angry I may be at my mother, I still love her more than anything in this world. Despite all the questions she'll have to answer, I know that when I see her, the only thing I'll want to do is hug her tighter than I've ever hugged anyone before. No matter how far apart we are, I know that everything I am, and every ounce of toughness I have, I owe to her.

"Whatever storm comes, we'll weather it together," Ara says, in a soothing tone, before caressing my hand. "Goodnight, Rion. Don't stay up too late." She plants a kiss on my cheek.

Our hands separate, and I smile while watching her pace back to our secluded cabin. As the sound of her footsteps disappear into the night air, my mind wonders about the Prophet Andromeda, the third Reader, and the Aural Clairvoyants I've yet to meet. I can only imagine what must be going through their minds while being so separated from all of this. Where are they? Do they know how dangerous Psyriin is? What will they think when they learn that Auriga is gone? What will their reaction be when they learn about me and a fifth strain?

I look up at the stars. I remember when they were the only things in my life that were consistent. That was before I discovered the other Clairvoyants. In meeting Aries and the Phantoms, I've gained more than friends. I've gained a family. For the first time in my life, I finally feel at home.

Nights like this...where the sky is as clear and deep as the ocean beneath it...will always take my breath away, no matter my circumstances. Nights like this remind me of the cool silence of the countryside, with Mom in the kitchen making dinner. She always told me

I'd need to find purpose and make my mark. Now, I finally understand what I was meant to do with my life.

I glance down at the newly cemented tattoo on my wrist. Sailors used to look up and use constellations to guide them home when they were out in the emptiness of the sea. You're out there, Mom. With the stars to guide me, I'm going to find you. Then I'm going to help defeat Felix Bard and Psyriin.

I'm going to make sure that my mother and the other Clairvoyants never have to live in fear again.

COMING SOON

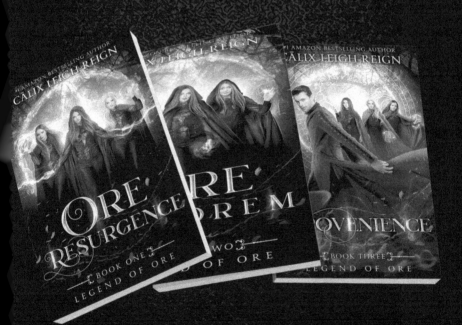

MORE READS

CayellePublishing.com

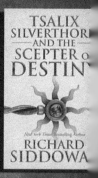

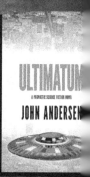

COMING SOON